THE FORBIDDEN WARRIORS

BOOK ONE OF THE FORBIDDEN SERIES

MOUD ADEL

MASTOPERIA BOOKS
WWW.MASTOPERIA.COM

First published by Mastoperia Books

Copyright © Mahmoud Hussin, 2019

The moral rights of the author has been asserted

All rights reserved. No part of this publication may be reproduced, stored or transmitted in any form or by any means, electronic, mechanical, photocopying, recording, scanning, or otherwise without written permission from the publisher. It is illegal to copy this book, post it to a website, or distribute it by any other means without permission.

First edition

Editing by Killing It Write
Cover Design by Christina P. Myrvold
Cartography by BMR Williams

ISBN-13: 9781698846323
ISBN-10: 1698846320

To Writing

For saving me from moments of darkness, for giving me hope and purpose, and for giving me a reason to wake up when all hope is lost

Books By Moud Adel

The Forbidden Series

War Remnants

The Last Seed

The Forbidden Warriors

Next in the Series

The Book of Salinda

THE FORBIDDEN WARRIORS
A TALES OF MASTOPERIA STORY

1

Amarin wrapped his fingers around one of the hot, steel bars centering the massive gate. The corner of his eyes sparkled as he spoke in a quiet voice. "I still remember every emotion that rolled through me when I first arrived at this gate. It was two hundred and fifty years ago, yet I remember as if it was yesterday." Amarin glanced up at the blistering sun. "I even remember how hot it was. How the sun vaporized my fluids, and my heart pumped hard as it tried to keep up with the blood racing through my veins. It was exciting."

"I know… I could hardly breathe when my faction nominated me, of all people, to become a royal guard." Takara sighed. "It was the greatest honor anyone could receive back then, and I was ecstatic. What a naïve girl I was!" She rubbed the back of her fingers against her beach-colored skin.

"It's still honorable." Amarin turned his head toward her.

"Debatable." Takara smiled.

Amarin looked into her eyes. "It doesn't matter, anyway. Our time is almost over. Once the new candidates finish their task, they will replace us, and we will be free to spend the rest of our lives together in peace."

"I hope it will be that easy. You know these things never go as planned."

"You worry too much, sometimes." Amarin playfully nudged her. "Plus, it wasn't always bad."

"No, you're right." Takara smiled and pulled the gate open before marching back to the palace. "At least I met you. So… Tell me about these new candidates. Who are they?"

"They are…" Amarin paused to remember their names. "Rondai of Kala, Evailen of Lunar, Kawan of Delphia, and Jihave of Averett."

Takara halted mid-step and reached for Amarin's arm. "I didn't mean their names. Tell me something about them. How they are? Who they are? Anything juicy." She wiggled her eyebrows with a wide grin.

"You always like to hear the gossip." Amarin shook his head.

"Please." Takara held both hands in front of her and faked an innocent smile.

"Fine." Amarin nodded and started down the cobblestone path again. "Rondai is the oldest of the bunch. He is twenty-six. Already a gate five master, and the Kalanian Council considered promoting him to their ranks before they chose to send him here instead.

"Evailen is a video game developer and a superb one at that. She is only twenty and—" He paused, his brown irises shifting to the side "—her only notable action was trying to expose the corruption of her enterprise. She showed no fear, and they couldn't contain her. I assume this was why they nominated her."

Takara reached for Amarin's arm with wide eyes and stopped his forward motion once again. "They wanted to get rid of her?"

"Yes." Amarin pulled Takara along the path as he gazed up at the highest tower of the palace centering the empty city. "The video game industry has strong lobbyists and a lot of influence in Lunar."

"I see." She lowered her gaze a moment before meeting Amarin's again. "And the others?"

"Kawan is the shortest. He is twenty-three. His peers call him The Invisible because he is quiet and spends most of his time practicing his power, ignoring all social life. Three Delphian magazines listed him among the top one hundred most powerful future tellers."

"Interesting." Takara's hazel eyes twinkled as she rubbed her hands together. "I want to see how powerful he truly is."

Amarin chuckled. "Finally, we have Jihave. He is twenty-five and answers to no one." Amarin turned his face away from her with his teeth clenched tight. "Jihave has collected the biggest number of Majestics anyone has ever seen at his age."

"Even more than you?" Takara asked in a high voice.

"Apparently." Amarin took a deep breath as he repainted the smile on his face. "But don't forget that I left my faction over two centuries ago, and we still had to deal with the wounds of our wars."

He nudged her forehead with his second finger. "Anyway, is that enough information for you?" He stared into her eyes.

"Yes, and soon, they will be here. Perhaps we can have some fun with these new candidates before they inherit our powers." Takara covered her wide grin with her hand.

2

Only Those Who Are Summoned Can Enter

The Four candidates inspected the grand port engraved with those words as they tried to shake off the residue of overwhelming emotions. Seeing their factions' symbols carved next to one another on the corridor leading to the grand hall sent a quick shiver through their bodies, but the main hall was something they couldn't anticipate.

It was the first time they had ever seen their colors grouped together to reflect harmony, instead of conflict. Delphian white, Kalanian yellow, Lunardis blue, and Averetti green decorated the western, northern, eastern, and southern walls respectively appearing as extended rays from the rainbow-colored ceiling. Words escaped them as they each turned in a circle to absorb the atmosphere.

When forty warriors came to join in, the four candidates positioned themselves at the core where the golden dome at the center of the rainbow ceiling reflected its light. They watched the warriors each take a seat near the northern wall in groups of ten that mirrored their factions before the Forbidden City leader appeared at their backs. The leader sat on a stone throne a few steps higher than everyone else, behind her, a shadow of a figure stood.

The first guard, Takara, tapped the floor twice with her sword as she appeared from the west side of the candidates. Her golden hair and classy white dress forced all eyes to fall upon her.

"No one told me we were attending a soiree." Jihave chuckled, revealing his big jaw, and a few missing teeth from prior battles.

The second guard, Amarin, tapped the floor three times with his spear as he appeared from the east. His tattooed, buffed-up body overshadowed Takara's dress. The candidates watched in near hypnotic amazement how the painted animals constantly moved over the guard's muscled arms.

"It's like his body is a universe of its own." Evailen shuffled her weight from foot to foot.

"How is that possible…?" Jihave dropped his jaw, thinking how dull his own body was in comparison. He carried more animal tattoos on his skin than Amarin, but Jihave's never moved—not like that.

The third guard, Radaman, tapped the floor four times with his double-sided ax. He sat on the floor facing the candidates, leaving his back exposed to the warriors, the leader, and the shadow. His silver arrowhead tattoo atop his bald head shone through his obsidian skin. He uttered nothing, and yet a quiver passed through their bodies.

Evailen's grin widened. "I knew this looked familiar."

Rondai tilted his head toward her and spoke in a near whisper. "In what way?"

"This entire scene reminds me of how ancient Egyptians believed their final journey through death would appear. Forty-two gods to witness and three gods to rule, or maybe, mmm… I'm not entirely sure, but there were forty-five and a bird! No, no, a feather. Yes, a feather against the heart." Evailen widened her smile.

"What are you rambling about?" Jihave raised his thick eyebrows.

"She's talking about a video game. I heard Lunardis are addicted to them." Kawan kept his gaze focused on his feet.

A muffled laugh escaped Rondai before he shook his head.

A moment of silence followed as if each waited for the other to talk until Jihave straightened his back, raised his head, and shouted, "Why did you summon us?" His voice echoed twice in the hall.

"No need to shout, my boy." The leader, Kalita paused, inspecting the candidates from afar before she continued. "You know that our world survived countless wars, three of which almost erased our existence, and because of that, our ancestors formed this city and the council present to keep the peace and govern with laws—"

"Stop your riddles Madame Old and answer my question," Jihave interrupted with his gaze locked on the dark-haired, blue-eyed, snow-skinned woman on the throne.

"Do I look old to you?" Kalita flexed her fingers repeatedly.

Jihave smirked. "You don't, but you do sound it."

Kalita's breathing grew louder, and her nostrils flared. "You are the Averetti, I assume. As usual, your words precede your thoughts."

"I—"

"Enough!" she shouted. "You are not here to debate my age." She paused and gazed toward the floor, tapping it repeatedly with her left foot. "The law states that every two hundred and fifty years, the Forbidden City Council must change its blood. That means a new ruler and three royal guards to carry the flame and lead this city's warriors."

"And those are to be us, I presume?" asked Jihave.

"Perhaps. Well?"

Jihave ignored Kalita and turned to the other candidates to ask, "Did any of you know about this?"

Rondai pretended not to hear the question and kept his gaze on the ruler. Only Evailen answered Jihave with her lips pursed into a fine line. "I didn't know..."

All three guards tapped the floor at the same time.

"All powers are forbidden within these walls, Delphian," Kalita said stressing each word but keeping her tone quiet.

Kawan moved his head in a slight nod indicating his apologies.

A cloud of silence hovered over the place. Rondai glanced sideways to witness the ghost of fear resting on Kawan's face. Evailen tried to fix the strip of hair that curtained her right eye, and Jihave struggled to stand still.

Kalita was the one to conquer the silence. "We will give you a task that will determine which of you will be the ruler of your group. The other three will become royal guards who must protect their leader and follow their orders. The task is—"

"Hold on, hold on," Jihave interrupted again. "At first you talk in riddles, and now you jump years ahead. Before telling us about the task, shouldn't we know more about the job you are offering so we can decide whether we want it?"

"Fine." Kalita sighed. "Your factions nominated the four of you to carry this tremendous honor, and—"

"Back to the riddles again. It feels like we're running in a circle." Jihave shook his head.

Kalita clenched her jaw. "I should have remembered that Averettis are a pain in the ass."

The three guards laughed, ushering some of the tension out of the hall.

"To make it easier for your simple mind," Kalita began, "you will replace me and the three guards you see around you. You will transcend beyond the boundaries of your factions to become a united front. The four of you—once appointed—will no longer be bound by your factions. Instead, you will look over the entire world as one, without favoring any single faction in particular. Your job will be to keep the peace at all costs. You will gain new powers, and the forty warriors you see here will be your soldiers."

Jihave didn't hesitate to verbalize his thoughts. "Now that's something I can get on board with. I'm ready to hear the task now."

"Finally, I satisfied your curiosity." Kalita sighed again. "Listen carefully then. We hid four artifacts in the outside world. Each within one of the four continents. Your task is to find them, but not together. You will search for them separately, and the one who returns carrying the highest number of artifacts shall be the new ruler."

Kawan cleared his throat. "Four contenders and four artifacts. What if each of us captures one?"

"Then, we shall give you a second and final task." Kalita narrowed her eyes, keeping Kawan in her field of vision.

Kawan heaved a heavy sigh. "If the second task is certain to be decisive, then why don't we start with that one?"

Kalita leaned forward on her throne. "We don't jump to conclusions and behave based on a what-if situation. First, you find the artifacts, and then we deal with the outcome."

She leaned back on the throne and relaxed. "Once the task begins, you are not to return until you have found all four artifacts. You will each have a device that will inform you when an artifact is no longer collectible because one of you have claimed it. You will also find within this device a map with a layout of the outside world and a small card on the back that you can use as currency. Is that clear?" Kalita formed her hands into loose fists.

The four candidates nodded in approval, their faces slightly tensed, hiding how they felt about visiting the outside world. Both Evailen and Jihave exhibited excitement over the chance to explore somewhere they have never seen, while the expressions of Rondai and Kawan showed concern over what was to come.

Kalita continued. "Each of you can choose three companions. Whoever you want from within your factions. You will have three nights to choose, and on the fourth sun, you are to return here to receive your devices." Kalita stood and waited until the warriors and the three guards nodded in respect before she left the hall.

The four candidates let out a breath of relief at the thought they could have companions they trusted to help them on their mission. But when they walked out of the city, they realized they were leaving with more questions than they had answers.

They knew only one thing. This would be the mission of their lives.

3

Evailen's over-thinking tormented her mind all the way back to her faction.

Lunar is the only place she ever experienced her entire life. Her eyes, like all Lunardis became used to the transparent energy field that surpassed her island, surrounding the entirety of lake Zuno. She strode off her lotus-shaped pod the moment she could step foot on the island.

Evailen liked to walk whenever her mind was heavy. However, before she could sink into her thoughts, the purple seed on the left side of her forehead blinked twice. She lifted her eyes and the air in front of her swirled like a micro-tornado before it took the shape of a person-like figure. First, the organs appeared colorless before the body took its final shape then colors cradled that piece of art. Within five seconds, the image was clear.

At five-feet-five-inches, the manifested woman stood an inch taller than Evailen. Her long blonde hair looked as smooth as a pure Arabian horse. She wasn't quite as slim as Evailen and had more curves. Her most notable feature, however, was her large nose that was out of proportion with the rest of her face, unlike Evailen who had tiny features that complimented each other. The woman's eyes were wide and green, and her skin was two shades paler than Evailen's.

She reflected a curious expression, moving her head from right to left then up and down like an ostrich while performing a circular dance around Evailen.

"What are you doing? You're embarrassing me," Evailen muttered to her closest friend who didn't stop her erratic movements and uttered nothing. "Cilia… *Cilia*… Cut it out!" Evailen's ears turned a little red.

"Okay, okay. So tell me, did they give you new powers? Did you receive an upgrade?" Cilia's nose wrinkled.

"Neither, nor." Evailen dipped her chin.

"Oh, keeping your answers short. That's so not like you. What are you hiding?"

"Don't you have somewhere to be?" Evailen crossed her arms against her chest.

"No way, you're even changing the subject! Okay, okay, I'll be at your place waiting for you."

Cilia's hologram vanished before Evailen could shape another word. She exhaled a sigh and continued her walk, ignoring the fact that her pod would take a few seconds to cover this fifty minutes of walking distance. A decision she revisited after realizing that everyone on the street eyed her. The change of heart came after she saw her full body reflected on a glass billboard that read, "A future in the making." That moment her head fell, followed by her short-black-curly hair.

She brushed the yellow seed on the top of her left arm, releasing a smaller seed that blossomed into a lotus flower before she sat inside and thought about her destination. At her house, the pod returned to its normal size and fell into Evailen's hand before she placed it inside her yellow seed.

Cilia opened the door before Evailen reached the handle, and launched herself toward her friend, locking her arms around a standing-still Evailen.

"Look at you. One success after another. So, tell me everything. Every. Little. Thing." Cilia's grin widened as she grabbed Evailen's arm and locked it with hers.

"Not now, I'm tired, and I want to sleep." Evailen dragged her feet around the house.

"What! No, no. Don't tell me you miss your video games more than you miss me."

"I was gone for one day, Cilia. I didn't miss anything. Please, I'm tired, and I need to regain my energy." Evailen freed her arm from Cilia's and carried her weight toward the stairs, ignoring her friend who stood frozen in the living room. Obviously, angry that her best friend was ignoring her, Cilia slammed the door on her way out.

In the privacy of her room, Evailen pressed her purple seed for a quick moment before she was able to pull out a smaller seed. She broke the small seed in half and stuck one on the black wall opposite her bed. While the wall turned into a screen, she pulled a joystick out of her nightstand and placed the second half in it. She watched a video of the planet Earth floating in space. When the planet stopped rotating, a menu appeared titled, "Return to Game." Using her joystick, she moved down a few options and chose "Select Your Era." On the following menu, she chose "Ancient Egypt" before clicking on one of the twelve avatars the game prompted her to choose from. She watched as her favorite in-game character went about her daily life.

Earth was one of few games made by Lantrix where players had little power over their avatars. Players had a limited number of options that enabled them to influence the lives of their avatars, but never fully control them. For that, players had to be smart and creative with their actions since the game didn't allow a do-over or save points even though the players could return to any point they wanted.

That day Evailen decided to do like most players and only watch her avatar explore the fantasy world of the game Earth. And as she watched, she allowed her thoughts to fall back into her mind.

Flashes of the Forbidden City took over her brain scrambling her thoughts until she heard two knocks on the door.

"Come in," she said, keeping her voice quiet.

Her father smiled as he walked in. "Is it true? You will be one of the royal guards?"

"You knew!" She tilted her head and paused. "Why didn't you tell me?"

"I thought you knew. It's time for new guards. Everyone knows that."

"Well, not me, apparently. I thought they wanted to talk to me about the corruption I found in Lantrix." She turned the game off and placed her joystick on the bed.

"Lantrix isn't important now." He moved closer to her and gently rubbed her head. "Were you nervous when you found out?"

"I wasn't at first, but now I am. Am I crazy, Dad?" She tilted her head and looked up at her father.

Her father laughed, and his brown eyes softened, reflecting the redness in them partially hidden by his blond hair. He sat on the bed next to his daughter, pushed a lock of her hair behind her ear to uncover her blue eyes, and asked her to tell him exactly what happened at the Forbidden City.

"But all of that didn't even bother me. The one thing I can't escape is how the other three looked. They appeared experienced and knowledgeable. Aware of everything surrounding them and as if they were calculating their words and movements. Even the guy who kept hammering the ruler with questions like a child didn't show the slightest intimidation. I, on the other hand, was just going with the flow and trying hard to appear natural, but I fear that I came across as naive and out of place." Evailen cradled her stomach with her hands when her stress turned into physical pain.

"You are young, my dear, but you are far from inexperienced. You follow what you want, and nothing persuades you off your path. Don't worry about the others, just focus on the task. You need to pick your team carefully. Choose those who will compliment you. All you can do is your best, and the rest will unveil itself as you go." Evailen's father held her hand and gently pressed on it.

"I already know who I will choose. I knew the moment they said there will be a journey that I would need to have a team and who I wanted on it."

"Great. Then, you have nothing to worry about. But don't waste time. Go speak to your choices, so they have time to prepare themselves, and let me know when you return home because tonight we will have your favorite meal." He planted a kiss on her forehead before he left the room.

Evailen's companions were happy to hear about going to the outside world on an authorized mission. To them, that world was the biggest enigma of their existence. There were legends about people who succeeded in going there and returning undetected, but their stories were just that, legends. After all, it was prohibited to go out of the continent of Mastoperia. It was also the only crime punishable by death.

4

"He is here. Open the gate," shouted the guard atop a rock wall before the gate scraped against the ground and sent hairs prickling on the backs of the two guards turning the wheel that pulled the gate open.

One would imagine that a city full of people who possess magic would be technologically advanced. At least, in the worst-case scenario, there would be many life hacks, but Kala was far from that. In fact, that city was more ancient than the word describing it. Everywhere were houses made of mud and hardened sand. Wooden merchant posts spread around the streets, and the signs of hard labor were visible on its inhabitants' faces. Magic was their point of pride, yet it was nowhere to be seen.

Rondai's eyes didn't once leave his feet as he roamed the sandy streets. His destination was the red temple—the holy ground where the city leaders spend the rest of their lives once appointed on the small council.

Two guards waited at the entrance. Their crossed spears moved to make way for the young man to enter. Twelve pillars shaped after ancient, powerful magic users paved the way to the temple's keep. Holy water filled the temple ground, leaving only a tiny passage. In the hall of the council, the light seemed to be artificial, but without any origin. Images of past Kalanian battles covered the stonewall, while the faction's sigil covered the entire floor of the round room.

Six council members stood in the middle of the hall, draped in colorful wide linen garments, scarfed and masked with nothing exposed but their eyes. They stood in identical poses with their legs and spine as straight as the stone walls behind them, and both arms crossed behind their backs.

"Were you called for the reason we expected?" asked a man with an elderly voice.

"Yes I was, but first I have a question." Rondai adjusted his stance to stand straight.

"What is it? Fear nothing, my child." The elder signaled him to move closer.

"The Forbidden Warriors said you nominated me which confuses me. I thought I heard you say they asked for me. Did my memory deceive me?"

"No, it didn't. Neither party is wrong," replied the elder. "The Forbidden Warriors asked for a nomination, so we asked the gatekeepers for guidance, and the answer was your name."

"Now, what did they ask of you?" questioned a woman who stood at the far right.

"They asked me to gather a team of three members who will go with me to the outside world on a task that will determine which of us will be the ruler and which will be the royal guards." Rondai paused and gazed at the details of his faction's symbol on the floor. "We have to collect four artifacts they have scattered across the world. Whoever captures more than the rest will become the leader."

The woman turned her head toward the elder. "That seems odd and different from all previous tasks. They have never sent a candidate outside Mastoperia before."

The elder turned to her. "It doesn't matter. He received a task, and he must complete it." To Rondai, he said, "We will choose the three members who will accompany you. Once the task begins, send each of them to a different location. This way, you can maximize your chances of becoming the ruler. Remember, it is imperative you succeed." The elder inhaled a heavy breath. "How long before you are to return?"

"Three days." Rondai shifted his feet.

"Then go to prepare. Return here before you leave on your journey back, and you will find your companions ready."

Rondai returned to his home, a one-room hut with no visible personal items except for a notebook that sat on an unstable bamboo desk and a candle. He sat on his bed and glanced around his room as if he were seeing it for the first time.

He acknowledged to himself that he was afraid of what was to come, but the thought that took over his mind was how he loved his simple room even with its tiny details. He looked at his coffee-scented candle and wondered how it remained lit for years, a question he asked himself every time he returned to his room after a mission. As usual, he raised his snub nose and inhaled the smell of coffee, then quickly discarded the thought, fearing he would jinx the candle and would no longer be able to enjoy its peaceful calming smell.

He used his thumb to trace an image of the number one around his heart to unlock the first gate as first gate magic gives him the power to control solid man-made objects. His blood rushed through his veins, signaling that the gate was now open. He then reached out toward his notebook, forcing it to fly directly to him. He held the notebook in his left hand and used the thumb of the other to again trace the number one around his heart, sealing the gate.

For the next thirty minutes, Rondai read before he could finally unlock another gate as different gates couldn't be opened within a thirty-minute interval. He used the same hand gesture again, only this time he traced the number three in the same place as the third gate allows him to manifest solid objects out of nothing.

He flipped to an empty page in his notebook and rested it on his legs. He then locked his arms behind his head and lay down before closing his almond-shaped gunmetal eyes. He imagined a musical beat playing in his mind and thought of words that rhymed with the melody. The words appeared on the notebook as he thought of them.

Too many laws,

Don't be stepping on their toes,

Don't go running to the gods,

Who no one really knows.

If you question your existence,

Is this really a resistance?

Can you tell me who I am?

Or will you always keep your distance?

I have always—

Three knocks sounded on the door interrupting his rhythm, and he closed the notebook.

"Who is it?" Rondai shouted, adjusting his position to sit up straight.

"It's Yasmina," She shouted in reply, although her voice reached Rondai on the other side of the door sounding quiet and calm.

"It's open, come in."

Yasmina hurried in, moving directly to the edge of Rondai's bed, a girl in her early twenties with dark hair woven into a braid down the middle of her exposed back. A simple white dress covered her dark skin that almost matched Rondai's. At five feet she stood only as tall as Rondai's shoulders. She had a fit body, small nose and lips, and low, thin brows that made her forehead appear almost as wide as Rondai's.

Yasmina held the edge of the bed frame with her hand, her face reflecting her inability to decide whether to sit or stand. "I heard you returned today, and I wanted to check on you."

"Thank you. I'm fine." Rondai leaned his head back.

"The council told me I will accompany you on a journey." Her grin widened.

"Okay." He focused his gaze on the ceiling.

Yasmina half sat next to him, keeping one leg on the floor. "I'm excited about spending more time with you."

"We will split up as soon as the task begins for optimum results." Rondai kept his expression neutral.

"Oh…okay. Do you want to train together?" She leaned back a little keeping her feet on the ground.

"My level is higher than yours. I will concentrate on my energy field, and I have to do that alone."

Rondai was one of the few gate five masters, which gave him the power to manifest and manipulate his inner aura at will. Yasmina had only mastered up to the fourth gate, which allowed her to manifest the elements of nature like earth and water with complete control over her creations.

"Okay, I will leave you to it then." Yasmina bit her inner lips and blinked back a tear in her round black eyes.

Rondai traced a five with his hand as she left and released a shield of invisible energy that surrounded his toned body, making his bald head appear shiny.

Having lost his train of thought, he could no longer add lyrics to his new song, so he switched to training mode to enlarge his aura as much as possible before his mission began.

5

"How did it feel?"

Jihave's grin widened. "My dear Salvanra, it was awesome yet disappointing. First, the wind was silent. The Forbidden Warriors have a giant palace with detailing that sucks the time out of anyone's life. Everyone dressed as if they will live forever, and the smell of Anarchy filled the air. But worst of all, there wasn't a single tree in sight." Jihave stepped off his tiger—a black beast with violet stripes and multi-colored eyes.

"It sounds awful. What was so awesome about it?" Salvanra locked her hazel eyes with the tiger matching her height of five-feet-two-inches before petting him.

"What's awesome?" he repeated. Grabbing her by the shoulders, he turned her to face him. "What's awesome is that we will finally realize our dream! The four of us will go on a journey to the continent beyond, armed with the Royals' blessing."

Salvanra asked Jihave two times if he was joking, and he assured her he wasn't. She tackled the air twice before jumping into his arms. She ruffled his long, straight silver hair with her hand and kissed both his brown cheeks and neck repeatedly before their lips passionately joined one another.

"Now we need to tell the brothers the great news," Jihave whispered into her tiny ears and tucked one of her braids behind it.

Salvanra untied the rest of her thick black braids before she placed herself on Jihave's tiger. She spread her arms, allowing the wind to flirt with her bronze skin as they rode past the gigantic trees of the Fantastic Forest. Flowers and plants seemed to follow them as they raced through like sunflowers tracking the sun.

They stopped at a house that occupied the space between two large trees. The moment the two of them stepped to the ground, the tiger jumped into Jihave's body, leaving a tiger-shaped tattoo covering his entire back. The Averettis power lay in their ability to capture and control Majestic animals that made their home in the Fantastic Forest. The captured Majestics lived the rest of their lives as a piece of art on their captor's body.

They climbed into a house made of boring planks of wood. Light could easily pass through the large gaps between that left the interior exposed.

Salvanra and Jihave banged their fists on the door while chuckling until they realized the door was open.

"Good, you are here. Let's eat together then," said Bofrat, who stood at six feet tall yet was two inches shorter than Jihave. Even though Bofrat was skinnier than his friend who had a built body, he lacked nothing in muscles as he stood slightly wider than Salvanra's athletic body. His eyes were dark brown like the original color of his hair which fell short between two long red braids.

Salvanra performed her famous excited-dance, a two-feet-at-once jump in the air. "Where is your brother? We have awesome news for you."

Bofrat mocked her by imitating her move. "He is away, trying to catch the inked elephant."

"That's not good." Jihave's eyebrows positioned themselves in a reversed V shape. "It could take him months before he returns. He has to be back before the next sun dies."

Jihave turned to face Salvanra who nodded before a golden-feathered eagle flew out of her top chest tattoo. She whispered a message to be delivered to Maringrad before the eagle vanished, scratching her chest afterward and adjusting her bra, the only thing covering the top of her body which matched her blue shorts.

Jihave cracked his neck as he moved toward the exit. "Let me know as soon he gets the message. I have to go speak to the elders now."

Jihave preferred running over riding his Majestics for transportation when he was in the Fantastic Forest because it allowed him to better experience his land. He enjoyed feeling the grass beneath his bare feet, the wind challenging his muscles and the smell of many life forms.

Two hours later, he arrived at the elders' rock, a rock formation that lay next to a lake so clear it appeared as if there were no water.

He poked one of his fingers and placed a drop of his blood on a tablet centering the formation. Nine members immediately appeared on the nine rocks surrounding him. Men and women covered only in shorts. Jihave glanced at them each, in turn, wishing he knew which Majestic gave them the power of teleportation so he could capture it himself. But he had asked many times, and they always refused to tell him.

"How can we help you?" Jihave's father inspected his son's Majestic tattoos from afar to see if he had added more to his collection.

"I'm going to the continent beyond with three of our members on a task to—"

"Stop right there," ordered one woman as she extended her palm in front of her. "We named you, but whatever comes next is up to you, and you alone."

Jihave spoke in a low and steady pitched voice. "I wanted to inform you that I plan to pursue the mission, but I shall also hunt for Afakan, and if my hunt denies me the leadership, so be it."

His father grinned. "Your actions are your own." The other eight elders disappeared before Jihave's father finished his sentence. "Good luck, my son," he said before he too vanished.

Jihave leaned toward the lake for a sip of water when Salvanra's eagle flew out of the ground and passed through his body. Jihave received the message; Maringrad was on his way back. He ran two more hours to return to the brothers and his partner. He thought about the moment he would capture Afakan and how the beast's tattoo would look on his body.

When he arrived at the house, the four gathered around a feast, eating, laughing, and drinking. The task occupied no space in their minds, only excitement for exploring uncharted territory. When night fell, they all headed out to a party at the Free Spirit Bar, a place frequented by music lovers. It sat inside a cave filled with Arachnocampa Luminosa—worms that glow blue in the dark, providing a magical atmosphere. At the center of the bar, lay a stage that housed different musical instruments made of wood and animal skins. Anyone could mount that stage to play their own music.

The four ordered one drink after another. One-eyed crocodile's milk is the strongest alcoholic drink they know, yet it takes at least three pints for a lightheaded Averetti to start feeling its effect.

Halfway into the night, the music went quiet, and the chatter became dominant. Jihave mounted the stage and drummed solo. He felt he was composing the notes of a lifetime.

"Get off the stage, get off the stage," someone shouted before the crowd gradually joined in, and the drunken player heard their voices.

"One last beat," Jihave shouted and continued randomly tapping with his drumsticks.

"No," the crowd responded in a unified voice.

"It's your loss." He cracked a pitched laugh, threw the drumsticks on the ground, and left the stage.

"Was I that bad?" he asked Salvanra.

"Not at all, my love. It's just that we are an ungrateful group that doesn't know how to appreciate your epic musical ear." She couldn't contain her loud laughter.

"Ouch." Jihave put his hands atop his heart and planted a quick kiss on her lips.

"So, what now?" Maringrad placed his arms on both of their shoulders. He had to lift one arm high to reach Jihave's while the other rested perfectly level on Salvanra's. Like his brother Bofrat, Maringrad had light brown skin and dark brown eyes. He had woven his long hair into complicated interconnecting braids that he painted green, blue, and red. He had strong, developed muscles, although his body appeared a little chubby.

Jihave almost lost his balance because of the added weight of his friend's arm, so he pushed him away. "Tonight, we dance. Tomorrow we rest, and after, we embark on the journey of our lives!" he shouted.

They all raised their glasses to that.

Near the end of the night, Jihave mounted the center stage one more time and addressed the crowd.

"Averett is the proud home of many Majestics. Nine of which are so rare that catching one makes you an elder, but one…" he continued, pausing as he tried to restore his balance, "one is a legend, only mentioned in our history but never seen. I believe the beast lives still, but in the continent beyond. It's my life's dream to tame him, and I finally have the chance. Woohoo!"

Jihave gathered all his focus to counter his unbalanced mind and blurry vision. He took one-step off the stage before he fell forward, landing on the ground face first, and losing consciousness.

6

Delphia is a city with glass skyscrapers and empty well-built streets that no one used. Upon entering the city, one had to take an elevator to the rooftop of the first tower. The building tops were where everything happened.

A sense of peace took over Kawan the moment he returned to his city of origin until he received a message on his smart wristwatch asking him to go directly to the Skeptic Room to meet the leadership. He didn't feel he was ready for a hearing, but he couldn't refuse.

At the main hall of the University of Delphia, he took a minute to gather his thoughts before one of the thousand quotes decorating the walls grabbed his attention.

"Sometimes, the world chooses you to carry its weight, so cry a lot and scream at the void because, from that moment forward, you will be alone." -Sikan Ron.

Kawan closed his hooded brown eyes and took a deep breath before moving toward the Skeptic door. He paused before he entered to fix his white suit and brown collar. He stretched his legs, hoping his skinny body would help him appear taller than his true height of five-feet-two-inches. Kawan fixed his short, smooth blue hair and gathered his courage before he moved inside.

Inside the Skeptic Room, two hundred and fifty scientists were present, surrounding him behind big round desks. They asked him about every little detail he witnessed while in the Forbidden City. Some questions were even repetitive and only purposed to catch different angles of what really happened. Once they finished their analysis, they told Kawan they would prepare fifteen suitable candidates for him to choose from for his companions.

After hours of questioning and analysis, Kawan was mentally exhausted. It was time to go home for a much-needed rest. He went out of the main door onto the roof. After taking a deep breath to cleanse himself of stress, he felt a need to grab the ledge. He believed his fatigue led him there to rest, but his mind disagreed. He looked down toward the empty streets and wondered. *Why did our first builders pave such beautiful streets? They must have always known we would end up using the rooftops to free-run everywhere. Why else would they build all entrances and exits through the roofs? So, why then did they waste resources on roads?*

He noticed a ladder at the far side of the building. As he approached it, the sign next to it became clearer. It read, "Use only if there is a fire." His recent journey revealed that there is a lot he didn't yet understand, and for the first time, Kawan wanted to experience the streets of his own city.

He heard a tapping sound, and as he moved closer to the ground that sound became louder, the rhythm clearer. It was music at a high volume. He had never listened to music that loud before—the Delphian leadership had banned it because of potential ear damage.

His mind said this was a mistake; he should go back up to the world he knows, but his feet followed the source.

They led him to a nearby park. Many were present, dressed in so many colors, not only white as the law dictated. Some were dancing, couples kissing, people smoking and others drinking.

"Hello there. Welcome to the underworld. Do you want something to drink?"

Kawan stared at the man who approached him. The first thing that grabbed his attention was the stranger's red shorts and painted tank top. They didn't match one another, yet felt refreshing to his eyes.

"You are obviously a first-timer." The stranger took a loud sip of his beverage, eyeing Kawan through the bottom of the glass. "I know it's a lot to take in at once, so let me give you a tour." The man signaled Kawan with his head to follow him. Kawan didn't really want to, but his body moved as if on autopilot.

"My name is Gabrin. Don't worry, I know first-timers like you don't know what to expect when they come down. Up there, you follow rules and routine. They tell you that life is about academics and using your power for the greater good. You learn how to see further into the future and increase your number of timeline possibilities. Then when the time comes, they will match you with a suitable partner." Gabrin paused to take another sip. "Your only escape of the day is when you free-run over the rooftops, but even that loses its magic after a while, and you get bored. Then, one day you stand at the edge of a building, wondering why did our predecessors build those streets if we would never use them? So, you come down and *voila*. You are talking to me." Gabrin stopped as his grin occupied the maximum space of his face before he looked at the puzzled, silent Kawan.

"Huh." Gabrin perked up, straightening his posture. "You are the first person to not wonder about how I knew all of this." He shook his head. "There goes my speech about how I was once like you and how I began all of this."

He started walking again. "Anyway, right here is the drinking station. One drink will cost you one silver coin but don't worry, your mind will float after two sips. It numbs your ability to see the future and allows you to relax for once. Over there is the smoking station. Highly addictive and comes in different power levels. Some people say the strongest types can make you see a future that isn't even your own, but who knows. The cost will vary between two pills of anxiety to a whole pack, depending on what you want. Then you will need to roll the product in a fresh tree leave to smoke it."

Kawan remained silent, listening, and looking at everything at once, taking it all in.

Gabrin stopped in front of the last stand. "Those are the seeds of insanity. I don't recommend them as they could lead to death if misused, but in our community, you have the right to try whatever you want. However, it will cost you a green lotus. If you could find any." Gabrin bowed with one arm behind his back like an actor who just finished his best performance.

Kawan ignored Gabrin's theatrical move and turned to absorb the market scenery more fully. He closed his eyes and extended his nose, seeking the mixture of smells surrounding him. He focused to feel the wind pressing on his sand-colored skin.

He opened his eyes and faced Gabrin once again. "Where do you get all of this?"

"So you do speak. I was wondering if you could." Gabrin smiled. "It's simple really. We trade with other factions. The higher-ups of all factions pretend to hate each other, but they trade among themselves in secrecy. We only took the idea and improved it. Each faction has secret groups like us. Well… except Averettis. They can do whatever the hell they want." Gabrin cracked a laugh. "Anyway, these little groups trade with each other, hence the prices. Averettis love silver coins. It helps them control their pets or whatever. We provide the silver in return for their crocodile milk. Kalangous make the best smokes, and they trade it for our anxiety pills. I heard it eases their pain after using magic. Lunardis are interested in the green Lotus, and only we can provide it since it grows nowhere else. That's how it all works. We are the best at it too. Since we can see the future, we can see the potential traps and find the safest routes, so everyone loves to deal with us."

Gabrin tilted his head with a small grin. "So what do you think? Did I blow your mind yet?"

"Does the smoking work?" Kawan hesitated before continuing. "You know, makes you see other's future, instead of only your own?"

"Whoa, bro. That's the only thing you think about after all I told you?" Gabrin raised his eyebrows.

Kawan pinched the skin at his throat. "Can you answer my question, please?"

"Fine." Gabrin blinked slowly. "I experienced none of that myself, but a few have claimed it to be true. I wouldn't recommend that you start with—"

Kawan left him mid-sentence to go back to his home and grab his stack of anxiety pills. He was no longer feeling tired.

7

For the Forbidden City, the day the candidates returned was nothing out of the ordinary. The wind still afraid to pass through the gates, no birds to sing and ghostly weather embracing the sun. The four nominees returned to the city with their companions, all feeling the tension dance around them as they passed through the giant ancient pillars paving the way from the city gate into the main hall of the palace one team after another.

The city was unguarded, yet mysteriously no one had the desire to explore it further. Evailen and her companions were the last to arrive amidst glares of frustration from those who waited.

Shortly after, the forty warriors strode in and took their seats before the Forbidden leader, her shadow following and seeming to appear out of nowhere.

Jihave said aloud although he appeared to be speaking only to himself, "Perhaps they were always here."

Still, the four teams could only recognize the leader, Kalita, as the shadow behind her remained mysterious. The three royal guards were the last to join them, a scene that overwhelmed the companions who stood inside the Forbidden City for the first time in their lives, which prompted them to converse with one another in hushed tones.

The leader broke their chatter. "Now that everyone is present, I will explain the competition one more time. Your mission is to retrieve four artifacts we have scattered around the four continents at the edge of the ocean. Your task will be to locate and recover them. Each of the four candidates will now receive an electronic map that has the complete outline of the outside world. It also has the details of the main cities, so as to help you navigate more easily. There is also a card that you can pull out from the side, which you can use as a method of payment if needed." Kalita paused while the guards handed out the maps.

"On the back of the maps, you will find the names of the artifacts you will look for. By clicking on the name, you will see what the corresponding artifact looks like."

Kalita paused again while the candidates inspected their new gadgets. "This is the only clue we will give you. How you locate and acquire the pieces is entirely up to you. Once one of you collects an artifact, it will disappear from the list, and you can only return home when all four have been gathered." Kalita allowed room for questions, but silence prevailed.

"Six of the Forbidden warriors will take you to the drop point using our private ship." Kalita paused again in case there were any questions to answer, but no one spoke. She wasn't sure if they were focused or stunned, so she shrugged and continued. "Once you step off the ship in the continent beyond the ocean and until one of you finds the last artifact, all of Mastoperia's laws are voided. We will enforce only one rule, and that is no stealing from one another. If the artifact disappears from the list, you can no longer claim that artifact, and fighting for it will result in the penalty of death."

Evailen's eyes widened, and her heart raced. "Does this mean we can fight for it *before* anyone claims it?"

"Yes, you can," Kalita answered. "If two teams meet in front of an artifact, then they may settle who claims it whichever way they see fit, but even if a fight breaks and in the middle of the fight someone claims the artifact, then the fight can no longer continue for it. If the other team continues to fight, they can't reclaim the piece even if they win the fight."

Cilia whispered in Evailen's ear, "I'm confused."

Takara, the royal guard who stood nearby grinned. "You are smart, Cilia. I'm sure you can figure it out."

Kalita continued. "This is all you need to know. Since you didn't take advantage of my earlier pauses, I won't answer questions about the mission now, nor will I repeat what I have said. And yes, those last words were for you Averetti."

Jihave squinted at her before she continued. "Tell me your companions' names. I want to know who they are."

Jihave was the first to speak after her snarky comment boiled his blood. "I will be accompanied by Salvanra of the enchanted tribe, and Maringrad and Bofrat of the bloom tribe. Together we will conquer the world."

Everyone laughed at how naive Jihave sounded, but he didn't seem bothered as his companions needed no further introduction. Both tribes were famous within Mastoperia as the only two tribes that fought the Kalangous council and lived to tell the tale.

Rondai felt heat rise in his face when he heard the names. He took a deep breath and faked a half-smile. "My assistants will be Yasmina, Rolakan, and Ryn." He paused for a second, then asked, "Do I need to elaborate?"

"No need, show off." Jihave gritted his teeth while he stared at an unshaken Rondai.

Rondai knew his message made it through. All Kalangous who possess names starting with the letter 'R' carry the purest blood and the strongest gate-magic, and the truth remained that both tribes survived their battles because there was no pureblood present to change that fact.

Kawan smelled tension in the air as he followed their unbroken stare with one another. He knew what the names represented, but his thoughts were elsewhere. He wanted to seize the chance and say what was on his mind. "My comrades will be Alinda, Terqwan, and Malani. However, we all know that—"

"Enough!" Kalita shouted. "You can't discuss further than that, not before we announce it."

Kawan sighed loudly as he realized that he wouldn't have a chance to warn the others about what was coming.

It was time for Evailen to speak and introduce her companions, but she stood silent with her eyes focused on the ground. She believed everyone had something to state about whom they chose except for her, causing her to feel out of place. Words remained caged within her thin lips until Cilia gave her a little nudge.

"My companions are Cilia, Enyo, and Naradia. They all come from Lunar, I guess." She rubbed her fingers together as she feared that her presentation was the weakest of all. She thought that even the Delphian who said nothing but names appeared to have more power in his words. She even noticed how the leader appeared to fear what she didn't give him a chance to say.

Evailen's fall into the cloud of doubt blinded her from seeing how everyone inspected her and her companions, including Rondai who portrayed a cold, powerful image.

The leader straightened her back. "Now that I know your names, there is one last thing you need to know. The companions you chose won't be part of your own team. Instead, we will decide your team formation through a draft."

Confusion haunted the faces of both the candidates and their companions. Only the Delphians remained calm wearing their smirking masks. Whispers maneuvered between the groups' lips as they revisited their tactics. Kalangous appeared to be surviving a sandstorm. Averettis were calmer but huddled together to negotiate strategies, while the Lunardis began to say their goodbyes to each other as if the end of the world was upon them, grabbing everyone's attention.

At that moment, Rondai, and Jihave realized that even though they would have to revisit their plans, this was the best thing that could have happened to them. Now every team could have a Lunardis in it, and it was in their best interest to keep those four separated because everyone knew what no Lunardis did. Lunardis portrayed self-doubt, fear, and even weakness, but when challenged, they are the toughest and most brutal.

8

When the sun centered the sky, the golden dome above the candidates shined like a mini star. The warmth of the new light allowed the candidates and their companions to calm down and focus their eyes on the Forbidden City leader in front of them. It was time for them to know how the Forbidden Warriors would decide the new team formation. They all stood in silence, anticipating what would happen next.

Shortly after, the air between them and the warriors swirled into a tiny tornado before it transformed into a solid board. Inside the board, three clickable square buttons appeared horizontally in three shades of black. Then, three other round vertical buttons appeared; colored red, yellow, and blue from top to bottom.

Yasmina took a step forward, pointed at the board, and shouted, "What's the meaning of this?"

Both Rondai and Jihave moved to her side. The first crossed his arms together while the latter shook his head.

The first and second of the royal guards tapped the ground with their relics.

"Order!" shouted the third guard.

Jihave's chest thrust out. "How do you expect us to remain calm when you are basing your method of choice on a technology that comes directly from Lunar."

Rondai planted his legs wide and bared his teeth as he quickly agreed with Jihave. "How do we know they didn't tamper with the technology?" He locked eyes with the leader. "I knew you would favor your original faction, but I thought you would be smarter than to use a device they built. At least make us think this will be fair."

Kalita tensed her fingers into claws as she stared back into Rondai's eyes before she took a deep breath and closed her own for a second. "This isn't the behavior I expected from those we consider the best of their factions, but I will let it slide considering you are young and perhaps inexperienced." She stressed on every word. "My predecessor made this device long before I became the leader. It does use Lunar technology to manifest, but there's more to it than that. We all know that the future is not set in stone and can change according to our choices. Since Delphians are the masters of choices and can bend the future at will, we couldn't allow them to use their abilities and arrange their decisions to manipulate the outcome of the draft. Therefore, the device will register the emotional choices you will make rather than what you think. The colors of the buttons you see have the same shades Averettis use to know their Majestics emotions. They will trigger certain feelings within you as you click on each button. Finally, what you don't see but Kalangous should be able to feel by now, is that there is a magic field around the device. Once any of you steps in it, nothing will matter except for the choices you make."

Jihave turned and faced Rondai. "Is it true? Can you feel it?"

"It just appeared, but yes, I can feel it now."

Jihave scratched the back of his head. "I confirm what she has said about the colors too." He moved his gaze from one candidate to the other and then to each of the companions. "But that doesn't mean we should trust them," he added, raising his voice.

Evailen scratched her elbow as she muttered, "It doesn't matter anyway. It's not like we can tell them what to do."

Rondai rubbed the back of his neck and kept his head down as he tried to sneak a look at the third royal guard, Radaman and the ten Forbidden Warriors who represent his faction. He clutched his hand when he saw that none of them moved a muscle. No one had used gate magic since entering the hall, and that confused him even more. It was the first time he saw magic operating on its own without a master manipulating it.

He looked at Yasmina and saw how she quietly tapped her foot as she gazed back at him. He understood that she felt the same way about the device, but her tapping was also a secret message to him. His fear was starting to appear obvious to those surrounding him, and he couldn't afford to show weakness. He nodded before he straightened his back and forced a smirk on his face.

Kawan's hands fluttered, and his skin flushed. He looked at the warriors and their leader behind them, and his heart raced. He knew that even though the council had few warriors in their ranks, everyone feared them. They successfully ended every war that broke down among the factions in the past two centuries, but he didn't want to believe they had this kind of power.

He saw the device for what it really was, a way to rip Delphians of their powers entirely. Delphians were neither the strongest fighters nor the smartest. Their power lies in being able to know the next move of their opponent and adjusting their decisions accordingly. If someone could take that away from them, they would be no more than ordinary people with a target painted on their backs.

He wiped away his uncontrollable sweat after he realized that although he knew the outcome of the draft, his actions and decisions could never change it.

He watched the Delphians surrounding him as they stood still, their faces vacant of expression. *Perhaps they didn't process what the device could do*, he thought. He then looked at the others and wondered if this was how they lived their lives, fearing what was to come.

Tears were about to escape his eyes, but he swam to his favorite place in his mind and screamed there instead. No one could see it, at least.

Jihave carried a smirk on his face. He believed he had figured it all out. He was familiar with the colors and the emotions they represented. When a captured Majestic missed the wilderness, its skin changed color. Through those colors, Averettis could decide their strategy to make sure the Majestic would conform to their orders and wouldn't escape captivity. He thought, with his knowledge of those colors, he could come up with a strategy that would allow him to manipulate the choices he makes so he could ensure that his faction brothers would fall within his group, but as he immersed himself in self-confidence, he neglected two parts. First, the magic field would have some kind of power over him, and second, he didn't really know what choices the colors corresponded to.

Evailen formed her hands into a steeple as her brows furrowed. Her blue seed, on the right side of her forehead, blinked as thoughts flooded her mind. She analyzed every word and saw why the leader called it a draft and not a lottery. There was nothing random about the choices, and when the random factor disappeared, then all that remained was a problem. Although she did believe she could solve it.

She theorized different systems and possible solutions, but in the end, she was more baffled because no matter how hard she tried, she couldn't factor magic into her equations. For her, it was the biggest mystery of all, and she was unable to come up with a solid strategy free of potential error.

The leader continued. "I want only the four candidates to step forward. When you hear your name, step into the magic field and click each of the three dark buttons in whichever order you see fit. Then wait for a minute before you click the other three buttons in whatever order you like."

The four stepped forward without saying a word and waited to hear their names. The mission was about to begin.

9

Kawan was the first to hear his name. The voice was deep and clear, and at first, he thought it was only in his head. His heartbeats increased with each step he took toward the device, and his feet became heavier and harder to control.

The moment he stepped inside the magic field, all his thoughts and confusion were no longer relevant. He forgot about the task and all that occupied his mind. All the tension in his body disappeared, and the worries that just before filled his brain were entirely absent. What took over him was a wave of emotions he didn't even know existed. Initially, he was afraid of Rondai, then a little troubled by all the Averettis, and finally he felt compassion toward Evailen. Each time an emotion struck him, he mindlessly clicked one of the three buttons. When he finished clicking the buttons, these emotions disappeared for a moment, leaving him standing as an empty shell until another emotional wave came over him. Only this time, he was ranking his companions.

He didn't know them well since he chose them out of the list the University of Delphia provided him. He based his decisions mainly on their life achievements, yet he realized at that moment that he had different emotions now. He worried about Alinda, felt a warmth toward Terqwan, and indifference when it came to Malani. After he mindlessly clicked the corresponding buttons again, he stepped away from the device like a robot that had finished its task and was returning to its charging base.

The moment he cleared away from the magic field, all his thoughts rushed back into his mind and his choices and feelings at the same time. Understanding how the machine worked frightened him even more. He knew it would probably work the same on the others as well, but that didn't make him feel better. In fact, that had him feeling worse and caused more questions to invade his mind, but as his free will returned to him, so did his power to predict the future and he remembered what he had seen the first time he entered the hall of the Forbidden City.

At that moment, the power of that little device seemed unimportant compared to what was to come.

The second to hear her name was Evailen. She moved toward the device and made her choices based on her feelings like Kawan before her, followed by both Jihave and Rondai. The four realized that all they did was categorize how they felt about the other factions and their own companions. They understood that this would be the deciding factor, and even though they didn't know how their categorization would affect the results, they understood deep down that; it was a fair process and that none of them could have been able to manipulate the outcome.

Once the machine registered their feelings, the buttons disappeared, and four lists appeared on the board. The names of each of the four candidates came first on each list, followed by their new teammates. As soon as the four saw the names below their own, the picture became complete. The machine placed their most trusted companion with their most feared opponent. The companion that alarmed them was placed with their least threatening opponent, and the third in the remaining group.

No one knew how each had ranked his opponents or companions. Therefore, there was no way to tell who feared them and who trusted them. The four candidates nodded at each other as they agreed implicitly that this was fair since it allowed all teams to have a member from each of the four factions.

Except for Kawan who stood in the back with his arms crossed. He believed he had the weakest of the bunch as he knew that everyone found his power non-threatening. However, it didn't matter how any of them felt about themselves or their new companions; it was time for them to cast their differences aside and figure out a way to work with one another.

Evailen joined her new companions with a smile on her face. Her eyes sparkled when she thought about the journey. Her grin widened as she realized that this mission would allow her to check many items off her bucket list as she would be able to see the mysterious world outside Mastoperia and learn about the other factions from her new team members at the same time.

Her companions, however, didn't share her vision. Bofrat's eyes glowed as he realized that the separation from his faction meant that capturing the Majestic Afakan was no longer a team effort, but a competition. He looked at Evailen and smiled but said nothing.

Yasmina had her arms crossed in front of her chest and lowered her head. Her mission was to support Rondai, not help a stranger from an enemy faction. She ignored Evailen entirely and focused on tapping the floor with her toes.

Malani fidgeted with his key chain behind his back. He was twenty-one, five-feet-six-inches with a military hair cut that matched the color of his long black eyes, and his muscles bulged out of his tight white shirt. He rocked his beige-colored shoulders left and right as if he was in his own world. He had placed himself where he stood long before the new team formations appeared as he knew this was where they would gather.

Rondai's eyebrows drew together as he inspected his new companions, approaching them with slow, calculated steps, giving himself the time to analyze them. He believed that on top of coming up with a new plan to implement, he needed to be wary of his new companions.

His first observation was how Salvanra stood too close to Jihave prior to the draft, and for that alone, he trusted her the least.

Terqwan locked eyes with Rondai when he noticed the candidate checking him out. They both uttered nothing, but a simple nod from Terqwan calmed Rondai who unlocked his crossed arms and let them fall next to his body.

Enyo started to hum quietly as his red seed above his heart blinked rapidly. He ignored Rondai's glare and focused on his chant. Rondai couldn't help but place Enyo in the threatening pile along with Salvanra. He was a Lunardis, and that was more than enough for Rondai to dislike him.

"There is one last thing for you to know," the leader announced, interrupting their gatherings. "The world you are about to see is different from ours. Those who live there don't have our powers, but that doesn't make them any less dangerous. They can be cruel and savage beyond your expectations. We ban traveling to their world not to keep them safe from us, but to protect ourselves from their monstrous nature. Be careful of showing your powers in public because if they capture you, we won't send rescue."

The leader paused. "The guards will now take you to the port. Good luck to you all and be safe."

10

The following morning, the group arrived at the ocean's shore. They had passed through hidden tunnels that lived under the massive mountains enveloping the entire continent of Mastoperia. It was the first time any of them saw the ocean. The waves on the water's surface stretched into the horizon and took their breaths away. And the blistering sun didn't feel quite so powerful against their skin as the wind brushed their bodies.

"What a sight!" Bofrat shouted as he sank his feet in the sand after they stepped off the hovercraft that carried them.

Evailen and Cilia couldn't contain their inner children and dipped their feet in the water. Enyo approached the girls from behind and slipped his foot into the waves. Then with a wicked grin, he lifted his foot and sprayed Cilia with salty water. Cilia and Evailen teamed up against him before Naradia evened the battlefield. Everyone stood on the shore watching as the Lunardis ran across the water, blasting each other with ocean ammunition.

Alinda was the first to surrender to her jealousy. She splashed Naradia hoping to find a place for herself in the game. The Lunardis froze taking a moment to interpret the sign of aggression before Evailen cupped the ocean between her legs and fired back at Alinda to reignite the fight, inspiring the others to take sides and participate in the epic war.

"The great water battle," Rondai muttered to himself before allowing himself a smile. Only he and Yasmina had remained ashore. He took a few steps forward to join then froze in his place. He repeated this movement several times but never brought himself to reach the battle.

Yasmina rubbed her chin. "Perhaps we can play a little?"

"It's time for reinforcements." His nose wrinkled as he nodded.

However, before they reached the fight, the ship's horn invaded their ears, grabbing everyone's attention. The sound brought them back to reality. It was time for them to board.

No one noticed the ghost of disappointment on Rondai's face who quickly donned his mask of callousness.

A large ship awaited them at an ancient dock with missing or misplaced wooded parts. Only the ship appeared new with shiny, fresh skin. The candidates and their companions ran toward the ship with uneven quickened steps.

A crewmember who stood atop the ship looked at the captain. "They remind me of my children when I took them to my faction's theme park for the first time."

🌀 🦔 🪷 🌑

Malani, Bofrat, Evailen, and Alinda lined themselves next to one another and held the side of the ship to watch as they embarked on their journey.

Evailen's eyes sparkled and gleamed. "I never thought I would actually see Mastoperia from outside."

"Me either," Malani said, the speed of his pulse increasing. "It feels strange to see it getting smaller and smaller.

Bofrat gave him a quick glance. "We aren't going that fast yet. It's still really big."

Alinda chuckled. "You know, he can see the future. He was talking about how it would look when we moved further away."

Bofrat stared at Alinda while keeping one hand on his stomach. "I would scold you for how you spoke, but I'm not feeling well right now, and I need to lie down." He brushed his shoulder against her as he left to search for his cabin.

"So, this is what the captain called seasickness," Alinda muttered to herself with a wide grin after she saw in her mind a future conversation with the captain where he explained to her why most of the companions felt sick.

At seventeen, Alinda was the youngest of the companions. She stood five feet tall and had a fit body. Her shoulder-length caramel hair had been pulled up into a bun, leaving a few strips to fall against her sunrise-colored back. Her round eyes were brown with a reddish tint to them.

◉ ❦ ✿ ◖

By the end of the seventh day, they were almost halfway to the outside world. The captain instructed them to strap themselves in their rooms as they would pass through a deadly tornado. Before the ship entered the tornado, the Captain flipped a lever in his wheelhouse to launch eight huge metal ropes that clanged into the bottom of the ocean. Each one heavier than a twelve-story building acted as an anchor. When the ship was secured in place, he ordered the crew to turn the wheel in the engine room before four metal legs found their way out of the sides and ambled through the tornado. Even though the ship could stand the weight of the wind pressing against it, the candidates and their companions still felt the pressure.

After twelve hours of being strapped in their seats, the storm finally calmed.

Naradia felt a sense of security and reached to unhook her seatbelt.

"Don't!" Kawan, her team leader shouted, but it was too late. She had freed herself.

Naradia stood at five-feet-four-inches, one hundred and fifty-four pounds with long curly chestnut hair, and fair skin. She was twenty-six with deep-set gray eyes.

The moment Naradia left her chair, the storm raged again, and she flew across the room, her body slamming against a wall before flying away and hitting another. Her other two companions whom she shared the room with watched her in silence.

Kawan saw the possibilities rush through his mind before he asked Ryn to control the seatbelt with his magic and bring her back safely to her seat, but Ryn ignored him. Maringrad glanced at Ryn who pretended to not hear Kawan before a glowing snake flew out of Maringrad's leg tattoo toward Naradia while it remained attached to him. The snake enveloped Naradia and brought her back to her seat. Only then did Ryn open the first gate using his hand gesture to strap Naradia back in the seatbelt.

🌀🐟🪷🌑

The storm lasted for another ten hours before the captain announced that it was clear for them to move.

Naradia stared at Ryn as she unhooked her seatbelt before she shouted, "You could have done something earlier if you wanted to help me!"

"I couldn't help you. I can't simply control your body. This isn't how my magic works." Ryn's chest thrust out as he held his elbows away from his body. "I can only control objects," he added, matching her tone.

"You could have controlled my clothing if that was your problem!" she shouted again.

"I didn't think about that at the time." His nostrils flared. "Let it go, you're safe already."

Naradia brushed her black seed to pull out her weapon. "I don't think I can work with someone I don't trust. This has to end now."

"Bring it on." Ryn opened the fourth gate of magic.

Jihave and his team ran toward Kawan's chamber when they heard the intense argument. They saw Kawan standing between Naradia who carried a see-through gun in one hand and a black round shield in the other, and Ryn who had a ball of fire surrounding his fist. Immediately both Rolakan and Cilia took offensive stances. Cilia's red seed blinked as she pulled out her hand-held cannon while Rolakan opened the fourth gate manifesting a mini lighting storm that spiraled around his left arm.

Both teammates sided with their faction members. However, before any of them could launch an attack, Jihave stepped in. Two large black Majestic apes, with jaguar skin, jumped out of his body and stood back to back amidst Cilia and Rolakan.

Jihave shifted his gaze between the two sides. "I don't care about the reasons behind this feud, but no team members of mine will fight against each other for the sake of their factions. This mission is more important than our origins. From this point, you will stand side by side against other teams. Even if that means you have to fight your own friends. Remember those words because if this ever happens again, I won't hesitate to kill you and continue the mission alone." Jihave's voice was so calm it scared everyone. Even Ryn and Naradia removed their weapons and took a few steps back.

Kawan let his arms drop to his sides as he centered the four. "What he said is true. We all need to remember that our teams no longer represent our factions, but who we are. All our factional rules are now void, and if we fight amongst ourselves, it's because we carry dark hearts. We can no longer blame anyone but ourselves for our actions. This mission should bring us closer together to understand that there are more important things in the world than our ancestors' conflicts."

A moment of silence reigned over the scene, but the message seemed to make it across. Ryn apologized to Naradia about his late response and promised to do his best if she was ever in danger again. Naradia nodded and forced a smile onto her face.

"This calls for a drink. I'm buying." After the Majestics returned to their home on Jihave's right side forming a two-headed-ape tattoo, he wrapped his arms around both Ryn and Naradia ignoring how their bodies trembled when they felt his arms on their shoulders.

🌀🐦🪷🌊

They spent another week sailing over calm waters. New friendships were forming, but still, the sensation of excitement was the overwhelming feeling.

When the captain announced they were almost at the docks, Evailen ran toward the front of the ship to see what it looked like. Her eyes sparkled as she stood at the edge of the ship, raised both of her arms to the sky and screamed at the top of her lungs. "Let the amazing race begin."

11

The ship's skeleton changed shape and color before it arrived at the port. It camouflaged itself to look like one of the trading ships of the world beyond. They docked at Matalia or the City of Light as its people call it.

An ancient style covered the buildings of the city even though its street looked almost as modern as the City of Lunar. However, the technology appeared different. Vessels that ran on wheels filled the city, residents carried little devices that they glued their eyes to, and a lighted billboard had been erected every ten meters.

Evailen bounced from foot to foot. "It's like I am inside the game," she muttered to herself.

"What's that?" Bofrat extended his ears forward and moved closer to her.

"Everything we see here matches the world of a video game I play. It's called Earth, and they have the exact same type of technology." She fanned herself.

"Maybe this is where they found the inspiration?"

"Probably. Anyway, this means I know the names of everything. Like those things on wheels, they call them cars, and that big one in the distance is a bus." She noticed how Bofrat shook his head before he walked away, but she continued talking to herself, naming everything she saw according to how it was inside her video game. "A phone, a streetlight, a tablet, a—"

Yasmina gave her a nudge. "The other teams left already. We are the only one still standing by the docks."

Evailen stepped toward the street and looked back with a wide grin. "I think we should explore the city first to know the world we are up against." She looked back at the street and smiled wickedly, thinking that they didn't notice her true desire was to simply experience the world.

🌀🐟🪷☯

After a few hours of exploring the city, Bofrat reminded Evailen that even though it was cool to discover, they still had a mission to complete and she agreed before they searched for a place to plan.

They chose a secluded beach. Evailen sat on the sand with the ocean to her back and the sun above her head. She checked her gadget to examine again what the artifacts looked like. She pinched the touch screen with her fingers to enlarge and rotate each of the artifacts, but after a careful inspection, she realized that she still had no clue about where they could be. Her first thought was to ask Malani for help.

"You can see the future. Why don't you tell me where we find the artifacts?"

Malani sighed a little before he sat next to her on the ground. "All right, I don't know what they teach you in school about us, but our power doesn't work like that."

Yasmina raised her thick brows as she crossed her legs together next to the others. "How does your power work then?"

Malani hesitated before sighing again. "First when we saite, we can't—"

Evailen raised her hand and shook it. "I'm sorry. What? Saite? What does that mean?"

"Saiting is… How do I explain this?" Malani scratched the edge of his forehead. "I guess you can say it's the name of our power. Not exactly though. When we try to see the future, we enter a state of saiting. It's the bond we create with time and the knowledge we receive. Does that make sense?"

"Not at all," they all answered in a unified voice with wide eyes.

Malani pinched his lips together. "Well, it takes years to learn how to saite and what it means. I'm not sure I can explain it that easily. All you need to know is that saiting means looking into the future. Okay?"

Evailen nodded. "I will leave it for now, but I'm curious about saiting and want to know more."

Malani took a deep breath. "When we saite, we don't see the future as concrete events. We see different timelines, and we search them for what could match the reality based on our decisions. Second—"

"Wait, wait, wait." Bofrat leaned closer to Malani. "I'm confused. What do you mean by 'based on decisions?' Do you decide how the future will be? Now I finally understand why the warriors came up with their device for the draft."

Yasmina displayed her smirk wide enough for Bofrat to see it. "Do you realize that not only did you not understand what he said, but you irrationally reached a conclusion based on false information?"

"I didn't know that a Kalangou could think rationally," Bofrat stared into her eyes.

"Kalangelle."

"Excuse me?" he said.

"Kalangou refers to a man, but a female from Kala is a Kalangelle." Yasmina met his stare.

"Well—"

"Enough," Evailen tapped her right knee with an open palm. "You are getting sidetracked. Continue Malani."

"We don't decide how the future will be, we only see it. Second, we only see our personal future. We can't see anyone else's. I will only see a part of your future if it will interact with mine."

Evailen asked, "Well, aren't we all sharing the same future right now? Shouldn't you be able to see what we will do next?"

"As I said, I see only possibilities, and in this case, the possibilities are endless."

"Can I ask you something?" Bofrat tilted his head.

"What now?"

"Why are you lying?"

The two girls raised their heads simultaneously.

"What are you talking about?" Malani looked at his feet.

"Actually, it does sound like you are lying." Evailen's blue seed blinked quickly. "Not only did you contradict yourself, but what you are saying means you can never know how the future will really be. If you see uncertain possibilities, then you're not seeing at all. Everyone knows that Delphians know what will happen and shape it at will. However, I don't have time to argue. If you won't help me, then I will find a way on my own."

She blinked and took a deep breath. "You can leave if you want since you're not considering yourself a member of my team." She shifted her sight toward Bofrat and Yasmina. "You can leave too if you don't want to use your powers for the sake of this team."

The few seconds of silence that followed felt like hours.

Bofrat's eagle slowly emerged out of the back of his neck, erasing its tattoo. "Perhaps if we can create a model of the artifact, my golden eagle can scan it with his analytic vision, and I can send him to look for it."

Evailen detached her purple seed from her forehead and held it in her fist. "I can create a hologram of the artifact if this is what you mean, but it will only be a three-dimensional image."

"That's not enough," said Bofrat. "It has to be a solid object so the eagle can understand it."

Yasmina opened and closed her mouth before she spoke. "I think I can materialize it." She looked at Evailen. "You create the hologram, and I will make it tangible by attracting the sand to its details."

"Would that work?" Evailen asked Bofrat.

"It should be fine," he nodded.

Malani placed his hands on the sand behind his back and used them to support himself as he watched his teammates in silence.

Evailen flipped her seed-holding fist and opened it. Colored tiny particles swirled around her hand before they moved in an artistic dance shaping the image Evailen had in her mind. Yasmina traced an invisible two on her chest to open the second gate, which allowed her to control natural elements already present around her and controlled the sand by waving her hand. The sand traced the hologram until it replaced all the particles. The eagle then scanned the shape before it faded away.

Evailen put her seed back in its place. "How long will it take for your bird to find it and fly back?"

Bofrat frowned. "First, he's not a bird, and he doesn't fly. When golden eagles identify a target, it's part of their hunt. They can sense the closest energy point to it. Even if that point was on the other side of the planet. They teleport from one point to the one after. Once they arrive at the targeted point, they merge with the air to reach their target. They only materialize when they are about to catch their prey. Second, his name is Marvaniard."

"That still doesn't answer my question. How long does Marvaniard need to find the artifact?" She smiled.

"I would say a few hours. I can't be sure since I don't have a clue about the actual distance."

"All right then, let's discover more of this world until Marvaniard returns." She clapped twice.

Evailen enjoyed their first real exchange. No one could contain her excitement as she explored the streets of Matalia. She had all that she wanted and couldn't wait for what was to come, but only Malani could see the future, and he chose to stay silent.

12

After four hours of exploration, the eagle returned to its nest on Bofrat's neck.

Feeling the return of his Majestic, Bofrat stood in the middle of a busy street and ignored the car honks hammering him to move until Evailen grabbed his arm and pulled him to the sidewalk.

"The artifact is on the southern continent," he said.

"It's too far," Evailen rubbed her fingers together. "We should try a different artifact. Maybe another is closer."

Bofrat nodded and led the team to an empty alley where they used the same technique to search for the second artifact.

While Marvaniard was away, they continued exploring the city. Evailen bought a digital camera like the one her avatars in the game used to save their memories. She and Bofrat took a picture of themselves with a part of the city every ten seconds. Yasmina and Malani followed them in silence shaking their heads every time the other two snapped a new photo.

When they had to send the eagle away for the third time, they took advantage of the time to taste anything they could put in their mouth. They sped from a restaurant to a kiosk, to a street cart.

"I can't do this anymore." Yasmina held her stomach in her hands as she leaned her shoulder against the wall of the fifth restaurant.

Malani bowed and grabbed his knees with his hands. "I agree with Yasmina. If I see anything more that is edible, I will throw up."

"Come on, guys." Evailen held the restaurant's door open. "Just one more meal." She grinned playfully keeping her gaze focused on Yasmina. Even though Malani had apologized to her while they roamed the streets of the city, she planned to wait and see his actions before giving him her attention again.

"No." Bofrat closed the door. "You said that two meals ago. I am going back to the beach to lie down until Marvaniard returns." He spoke in a wavering voice.

Evailen frowned and her shoulders dropped when she saw Yasmina and Malani followed Bofrat. She sighed heavily and dragged her feet as she walked behind them.

As soon as they returned to the beach, Malani spread his body on the sand and closed his eyes with the intention of taking a nap. Yasmina and Bofrat accompanied Evailen for a quick walk around the beach to cheer her up before they sided Malani to rest.

A few minutes later, Bofrat opened his eyes. "Can you sleep?"

Yasmina sat up. "Not really. It's like my body is dead, but my brain is in a carnival."

"Do you want to sit by the water? I would like to chat, but I don't want to annoy Malani."

Yasmina nodded and followed him to the edge of the ocean.

"And this one is called Apooh." Bofrat pointed at his bear tattoo on his calf. "I don't use him a lot in fighting because of his attitude, but we like to play together whenever we have a chance."

"Attitude?" Yasmina raised her brows. "I thought you could control your Majestics."

Bofrat smiled. "It all depends on the Majestic."

Yasmina tilted her head. "Aren't all Majestics the same?"

Bofrat chuckled and crossed his legs together. "No, they aren't. They differ from one another even if they are of the same species. Like us, they have personalities and unique abilities. Usually, they have general abilities and physical constraints that they all share, but the environment they grew up in affects their personality and strength and can give them small additional powers. Their age also makes a difference. How old they were when we captured them is another element."

He looked at his snake tattoo on his arm and gently rubbed it. "When I captured Atina, she was three years old, and she had two baby brothers. I was actually going for one of the babies, but she put up a hell of a fight; I had no choice but to capture her instead." Atina freed herself from her tattoo and slowly crawled Bofrat's arm toward his neck. "Usually, Majestics change genders to match that of their master, but she didn't. She defied everything I know about Majestics. She is also very protective of me. I think she feels responsible for me."

"Maybe she is grateful you left her brothers in peace."

"Could be." Bofrat smiled before he saw his eagle materialize and fly back to his neck. "Tell Evailen to get out of the water, and I will wake Malani. This artifact is close."

🌀🐢🪷☯

The four of them sat in a circle.

Evailen pulled up her gadget and checked the world map. "The coordinates you gave me are in this city here." She zoomed in on the city of Zaman. "It's thirteen hundred miles away.

"It's not that far, and it took us a full day to find it. I fear that others may be on their way already." Bofrat scratched his neck to ease the burn his eagle leaves every time it detached and reattached itself.

Evailen gazed toward the train station opposite the beach. "Maybe we should try the transportation of this world."

Yasmina's mouth fell open. "Is this your response to what he just said? Perhaps you should act less of a child and more of a leader. We don't know how trustworthy these things are. We need to stick to our traditions for this mission and not get distracted by this world."

"Yes, this is my response." Evailen stared at Yasmina. "The artifact is still on the list, and if someone is already there, then we won't catch up with them in time anyway."

Her hands clenched. "We know nothing about where we are going or what is waiting for us. Would you rather we use our powers and get there exhausted or sit on the train and come up with a plan while we try to find out more about our destination?" She sighed heavily. "Not to mention that the guards told us to be careful when we show our powers."

Yasmina crossed her arms in front of her chest. "It's not as if you look like a normal person. You have six seeds glued to your skin. Don't you think you look suspicious enough?"

"My seeds are who I am, not a fashion choice."

Malani leaned toward the center of the circle. "I prefer the train idea. It will help us come up with a plan. Anything is possible when you have a plan."

Bofrat narrowed his eyes as he looked at Malani. "Do you know something or are you trying to mess with us?"

"I don't need to explain myself to you every time I say something."

"Stop this. We will take the train. It's my decision." Evailen forced her face to look serious but failed. They all laughed when they saw how her chilled mouth didn't match her wrinkled nose, but she ignored them and continued.

"According to the information I found, the next train leaves in forty minutes. That gives us roughly six hours to get there." She stood up. "Let's go to the station. We can figure out our next move on the way." Evailen moved with a double step. Her enthusiasm confused everyone. They couldn't tell if she really cared about this mission or not.

🌀 🐦 🪷 ⚫

Evailen easily tapped into the world's network after she realized that it was similar to the one she shared with her faction members through their seeds. Only in this part of the world, people accessed the network through devices separate from their bodies.

As soon as she sat on the train, she looked up all the information she could find about their destination. Zaman was the center of information and technology of the outside world. It was a harbor of scientists and developers. Almost all inventions came out of there. The more she read about it, the more she felt she was returning home, which disturbed her.

In the meantime, Yasmina took a walk on the train to enjoy her first ride. A decision that Evailen applauded. Standing at the rear of the train, Yasmina searched for an empty seat that sided a window. Her gaze scanned the blue sky, contemplating what to do next. A few moments later, she traced a three against her chest to open the third gate before she placed her right palm on the glass. On the other side of the glass, dirt from the ground accumulated and formed a message in the Kalanian language before the wind swept it away.

🌀 🐦 🪷 ⚫

Evailen switched off her device and sat straight. "Now that Yasmina is back, I can tell you what I found so far." The others fixed their seating positions and stared at her in silence. "The location we have for the artifact appears to be the headquarters for a video game company called Lantrix."

Malani's eyes widened as they met Evailen's. "That's interesting."

"Exactly." She nodded.

Bofrat leaned forward. "No, no, hold on. Why is that interesting?"

"Lantrix is also the name of a video game company in Lunar. I used to work there before they sent me to the Forbidden City. They are also the makers of Earth, the game I told you about."

Yasmina squinted. "Do you mean to say your faction planted roots here already?"

"I don't know, but I don't think it's a coincidence. There are too many similarities. It's not just the name, but the layout of the building is interesting too."

Bofrat crossed his arms, rested his back against his seat, and looked at Malani with a sideways glance. "Oh man, now is the time for you to saite or whatever and tell us what we are getting into."

"I can't." Malani heavily sighed. "All right, the truth is, I don't know. While we were on the ship, I tried to see as many timelines as I could. I could see us plan and search, but each time it looked promising, the future went blank, and I couldn't see anything. This has never happened to me before. Even when I failed to see the future, I always saw something. I don't know what to do."

"Huh." Bofrat rested his head back "I really don't understand how your power works."

"Actually," Evailen broke in, "I wouldn't expect any less. Getting this artifact can't be easy. Otherwise, it would be like a walk in the park for us."

Yasmina bared her teeth. "So, what now? I still don't see a plan."

"The Plan!" Evailen rested her head on her hand and tapped her forehead with her middle finger repeatedly. "I guess the plan is that there will be no plan. We don't know enough. All we can do is prepare ourselves for the worst and hope for the best. I wish I had something better to tell you, but if any of you has a better idea, I'm listening."

Yasmina bit her lower lip before she stood up and looked at Evailen. "Can I talk to you in private?"

The other two said nothing and rested their heads against their seats. Bofrat grabbed the headphones he found in his armrest and connected them to the only jack opening visible. "I would like to figure out what kind of music this world has," he said before he put the headphones on his ears and closed his eyes.

13

Evailen and her team stood across the street from a blue four-story building that differed from any other building they saw since arriving in the new world. Only Evailen recognized the shape of the building that resembled Lunar's most sacred flower, the lotus.

"The artifact is at the center of the second floor." Bofrat cracked his neck twice after his eagle returned.

"So, do we have a plan now?" Yasmina tilted her head left and right to examine the building.

Evailen repeatedly snapped her fingers behind her back as both her blue and red seeds blinked rapidly. When the blue seed blinked, her brain functions evolved beyond genius, but when the red did the same, it showed that her emotions were imbalanced. The conflict prevented her from forming a proper strategy. She clenched her jaw and heavily sighed before she felt her consciousness fade away.

A calm musical note played in her head. The nothingness she fell into, vanished as she reclaimed perspective. A cold touch explored her body, leading her to rub her left arm in an attempt to restore the warmth. A quick shiver passed through her before she pivoted toward Bofrat who had his palm placed on her back with his snake crawling away from her shoulder to his arm.

"What did you do?" she asked.

"Relax. You seemed lost in your mind, so I calmed you down."

"How?"

"Not important. You need to focus on the task ahead." Bofrat's tone grew sharper. "Come up with a plan."

Evailen closed her eyes for a few seconds to concentrate and opened them with determination. "This building's layout matches Lunar's headquarter. It can't be a coincidence. I think it's safe to assume that it will have the same interior design."

"I can confirm the layout structure. I will send one of my Majestics to—"

"No. there's no need. I'm almost certain."

Yasmina stepped closer to her and raised her voice. "Are you going to risk everything based on an almost?"

"Sometimes, it's better to leave room for error if it will give you the element of surprise." Evailen kept her gaze focused on the building.

"What are you afraid of?" asked Malani.

"It doesn't matter right now. There's no point in worrying about what may not happen."

"You know that I come from a faction that survives based on worrying about—"

"Enough Malani. I don't want to be distracted right now. I've come up with a plan."

Evailen explained the plan to her teammates. She then took her red seed out and gave it to Bofrat before she asked him to guard it with his life. The absence of her red seed ripped her of all emotions.

She straightened her back and walked toward the main entrance. She approached the security guards who stood by a metal detector with steady feet and rested her palm on a device that read her fingerprints. She was acting as if she passed through these gates hundreds of times.

Usually, the device would blink in red or green to deny or give access, but this time it blinked blue.

"Step back," said one guard while the other inspected her seeds.

"What is your business here?" asked the second guard as soon as he noticed she was missing her red seed.

"I'm here for my initiation." Evailen looked around her and knew that it didn't matter what she said, they were playing a game, and she needed only to take part. The guard pointed toward the elevator and instructed her to go to the second floor.

She nodded and continued on her path. On the second floor, she examined the doors one by one until she found a fingerprint style lock. She placed her palm on the lock screen and watched as the door unlocked almost immediately.

At the center of the white-metal room a large control panel surrounded the glass protecting the artifact. When she inspected the panel, she noticed five empty slots matching the size and shape of her seeds. She pulled out her blue seed, placed it in the slot next to the control screen, and watched as several functions appeared in front of her. She scrolled down until she found a command titled "Roof." She pressed it and watched the ceiling open like a blooming flower before her three companions jumped in on the back of Bofrat's Majestic tiger.

"That was too easy. How did you know you could do all of that?" Bofrat's tiger made its way to his back.

"Don't lose focus. Lunardis make it easy for anyone to break in and reach their goal. The real problem will be to get out." Evailen grabbed her red seed and placed it back on the top of her heart.

"Can't we go out the same way we came in?" asked Yasmina.

"Let's see what will happen." Evailen's heart raced, and sweat poured from her body as she removed her other four seeds and placed them at the remaining empty slots around the artifact. Bofrat noticed her anxiety and tried to interfere, but she didn't give him a chance. She knew that if anything distracted her, she might question her decision of taking five of her six seeds out of her body at one time.

Once she placed the last seed, the glass slid down, exposing the artifact. Yasmina used third gate magic to dissolve the artifact, making her the only one able to put it back together. Once secured, Evailen quickly reached for her seeds and replaced them on her body one by one, but when she tried to pull out the last seed, she couldn't. A metal belt surrounded her blue seed securing it in its place while the ceiling slowly closed.

Malani moved his gaze between the ceiling and Evailen. "What are you doing? We need to go Evailen!" he shouted.

"I can't leave without my seed." Her eyes accumulated tears.

Yasmina moved closer to her. "Let me use my magic to free it."

"No," Evailen answered quickly. "I don't want any of you to use your powers on my seed. I can't risk damaging it."

Bofrat placed his hands on Evailen's. "Don't worry. We will take it out."

"We have another problem!" Malani shouted.

They glanced at him and saw the floor closing in on them like a flower going to sleep.

Bofrat looked at Yasmina and shouted, "Dissolve it like you did the artifact, and I will help Evailen!"

Yasmina tensed her fingers as she pointed her arm toward one of the panels. "I can't." She struggled to catch her breath. "The floor must have natural elements infused in it or something. I can't control it."

"How is that possible? You just did it to the artifact." Malani pushed against the boards, hoping that his weight would slow them down.

"The artifact wasn't made of a natural element. I need a different gate to control the boards." She grabbed her knees and tried to regulate her breathing.

"So, open the gate you need! What are you waiting for?" Bofrat shouted.

"I need at least thirty minutes to switch gates. I can't just do it."

"Well do *something*!"

Yasmina materialized a room-wide set of thick iron bars to block the movement of the boards, but they continued to fold, bending the iron in the process. She gradually added thickness to the bars hoping to find a balance.

"Stop that!" Malani shouted. "If you make it any thicker, it will break and hurt Evailen and me."

"If you saw that, then tell me what I need to do!" she shouted with her palms pointing toward the bar to control it.

"I didn't find the right timeline yet. Just keep doing something until I know."

Bofrat glanced at the situation one more time and freed a fire-skinned ape out of his side. The ape elongated its arms to push against the panels from both sides. Both the ape and Yasmina's iron bars combined slowed down the boards' movement but couldn't bring it to a full stop.

"It's working," Yasmina shouted, "we just need more power!" She looked at Malani. "Can I at least add more bars?"

"Don't bother." His voice trembled as he lowered his chin to his chest and stared at his feet. "It's the end anyway."

The floor trapped them, but before they could catch a breath or think about their next move, the wall turned transparent, and a group of Lunardis appeared on the other side.

The only thing separating them from those who lived in Lunar was their blood-red-eyes—a side effect to the permanent removal of the red seed.

One of the red-eyed Lunardis approached the wall and placed his palm on it. "Don't worry." He smirked. "The gas filling up the chamber will cause you no pain, and you will die quickly. After all, we're not savages."

14

As soon as Rondai and his team stepped off the ship, he led them away from everyone else. When they reached a secluded area, he opened the third gate and materialized a small car similar to one of those he saw on the street. His companions joined him inside the car before he used his magic to move it. Rondai followed the streets in a random fashion. After avoiding several dangerous collisions in the nick of time, he concentrated his attention on everything that moved close to them. He didn't stop until the sun began to set. Only then did he realize they were no longer in the same city.

"This looks calm enough." Rondai brought the car to a halt, and everyone climbed out. He waved his hand, and the car faded away before he turned around to face his companions.

"Let me be clear from the beginning." His eyes narrowed and brows wrinkled. "I trust none of you, and I can carry this entire mission on my own. However, I will give you the benefit of the doubt. If you promise me your loyalty, then I will consider it a base to earn my trust. If not, you are welcome to leave and join whichever team you like. I won't judge you." He cleared his throat. "In fact, I don't expect you to change your life-built loyalty overnight, but if you stay and betray me for any reason, then I will kill you." Rondai spread his legs wide and studied his companions.

Salvanra took a step closer to him and looked into his eyes. "I will promise you my loyalty and help you to the extent of my power if you promise me one thing."

"Which is?" Rondai pivoted toward her.

She pointed to her tattooed body and smiled. "To give me enough time to capture Afakan so I can add him to my collection before we return to Mastoperia."

"Who?" Rondai raised his brows.

"Afakan, the last beast of the old world. He's the father of all the Majestics in our forest. The legend says the first civilization created him to end the war of the ages, but the beast was too strong and ended their world instead."

"The first civilization? The one that existed long before our factions?" Terqwan perked up. He stood six feet tall, with a fit body and off-white skin tone. He had short black hair and small green eyes that matched the color of his collar.

"Yes," she said.

He shook his head. "Then what you are asking is impossible. There's nothing left from the first civilization. The great explosion wiped everything. Nothing survived."

"You're wrong." Enyo stood next to Salvanra. "The explosion destroyed only the heart of Mastoperia, but the other continents survived."

"That doesn't even make sense." Terqwan's eyes bulged. "There were no other continents back then. The explosion is what broke the land into five continents. How do you explain that?"

Enyo locked his arms behind his back. "I find it strange that you would think nothing survived. Your entire faction relies on education and logical analysis. The explosion did break the world, and wiped all trace of their civilization, but if nothing survived, then how do you explain us? How do you explain this conversation?"

Terqwan felt his cheeks burning. He wasn't ashamed because he failed to construct a logical conclusion to his history classes, but because he didn't use his power of saiting which enabled him to see the future to avoid himself the embarrassment.

Rondai grinned and gave her a small nod. "If your beast exists in this world, then I will help you capture him. It's a small price to pay if you offer me your loyalty."

"Do you know how to find that beast?" Terqwan asked Salvanra.

"There is a technique I believe will lead us to him." She scratched her neck.

"Then, I will stick around. I'm interested to see that beast. I guess this means you have earned my loyalty." Terqwan locked eyes with Rondai who nodded in silence.

"And you Enyo, what is your answer?" asked Rondai.

"Evailen is a good friend of mine, but I know she won't accept that I join her and will lecture me about the importance of following the rules or why it would benefit me to stay with my team." He smiled. "Even if I evaded that, she would give me the equality speech and remind me every ten seconds that she can handle herself without my help. I think it's more peaceful, and perhaps safer to stay with you."

Rondai's tentative smile grew as he realized how quickly they offered him their loyalty. He stroked his chin and wondered if he would have done the same had the roles been different.

He told himself that he still needed to be wary of them, but it was time he eased up and saw them as companions rather than enemies from another faction. The concept of all factions working together tickled his mind, and he couldn't help but turn his smile into a wide grin. "A single exchange doesn't erase the past," he muttered to himself hoping to find strength in his words.

"Don't worry." Salvanra placed her hand on his shoulder.

"What?" Rondai quickly turned his head toward her.

"I know that in your culture, caution comes first. You prepare your entire life for the worst scenario possible. I understand how important this mission is to you, too, and it's natural to expect that our allegiance falls with our faction members, but we also understand the concept of duty, and if not, then find solace in the fact that none of us would want to piss off the Forbidden Warriors."

She rubbed his shoulders. "I won't deny that I'm rooting for Jihave to win. He is my partner, after all, but he also has a team like us, and I know that he will win them over." Her face softened. "We promised to do our best to help you and know that Averettis are a competitive bunch. I want none of them to rub it in my face that I lost. So, relax, live a little, and enjoy the experience. It will be fun." She displayed a genuine smile.

"Last I checked you weren't the one who could see the future." Rondai briefly lowered his head as he realized that his words failed to relay his feelings.

"Come on. I don't need to see the future to know that this will be fun." Salvanra laughed out loud.

Rondai's smile stopped halfway when he saw the other two laughing as well. He wasn't sure if they laughed at him or Salvanra's words.

"All right guys, the fun is over." Rondai straightened. "It's time to discover our first step." He told himself that perhaps Salvanra was right, and he needed to enjoy the journey. He took a deep breath and thought about how it would be in Mastoperia if life between their factions were as easy as this little interaction with his companions, but then he remembered his faction and the price they have to pay for their magic before he snapped himself out of that ridiculous dream.

15

Rondai's eyes sparkled as he rubbed his hands together in front of his chest. "First order of business is to locate all the artifacts, then decide which one we will hunt first."

Terqwan stood slacked-jawed while he adjusted his white suit. "I have to say I tried to see the locations of the artifacts, but something is blocking me. I guess the Forbidden City is using the same technology they used for the draft to block my ability." He scratched his head, trying to find a better explanation but couldn't.

"Don't worry about it." Rondai opened the fourth gate. "I will send out a wave of planetary wind. Soon enough, we will know."

"How does that work?" asked Salvanra.

"Using the power of the fourth gate, I can conjure any natural element. Elements I create are connected to my heart through the power of the gate. I can feel everything they feel, see everything they see, and a lot more." Rondai bit his tongue intentionally to hold it from revealing more secrets.

Enyo cupped his skinny white elbow with one hand while tapping his lips with the other. "How long will that take? You have to search the whole planet I assume."

"Several days, but we will know the locations of all the artifacts."

"I might have a faster way."

Rondai's eyes widened as he looked at Enyo. He turned his face upward, and he smiled, amused by how they were all keeping their promise until Enyo's words forced him to quickly shake his head and return to reality.

"In this world, they use technology for everything and connect it all with something they call the internet."

Terqwan tilted his head. "How does this help us?"

Enyo fixed his perfect cut short brown hair, "The internet is a basic network used to transfer information all over the globe. I can easily tap into it and explore their secrets. Their security protocols are outdated, and not even first Gen."

Rondai chuckled inwardly and crossed his arms. "I understood nothing of your words. Just tell me how we can use that internet thing to find the artifacts?"

"Just give me one hour, and I will see what I can find. If I fail, then we've lost only an hour, but if I succeed, then we've gained a lot of time."

Rondai nodded before Enyo sat on the ground and crossed his legs. Enyo placed both his index fingers on the two seeds that side his forehead before they blinked simultaneously. Then, he closed his eyes.

Rondai paced back and forth in a pattern that steadily increased.

"Shh, shh." Salvanra placed her palm on Rondai's back, bringing him to a full stop. "Close your eyes," she whispered. Her voice echoed in his head before he blindly complied with her words.

She continued. "Listen to the world around you. Can you hear it? The birds in the trees, singing in harmony. The leaves dancing with the wind. Can you hear it? Smell the air. The euphoria coming out of the plants to purify the atmosphere as they sunbathe. The—"

"Coffee?" Rondai opened his eyes, interrupting her. He felt a movement on his skin and quickly shivered to shake it off. He glanced behind him and noticed a snake crawl back into Salvanra's arm.

"How...? What...? Coffee. I smell coffee." Rondai took a deep breath to gather his thoughts. He didn't understand how he could feel and hear a forest around him when they stationed themselves under a bridge where all they could hear was the noise of moving vehicles speeding above them. But the scent of coffee was all he could think about. He felt his cells gravitate toward the smell and couldn't control them any longer. "Would either of you care to join me for a side quest?"

"To do what exactly?" Terqwan quickly saited to see the future. "Oh… That taste is definitely interesting."

"Did you taste it?" Rondai understood that Terqwan looked into the future, but his choice of words confused him.

Terqwan smiled. "You will see. Let's go."

Rondai shrugged. "All right then, so we are going." He pivoted to face Salvanra. "And what about you?"

"Yes, yes, I am in." Salvanra had been lost in her mind. She knew her silver mamba is one of the strongest mambas in her forest. Her snake's hypnotic ability even surpassed some of her elders', yet Rondai broke free easily. For a moment, she thought about how powerful Rondai could be. The thought scared her enough that she fell into the darkness of her mind. She moved first so she could keep the fear from showing on her face.

"Salvanra!" Rondai shouted. "Salvanra!"

"What!" She spoke fast and loud before she rotated to face him, wondering if he noticed how he frightened her. She wanted to neither explain her fear nor ask him how he escaped the hypnosis. Instead, she wanted time to think. Numerous thoughts passed through her mind in a fraction of a second. She feared he would ask her about her snake, so she prepared different answers, hoping she would land the one that didn't reveal how scared of him she was.

Rondai noted her gaze moving in all directions, but never meeting his. "The smell of coffee is coming from the other side, you know." He smiled and pointed in the direction opposite to where she was headed.

Salvanra took a deep breath to calm her racing heart and cursed herself for letting her overthinking get the better of her. She believed herself to be wiser than that.

16

Terqwan's pupils dilated after he finished his third cup of coffee. "This drink is amazing. It makes me feel alive. I have to admit, it's even better in reality than in my saites." He placed his cup on the table and looked at Rondai. "How did you know about it? Does it exist in Kala?"

"I inherited a coffee-scented candle from my father. It was the only thing he left me." Rondai blinked back a single tear before anyone could notice. "No one knows where it came from or anything about it. The only clue I had was the word coffee engraved on the side. Before today I didn't know it was a drink." Rondai closed his eyes and took a deep breath.

Salvanra studied Rondai's face in silence. When she noticed Terqwan's mouth open, she feared he would ask inappropriate questions and beat his words with hers. "I think we should leave. Enyo should be finished by now."

"Okay." Terqwan smiled. "Let me just buy some grains to take back to my faction." He stood up and moved to the bar.

"Thank you." Rondai opened his eyes and turned to face Salvanra, who nodded in silence. When they returned to Enyo, he had his left palm extended in front of him with a hologram of the planet beaming out of a purple seed in his hand, the one seed that matched the color of his eyes. They sat next to him and looked at the rotating planet, noticing several marked locations.

"Did you find them?" Rondai leaned toward the hologram.

Enyo kept his eyes focused on the hologram. "Not exactly. The nine locations I marked are mysterious. I couldn't find out anything about them, but I think the artifacts will most likely be among them."

"Mysterious in what way?" asked Salvanra.

"This part of the world has satellites that scan every inch of the planet to create maps for military divisions that combat terrorism. They hide it from the public because they map not only streets but inside the buildings as well. They monitor everyone all the time. I checked the live feed and all the data they have on the project. The satellites are blind against the entire continent of Mastoperia. I'm not sure if we do this on purpose or not, but they can't see us."

"What does this have to do with the artifacts?" Terqwan asked.

"These nine locations are also blind spots for the satellites. If we're using technology to keep ourselves hidden, then most likely whoever hid the artifacts used the same equipment to make sure no one from this world found them."

"It makes sense that the same people who blocked me from saiting the artifacts can blind a machine." Terqwan looked toward the sky. "I want to try something."

They all looked at him with wondering eyes.

"When I was looking for the artifacts, I was searching for the timeline through which we would succeed to find them, but each time I got close, I felt as if someone was forcing me out of my saite. However, without knowing their locations, the possibilities were endless. This never happened to me before, and I want to know if I can't saite the artifacts because I've been blocked from doing so or if something is wrong with me in general."

"You want to see what lies in these locations?" Enyo squinted.

Terqwan crossed his legs and placed his fists on his knees. "Exactly. I won't saite to see the artifacts, but the places you marked, and I will do it completely focused this time."

Terqwan closed his eyes, now in his full meditative position, he was able to boost his power of saiting further to see more of the future than what he could see when he saites on the go. After a few minutes he opened them again, and pressed his lips tight into a grimace. "I couldn't see anything. No matter how hard I tried, I could reach none of the locations. All nine places are blind spots for me too." His shoulders tightened, and his lips and chin trembled slightly as the thought that he could no longer saite scared the sweat out of his body.

Rondai noticed the horror in Terqwan's eyes. He didn't know much about saiting, but he knew how much it would scare him to find out that someone could rid him of his power.

For a moment, he felt superior. He was now sure that Delphians had a weakness and if he could find how these devices worked, then he could offer his faction a way to enslave them. However, his brain ached from the idea after his heart pumped guilt into his veins. *How dare I think about the demise of my friend?* And *when did Terqwan become a friend?*

His mind fought against itself with questions until he realized that in order to get out of this maze, he needed to focus on his mission only.

"This isn't entirely bad." Rondai looked at Terqwan. "If you can't see them, we can safely assume that Enyo is correct. These locations are somehow connected to Mastoperia, and the artifacts will be in four of them."

Salvanra raised her chin. "They are spread out across the globe, though. Perhaps you can do as you said earlier and send this planetary wind now. Wouldn't it be faster since you are focusing on certain locations?"

"It would be, but I'm no longer sure this method will work. If they went through all this trouble to block sky-eyes and the Delphians vision, then why wouldn't they try to block my powers?"

"I disagree." Enyo cracked his fingers. "While Terqwan saited, I tried something too. I checked simpler navigation apps that they use here to find their way. I didn't do it at first because I thought it would be too easy."

"You don't need to explain yourself. Just tell us what you found," Rondai countered.

"One of the applications doesn't use satellites. Instead, it uses drones that fly over the streets and registers three-dimensional images. The application is operational only in the continent of Profectus, which we are on right now, but they do have a road map with street view of the three locations on this content."

Enyo waved his hand before the hologram changed from the shape of the planet to the three locations he mentioned. "As you see, there is life there." He snapped his finger, and one of the locations turned into a live feed. "This is a streetlight camera. Those people don't look military-grade, and the cameras can see them without a problem."

Salvanra tilted her head to the side. "What are you trying to say?"

"Whatever it is that blinds the artifact and Terqwan's power isn't disrupting everything."

"It's affecting only what can see it," Rondai clarified for him, narrowing his eyes.

"Exactly." Enyo nodded. "The military satellites can see through walls."

Terqwan shook his head. "What about me? I can't see through walls or scan anything."

"But your power still works on a frequency." Enyo looked at him. "I won't pretend that I understand your power, but the only logical conclusion I could find is that the artifacts or whatever it is can defend itself against certain frequencies."

"This seems like speculation unless you have proof," said Rondai.

"I don't, it's only a theory." Enyo turned his face to Rondai. "All I wanted to say was that the power you described sounds like a natural occurrence to me. I don't think that artifacts would block the wind from running its natural course, would they?" He raised his brows.

Terqwan raised his shoulders. "Unless his wind carries a magical signature. Wouldn't that be a type of frequency too?"

Enyo nodded in agreement. "I think we should still try it. At least with one of the locations."

At that moment, Rondai noticed a certain blackbird in the sky, familiar only to his people. "I will be back," he said.

He moved toward the bird and watched it land on a rock close to him. He opened the first gate and waved his hand to raise the bird in the air and crash it into the ground. The crash turned the bird into dust that shaped a message directed only to him.

Rondai quickly erased the message and returned to his friends. "Let's go."

"Where to?" asked Salvanra.

"To capture the first artifact." Rondai ran in the artifact's direction without taking the time to devise a plan or think about what awaited them.

17

"Do you realize that we're just running toward the artifact? Is it that close?" Terqwan contained a little laugh when Rondai halted bringing everyone to a complete stop.

"That was stupid. I apologize." Rondai stared at his feet but smiled when he heard the others laugh.

"Is it in one of the locations I marked?" Enyo wondered.

"Yes, the one in Zaman."

Silence prevailed for a moment when none of them dared to ask him how he knew.

Terqwan twisted his lips to the side. "It's a bit far and would take us a lot of time to get there if we moved along the streets like we did to get here."

Enyo scratched the back of his head. "I would propose my Lotus pod. It's fast and can fly above the clouds, but it's small, and there's no space for anyone but me. I'm five-feet-eight-inches tall, you know."

"My tigress can carry us, but we have to find a way to move without being seen. She is too unique for this part of the world," said Salvanra.

Rondai opened the third gate. "Don't worry, I will take care of transportation." He conjured a plank of wood on the ground. "Everyone, get on." He sat in one corner and crossed his legs.

"Are we going to slide there? Or will we wait for the planet's rotation to bring the location to us?" Terqwan pitched a laugh.

Salvanra punched his shoulder. "Stop being a smart ass and do as he says."

When the other three positioned themselves on the wood, Rondai controlled the plank and raised it above the clouds before steering it toward the artifact. Terqwan kept sneaking a peek of the world below every few seconds.

"Sit still, Terqwan. You don't want to fall." Enyo stared at him as he did it one more time.

"Forgive me, but I have never flown before. We consider flying to be of high risk, so we never do it."

"Yet you seem eager to die." Enyo kept his stare unbroken.

"Stop your bickering." Salvanra scratched her arm tattoo in wariness. "We need to figure out what we are getting into here."

"I scavenged the internet and vaguely constructed the place from posted pictures of people who tagged themselves anywhere near the area and found something interesting." Enyo detached his purple seed and placed it in his hand before beaming a hologram of a building.

"When did you do that? You know what, never mind. I don't want to know." Salvanra raised her brows in a quick move. "How do you know the exact building we are going to, though?"

Terqwan moved closer to the hologram and rubbed his eyes. "Does that look like—"

"Yes," Enyo interrupted him. "A lotus-shaped building can only mean one thing; my people built it."

"Could it be a coincidence?" Salvanra narrowed her eyes.

"Unlikely. It was Mastoperians who made and hid those artifacts so it can't be a coincidence."

She looked at the two men with her eyes popping out. "Why do I feel that the shape of the building isn't the worst thing?"

"This building wasn't built overnight. The artifacts have been here for some time." Terqwan threw his back on the wood.

Enyo zoomed in on the building and rotated it from one side to the other using his fingers "What he means to say is that there is a big chance that Mastoperians guard the building or at least the artifact, and based on the shape, I would say we need to prepare for a fight against Lunardis."

Terqwan turned his head toward Enyo and asked calmly, "Will you be able to fight against your own people?"

"Would they be my people, though?" Enyo looked back at him. "Judging from the size of the building, the material, and its integration with the surroundings, I can easily conclude that they have been here for quite some time. We've evolved a lot in the last few centuries alone. Who's to say they are anything like me?"

"It's not necessarily so that the guards have lived here for generations." Terqwan rubbed his chin. "They are clearly in contact with the Forbidden Warriors since they are helping them for the ascension."

"Unless..." Salvanra watched as the other two turned their eyes toward her. "What if the guards lied and they didn't hide the artifacts at all? What if they sent us to do their dirty work?"

"Unlikely," both Enyo and Terqwan said at the same time.

Enyo shook his head. "This is the right time for ascension, and it's customary to give the candidates a mission that tests their limits. They need to know the new generation is worthy of the power they will receive and would use it wisely. It's natural the mission would have some controversy."

Terqwan quickly added, "Not to mention our involvement. We will return to our factions after we complete this mission. Only the candidates will return to the Forbidden City. If they wanted them to do their dirty work, they wouldn't risk making us tag along. They have a reputation to consider, and it won't be easy to silence all twelve companions who come from different factions. I'm sure they know we have our own weight in our individual factions."

Salvanra crossed her arms over her chest as she looked at Enyo. "Then how do you explain all you said about your faction's existence in this part of the world."

"I don't know yet. I was just making the observation, but we can't jump to conclusions before we have the full picture."

Salvanra turned her head toward Rondai who had stayed silent the whole time with his back facing them. "I would love to know his take on all of this. He has been silent since we left, and I don't think controlling this piece of wood requires that he keeps his mouth shut and his eyes closed."

"Perhaps he knows something we don't." Terqwan sighed and placed his hands beneath his head.

Enyo imitated Terqwan and leaned his back against the wood's surface. "He definitely knows several things, not just one. Like how did he know for sure that this is the location of the first artifact? We didn't see him use his wind magic, nor did he have the time to do so. He's also focusing on something, in particular, so at least one thing has changed. Twenty minutes ago, he doubled our speed."

"I felt that too," said Salvanra.

"I guess we'll just have to wait and see." Enyo closed his eyes and thought about what it all meant. Seeing his faction's sigil in this part of the world opened the door to memories he had locked away a long time ago.

A few moments later, Rondai opened his eyes and blinked back a tear. "We are too late," he said.

18

Evailen and her team couldn't see the invisible gas filling the room, but they could smell it. Malani immediately covered his mouth and nose, while Yasmina and Bofrat tried to use their powers to protect themselves. Only Evailen ignored the threat entirely. Her blue seed never once left her sight or the grip of her hand. Even when she knew her end was near, she cared about nothing else.

Malani was the first to suffer from the gas. He felt his heart race and his vision slowly blur before everything around him disappeared. His body was still, but in his head, he was running aimlessly in a white circle. He tried to force his body to stop but couldn't control his actions, and each time he fought his movements, he sped up. His mind believed that he ran for hours and pushed his body into fatigue, forcing him to fall unconscious.

Yasmina saw him fall toward the floor in what seemed to her as slow motion. She tried to reach him, but her body couldn't move either. Remembering she had the third gate open, the thought of materializing a small rope to attach around his arms and pull him to her struck her. But Yasmina struggled to move her fingers in order to weave her magic.

She screamed as she felt her blood rush backward in her veins until she managed to manifest and secure the rope. She clenched her fists as she tried to bring Malani closer, but with every inch she pulled, she felt the room expand, and the distance between them grow. Moving closer to him wasn't an option either after she lost the connection between her brain and her legs.

She paused for a second to question her power. She had mastered four of the magic gates and trained both her body and mind to withstand all terrors. She believed she could overcome any mental exploitation, but this time she doubted herself, unaware that the manipulation came from her mind after it lost all perspective.

A single tear escaped her eyes as her surroundings faded away, and a figure materialized. "I'm sorry, Father. I failed you," she said and gave in to the gas before her body collapsed in the same way Malani's did.

Bofrat still had the power to fight. The moment he knew the enemy had launched a toxic gas upon them, a transparent blue jellyfish detached from his left ankle and floated in the room for a moment before settling on his head. The fish covered Bofrat's face creating a see-through-mask. He sat on the ground to catch his breath as his Majestic ape pounded over and over upon the glass, separating them from freedom. Each time the ape failed to achieve its goal of breaking the glass, the following punch became automatically stronger. But after nearly fifty hits, Bofrat absorbed the ape back into his body as not even a crack had been generated. The ape hadn't gotten tired, but Bofrat struggled to keep his eyes open.

Eventually, the jellyfish retreated to its tattoo after Bofrat lost the power to control any of his Majestics. He didn't know that the gas needed only touch his body to spread its cancer within him. However, it took more time to assume full control on Bofrat as it couldn't integrate with his cells as fast by touch. In the end, the gas took away his consciousness like his companions before him.

When Evailen heard the word gas, she quickly brushed her black seed before her armor crawled out of it and surrounded her entire body, but that was all she did. She could probably have been able to battle the gas and save her team had her blue seed been in place. With her brain functions boosted, she would have managed to analyze the situation and form a counter plan. However, all Lunardis knew the importance of the blue seed, so they made sure if one of them attacked the artifact, they would lose the ability to think properly.

Evailen focused only on reconnecting the seed stuck in the panel with her body. After failing to free it peacefully, she thought about destroying the panel holding it in place. She drew force into her arms by raising them above her head but then couldn't bring herself to bring them back down for fear of damaging the seed.

The consequences of losing one of her seeds forever were severe. Each seed contained a part of her soul along with the ability that correlated with that seed. The blue seed controlled the right side of her brain. Losing it meant she would say goodbye to her analytical abilities, creativity, and imagination. Her intuition would no longer exist, she would no longer be able to think properly and would feel empty for the rest of her life.

Evailen knew she would rather die than spend a lifetime searching for something she would never find. She didn't want to become one of those underground addicts that lost their original seeds and either spent the rest of their lives using fake ones that carried no power or lived in hiding from the Lunardis guards after they became nothing but empty shells with dead souls.

In a moment of despair, she let her body armor retreat into her black seed and inhaled the gas. She took a final look at her fallen companions before she slammed her head against the blocked seed as strongly as she could. All she could hope for now was to reunite the seed with her body before she died. Lunardis believed that if they died missing even one of their seeds, their souls wouldn't return to the heart of the white lotus and their spirits would forever roam a strange world tortured by the worst of punishments: a lack of purpose.

🌀🐦🪷☯

The leader of the red-eyed Lunardis waited until he saw Evailen fall before he pushed a button on the wall to reopen the sealed room. He walked toward Evailen, carefully stepping around the small strip of blood leaking out of her head. He grabbed her hair with one hand and tried to pull her head off the panel but couldn't. Her seed had returned to her body, but the two remained attached to the metal board. The man searched for the artifact within the room to place it back at its original location. It was the only way to free the seed, but the artifact was nowhere to be found.

He faced his men who stood by in full armor carrying beam guns. "Find the artifact!" he shouted.

The guards didn't know where to begin since no one had left the room, but they chaotically scattered themselves. After searching the room thoroughly, they still found nothing. Their leader's veins popped in his forehead, and his face turned red when he remembered they couldn't place cameras in the room because of the artifact.

"Take their bodies to the examination rooms," the leader ordered, ignoring his trembling fingers. "There is no way the artifact left the building. One of them is hiding it with their ability. Find out which ability can remain active after the death of its owner. And as for her," he continued pointing at Evailen, "cut her head off if you need to examine her too and bring me her seeds."

19

Rondai stood atop the flying plank of wood, looking down upon the lotus building. His heartbeat raced against itself. Tears ran down his face while his companions understood nothing.

"What's wrong, Rondai? Talk to us." Salvanra placed both her palms on his shoulders as she looked into the eyes of a lost Rondai.

Rondai slowly pushed her hands away, took a step backward, and traced a three around his heart to close the third gate followed by a five to open the fifth without uttering a word. A transparent aura surrounded his body. It was clear as water, yet it reflected darkness. He flew into the air and launched himself toward the top center of the building, leaving the wooden plank in free-fall and with it, his companions.

As Rondai sped toward the building, he focused his aura into his hands and released a missile-power-blow toward the roof. The explosion preceded him by seconds as he slipped through the smoke into a scene he didn't want to see.

Salvanra acted the moment she noticed the absence of support by freeing both her tigress and silver snake at the same time. She rested on the back of her tigress while her snake grabbed Enyo and Terqwan, bringing them to rest on the Majestic.

Enyo realized that they weren't slowing down and quickly brushed his yellow seed, launching his lotus pod. He placed it under the two front feet of the tigress as they all shifted their weight toward the front. The pod slowed their descent, but the speed remained dangerous. The impact could still kill them.

Terqwan quickly saited to find a better solution before he jumped off the back of the tigress toward the pod, grabbing its decorative flower leaves and leaving his body hanging in the air. The others understood the plan and did the same allowing Salvanra to lock her tigress back in its tattoo. Without the added weight, the pod could carry them, and Enyo was able to slow it down for a safe landing on the roof.

As Salvanra rested her feet on the roof, she wondered if Rondai was trying to kill them, but the thought didn't have time to take hold in her mind as she saw Terqwan rush inside behind him without his usual questioning.

Once the smoke cleared, she saw what was happening. The fight had already begun. Rondai and Terqwan versus twenty heavily armored Lunardis look-alikes, and four bodies scattered across the room. Among them, she saw Bofrat.

Enyo pressed his black seed to release his body armor. He grabbed his double-barrel long gun out of the armor and dove into the center of the battle followed by Salvanra.

Rondai transformed his aura into a transparent shield that enabled him to block all attacks and fire aura bullets toward the enemy at the same time. His anger blinded him from devising a strategy. He fired at everyone randomly prolonging a fight that could have ended in seconds with just a little focus.

Enyo fired compressed energy shells that exploded upon contact out of his gun, but so did the enemy, and as his armor could withstand the power of his bullets, so could theirs. Lunardis build their weapons and armors in a specific manner to ensure that they could never be used against them. After realizing that it was useless for him to fight, he opted to help Terqwan check on the fallen bodies, leaving the fight to both Rondai and Salvanra.

Salvanra started by using her tigress but had to reevaluate her plan after the enemy cornered both of them. The room was tight, and she couldn't allow a full rampage fearing that she would hurt her companions. So instead, she freed her mantis out of her left thigh. The mantis carried a two-meter-long scepter that could cut through the enemies' armor. With Salvanra's support, Rondai's shots gradually became stronger as they focused on fewer enemies. Together they wiped out the enemy in less than fifteen minutes.

Terqwan and Enyo assessed the state of Evailen's team. Three of the four still had a faint pulse, but too weak to generate hope. Terqwan started to treat Bofrat first. He connected both of their hearts using a Delphian device. The device matched both hearts together forcing Bofrat's to beat at the same rate as his. However, the process sent Bofrat into shock, and Terqwan had to stabilize him several times before re-starting the process.

Rondai raced toward Yasmina and held her in his arms as tears ran down his face.

"You need to unclog their veins and liberate the blood circulation," Terqwan shouted without shifting his eyes away from Bofrat.

Rondai nodded before he extended his aura to surround Yasmina's body. He closed his eyes and focused on her blood until he could feel it begin to move. He infused his aura with her blood, sensing the gas particles clogging the path and slowly defused them. After the blood could circulate easily, her heart regained strength, although at a slow pace, and she showed signs of regaining consciousness.

Once Rondai believed she would be okay, he handed her to Salvanra, then approached Malani and revived him as he did Yasmina before moving on to Bofrat.

"Let me help him." Rondai knelt next to Terqwan and Bofrat.

"Your way won't work with him. Malani and Yasmina inhaled the gas, but he didn't. The particles merged with his heart tissue." Terqwan felt Bofrat's heart stabilize at that moment, "It's fine. He will be okay." He sighed.

Rondai rushed toward Evailen whose head still remained stuck to the panel. He prepared his aura to treat her like he did the others.

"Don't," Enyo muttered through his tears. "Her heart has already stopped."

Rondai sat on the floor next to Evailen and looked at her closed eyes. He didn't know her well but seeing her face stuck in that panel troubled his heart. He thought she was funny and spontaneous. He liked how she rambled about her video game the first time they met, and how she started the water fight on the beach. He didn't enjoy seeing her like this and turned his aura into a sharp blade to cut the panel around her head so she could be free, but before he touched the board, it turned into ashes.

Rondai glanced behind him and saw Yasmina waving her hand. She used the first gate to free Evailen by dissolving the panel.

"Bring her to Bofrat." Yasmina struggled to reach Enyo with her voice.

"What did you do?" Enyo whispered in Evailen's ear as he carried her to Bofrat.

Bofrat used his hands and legs to seat himself and held Evailen's hand. A scarab moved out of his chest and marched atop her arm. They all surrounded Evailen watching as the scarab reached her heart, plunging its feet into her skin. The scarab changed color several times before turning counter-clockwise.

"Is it going to work?" Salvanra knew the scarab's power.

"I don't know. I hope it's not too late." Bofrat pressed on Evailen's hand.

20

Earlier on the Train

Yasmina bit her lower lip before she stood up and looked at Evailen. "Can I talk to you in private?"

Bofrat and Malani uttered nothing and rested their heads against their seats. Bofrat grabbed the headphones he found in his armrest and connected them to the only jack opening visible.

Yasmina and Evailen moved to a different wagon.

"What's wrong?" Evailen's eyes widened.

"I did something I now regret." Yasmina crossed her arms against her chest.

"What is it? Don't worry. You can tell me anything." Evailen rubbed her palm on Yasmina's arm.

"My faction puts a lot on this mission, and it's very important for us that Rondai becomes the chosen one."

Evailen struggled to contain a chuckle when she heard the words "the chosen one."

Yasmina didn't pay attention and continued. "We had a plan prepared, and orders to follow, but it all fell apart the moment our teams changed up." The corners of Yasmina's mouth turned down.

"What did you do?" Evailen raised her brows.

"I… I…betrayed you. I sent a message to Rondai and told him the location of the artifact. I'm sorry. Malani's behavior made me think he was going to betray you, too, and it motivated me to do the same. But I see how awful it was now. I know Rondai won't accept that from me either. He wouldn't accept betrayal even if it were for his own benefit. However, now that it has been done, he wouldn't pass up the chance to get the artifact." Yasmina's eyes accumulated tears.

Evailen's blue seed blinked quickly as she stared into nothingness in silence.

"Say something, please." Yasmina's voice cracked.

Evailen shifted her eyes to Yasmina's. "When did you send the message?"

"Earlier when I went for a walk on the train."

Evailen turned around and moved quickly toward their seats. Yasmina matched her pace.

"Evailen, talk to me. Please."

Evailen pivoted toward Yasmina. "Don't worry. I understand why you did it, and I'm not mad at you. In fact, this might be the best thing to happen to us." Evailen continued her walk back.

"Malani, I need you to see something for me." Evailen sat back in her seat.

"I told you—"

"It's not about the artifact. I need you to see where Rondai is. Exactly."

"My power doesn't work like that. I can only see my future, not everything."

"Can you at least figure out when they will arrive at our destination?"

"That I might be able to work with. So, you are sure Rondai and his team are going to the same destination as us?"

"Yes."

"Good. It should be doable then. Give me a minute." Malani closed his eyes and saw different situations where they could intercept Rondai the moment he arrived. "They will arrive two hours after us."

"So, we have two hours to capture the artifact." Evailen's blue seed blinked faster and faster.

Bofrat leaned forward. "That's not good. Two hours are not enough to come up with a plan and execute it."

"I agree with Bofrat. We have to—" Yasmina tried to express her thoughts before Evailen interrupted her.

"My question to you all is this. Do you trust your faction members with your lives?"

Bofrat and Yasmina didn't hesitate to say yes, while Malani said nothing.

"And you Malani. Don't you trust Terqwan?"

"It's not about trust. We didn't really know each other before this mission. I trust that he wouldn't let me die if he could do something about it, but without knowing where you're going with this, I can't judge."

"Fair enough." Evailen nodded. "Listen. I have a plan, but it's dangerous, and requires that we put our fate in the hands of our rivals without them even knowing the plan."

"That doesn't sound like a good plan." Malani shook his head. "Not even a semi-good plan. In fact," his voice squeaked, "why should our fate be in any plan at all?"

Bofrat's grin widened. "I'm actually interested to hear about it."

"I will tell you my plan then we can decide together whether we do it."

"Now, that sounds like a good plan." Malani chuckled.

"What we know so far is that the artifact is guarded in a building that resembles my faction's sigil. Based on all the signs, I will assume they are following Lunar's protocol to guard objects, which would give us an advantage. They will want to trap us. Make it easy for us to go in so they could place us exactly where they want us to be." Evailen's shoulders tightened. "No matter what mechanism they will use to trap us, it won't trigger until we capture the artifact."

"That sounds stupid," said Yasmina.

Bofrat half-smiled. "It actually sounds fair. They don't judge until the action happens."

"Now is not the time to discuss my faction's morals," Evailen interrupted. "I don't know the nature of the trap, but I can assure you it will be lethal, and it will be impossible for us to survive."

Malani's mouth slackened. "So what you are saying is that we die?"

"I'm saying that we use the other team to our advantage."

"How?" Yasmina asked.

"Once we bite the bait and we appear dead, whoever watches over the artifact will lower their guard. Then—"

"So, we pretend to be dead?" Malani interrupted.

"We cannot pretend to be dead. They will know. Listen. Whatever method they use, it will aim to stop our hearts. At least that is how we Lunardis do it. But they will try their best to keep our bodies intact. What we need to do is to keep our body functions working even after our hearts stop beating to give Rondai and his team the chance to revive us." Evailen grabbed two vials out of her thigh pouch. "This is a serum that comes from the white lotus. It contains life energy and will allow our bodies to function for four hours even when our hearts stop. If they revived us within that time, then it will be like our hearts never stopped."

"Why did you pack such a serum for this mission?" Yasmina raised her brows.

"What are you talking about?" Evailen stared into their blank eyes then continued. "Right. Every Lunardis carries this serum at all times when they leave the faction. It allows us to boost our energy and combat fatigue." Evailen noticed how their stares remained vacant. "It's also helpful if we want to preserve our bodies for a longer time in case we sustain injuries that no one can treat on-site." Evailen sighed.

Bofrat locked his arms together. "I see. So how will Rondai and his team know that they need to revive us?"

"First, we will have to hide the artifact as soon as we get it. Somewhere inaccessible. This way we can allow Terqwan to see the situation, assuming the artifact is blinding his visions too."

Yasmina scratched her jaw. "Will you trust someone that's not even from your faction?"

"I'm putting my trust in you and your connection with your faction mates. I know that Enyo won't let me die over the artifact no matter what, and I hope your mates will do the same."

Bofrat's grin widened. "This plan of yours is dangerous, indeed. I like it."

Yasmina thought even if they were to die, that would allow Rondai to get the artifact and bypass the enemy's traps. A small price to pay. She said, "I Trust Rondai with my life. He will do all he can to revive me. I'm in."

Malani pressed his lips together in a slight grimace. "I don't like this plan one bit. It's risky, foolish, and counts on factors we can't control. But I have to say I never felt this much life coursing in my veins. I must be turning stupid, but I think I'm in too."

"One last thing. It's possible that eyes will be on us the moment we set foot in the city. If they are watching for attacks, they will have detection systems everywhere, and will know we don't belong to this part of the world." Evailen paused for a long period, ignoring the stares of her companions before she continued. "I will have to erase the last hour out of my mind in case they try to remotely hack my brain. It would be best if I knew nothing."

Their eyes widened, but only Bofrat dared to ask, "You can do that?"

"Yes," she replied with a definitive nod. "I would say I'm amazed by how little you know about my faction, but then, I don't know that much about yours either."

Bofrat smiled. "It's not like we have a class on other factions. All of our knowledge comes from the older generation and their war stories."

"You don't?" Malani turned his head toward Bofrat. "We have such a class. It's fun. You should suggest to your minister of education to add one in your curriculum." He winked.

"We don't exactly have ministers."

"Okay, okay." Evailen raised her palms. "All you need to know now is that all of my body functions are directly connected to my seeds; thus I can control my internal brain and body functions as long as I control my seeds."

"So basically, you can do to your body, what we can do to ours with medicine." Malani ran his fingers through his hair. "That means you can prevent yourself from ever getting sick."

"It's something like that, but this subject is too complicated to be had right now." Evailen didn't feel comfortable sharing too much about herself and decided to abandon that conversation.

"So, here is your serum. Take it only when we arrive, but I will have to take mine now."

Bofrat tried to speak before Evailen added, "I know that it means I have one hour less than all of you, but I can't risk endangering a dangerous plan."

"Then take this." Bofrat extended his arm as a tiny scarab crawled down his arm into his palm.

"What is it?" Evailen asked.

"It's a female scarab. Place it on your heart, and it will crawl inside and record your heart's activity at this moment. If all falls apart for you, then I can use the male to reverse time for your heart only. If I survive, then I can revive you too." Bofrat didn't tell her that the scarab too had a time limit. He wanted to give her hope.

"Do you have one for me too?" Malani asked.

"Sorry man, your chances will have to be exactly like mine."

Evailen grabbed the scarab and placed it below her red seed, clenching as she felt the small Majestic cut through her skin to reach her heart before she pressed her black seed to heal her body.

21

Rondai, Terqwan, Malani, Yasmina, and Salvanra stood in silence watching as Enyo sat next to Evailen's body lying on the floor holding her hand while Bofrat placed his palm on her heart hiding the scarab below it.

"So?" Yasmina asked.

Bofrat shook his head. "The scarabs didn't sync together yet."

Salvanra took a step closer to Bofrat with her arms crossed against her chest. "Is the male still alive."

Bofrat nodded.

"Good." Salvanra noticed how the others looked at her and understood that they wanted an explanation. "Scarabs can only eat live animals, but the ones they eat happen to be dangerous to them. When they identify a prey, the male latches on to it and releases a chemical that spreads in the heart before the rest of the hoard kills the animal. They then proceed to secure their dead prey by destroying the limbs and the jaw. After that the female syncs with the male latched onto the dead animal and revives it by rewinding the time of that animal's heart to the moment the male attached itself to it, giving them a meal of an alive, immobilized predator. However, the scarabs can't sync with one another after a certain period of time, in which case, the male will die too. Since Bofrat said the male is still alive, there's still a chance that the female will manage the sync."

At that moment, they heard Evailen's gasp for air. Enyo quickly leaned in to hug her, but Bofrat held him back by his shoulder.

"It's not finished yet. She will be okay, but the scarabs have to get out of her first." Bofrat kept his other hand on Evailen's heart until the two scarabs crawled back to his chest through his arm.

"Is it okay now?" Enyo asked the moment Bofrat moved his hand away from her.

When he saw Bofrat's nod, Enyo pulled Evailen into his arms.

"Too tight," Evailen said around her cough, her voice cracking, but Enyo ignored her.

Yasmina moved next to Bofrat and bent down on one knee. She looked at Evailen with a smile on her face and waited until Enyo freed her. "I can't believe you pulled it off."

"We did it together." Evailen grinned as she looked at Rondai. "Thank you."

Rondai nodded in silence, but his eyes never once left Evailen, even after she stood up and hugged everyone on both her team and his. When she approached him, he quickly extended his hand for a shake. She looked at his hand and smiled before cradling it between her palms.

The eight Mastoperians walked out of the building smoothly after the guards fled, fearing they were out powered. Enyo and Malani wanted to stay longer and search the building, hoping to understand more about the existence of such a corporation and how Lunardis could exist in this part of the world. But Evailen claimed they would find nothing, and that Lunardis knew how to cover their tracks well. They both disapproved, however, the rest of the group seemed to be on Evailen's side, so they accepted the majority's decision and agreed to relocate to a nearby café where Evailen and her team told the others their entire plan.

Once the truth was out, Rondai asked Yasmina to talk in private.

"I need to tell you something first," Evailen said, grabbing his arm before they moved away.

"What?" Rondai looked at her hand before meeting her eyes.

"I was the one who asked Yasmina to send you the message. Without it, our plan would have failed."

"We will talk about that later, but I still need to speak with Yasmina." Rondai pulled his arm from Evailen's grasp and led Yasmina to a corner, away from the group.

"Is it true?" he calmly asked.

"Is what true?" Yasmina raised her brows.

"Did she ask you to send me the message?"

Yasmina's voice shook as she said, "No, she didn't. I did it behind her back, but I couldn't keep lying to my team leader. I couldn't continue betraying her faith in me, so I told her the truth, and that's when she came up with the plan."

Rondai leaned over Yasmina's shoulders to look at Evailen from afar. "She's crazy that one." He smiled and started toward the table.

Yasmina froze as she needed time to grasp what he really meant. Her face grew red as she contemplated what his smile could entail.

When Rondai reached the table, he stood behind Evailen and placed a hand on her left shoulder. "Would you care to go for a short walk with me?"

Evailen placed her hand on top of his and imitated his serious tone. "I would love to," she replied, making everyone laugh.

Rondai locked both his hands together behind his back as they marched down a narrow street. "I admire that you took a stand for Yasmina, but you had to know that she would tell me the truth."

"I have no idea what you're talking about." Evailen closed her eyes. Sealed her lips and moved her entire face away from him in a childlike move, causing Rondai to laugh out loud at her reaction.

"Look at that. He *can* laugh!"

"What is that supposed to mean?" Rondai tried to force his serious face back in place but couldn't.

"I thought maybe you didn't know how to smile. Don't get me wrong, I wasn't trying to judge, but I thought maybe at Kala they never teach the men how to smile. After all, I don't know many Kalangous." Evailen hid her smile with her hand.

"No, they don't; it's a skill we have to learn on our own. So, forgive me if I was not that good at it."

"Did you make a joke?" Evailen raised her brows as she pivoted toward him.

"Me? Never." Rondai wore his serious face.

Evailen's red seed blinked as she froze in place. She snapped herself out of the confusion when she noticed that he was a few steps ahead of her now. Quickening her pace, she returned to his side. "I'm sorry. I'm such an awful judge of character."

"Don't apologize. I don't blame you. I know I can be mean sometimes." He paused when he realized how at ease he felt next to her. A feeling he deeply missed in Kala, yet he had experienced it more than once in the last few days. "I assume you have the first artifact. I won't say you used us because

I think you acted brilliantly, despite how crazy that plan of yours was. I just want you to remember that during the hunt for the other artifacts we are still rivals, and I won't go easy on you because we are friends now." Rondai smiled as his gaze followed his moving feet.

"Oh… We are friends?"

Rondai glanced at her from the corners of his eyes as his smile continued to inhabit his face, but he ignored her question. "We have to go. I can't waste more time here. The other teams have clearly gone after different artifacts."

Evailen nodded. "I think we will rest for a day or two. Returning from death is tiring." She didn't need to tell Rondai that, but he understood the message. She was giving him a head start as a thank you for his help.

22

"Are we going to keep running aimlessly for much longer?" Alinda stopped and sat on the grass before she shifted her eyes across the endless field surrounding them.

Jihave brought his tiger to a stop before turning his face down to see her. "What do you mean running aimlessly? Didn't you enjoy your time at the theme park? The boat ride? The walk among the skyscrapers?"

"No, I didn't. You are the one who enjoyed all those things. We have been running for two days at high speed. Correction, I'm the one who has been running at high speed. You are dangling on the back of your…" she paused to point at the tiger, "I don't know what that thing is. Cilia is using her pod, and Rolakan made himself what looks like a flying piece of wood. I'm tired, and we have no clue where we are going or when will we get there." Alinda took a deep breath to regulate her heartbeat.

Jihave sighed. "That *thing* is the greatest tiger of all time, and I told you to get on his back with me. You are the one who refused."

"I don't want to get on it. I don't like animals."

"Who doesn't like animals?" Cilia asked, quickly shifting her gaze toward her, legs crossed over her lotus-shaped pod.

Alinda scowled. "Well, I don't. Excuse me for not falling into your set of expectations."

Cilia rolled her eyes. "You're being rude, Alinda. You also refused to get on the flying wood with Rolakan. One could argue that you're the one who's slowing us down."

"That doesn't look safe either." Alinda threw her back on the ground.

Jihave's tiger moved between Cilia and Alinda with him on its back, looking at Cilia. "Alright girls, cut it out. She isn't slowing us down." He turned to Alinda. "But we can't come to a full stop either. We have to keep moving."

"Ugh… I'm exhausted. Can't we rest a little while you tell us where we're going? Motivate us. We didn't even search for the location of the artifacts." Alinda kept the clear sky within her eyesight.

"I don't know where we're going exactly, but I assure you that we're moving toward one of the artifacts."

Jihave patted the tiger, who moved around before he turned to face Alinda one more time. "If you don't move, then I will leave without you."

Rolakan waved his hand and the wooden tablet he sat on moved closer to Alinda before he extended his arm to her. "If security is your only concern, I will add sidebars to secure you."

Alinda sighed before she nodded. "You could have offered this from the beginning." Her body was failing her, and she could no longer run. She took his arm and placed herself behind him before wrapping her arm around his waist.

Rolakan said nothing. He was five-feet-five-inches, dark-skinned with a built body, bald head, and wide brown eyes.

"You don't talk much do you," Alinda asked.

"I never thought about it, actually. I guess it's because in my faction they teach us to never overdo anything. Perhaps that has also extended to my speaking ability." Rolakan smiled.

"That sounds strange." Alinda laid her head on Rolakan's back to hide from the wind, not noticing how Rolakan shook his head in disapproval when he felt her head on his back.

"What about you? You come from an advanced faction. How is it possible the Delphians have never made something to use for transportation?"

"I complain about that same thing all the time. It would have been useful now. However, we are more of academics than we are inventors. Lunardis are the ones who invent, and sometimes we take their inventions. Did you know that it was Lunardis contractors who built Delphia? I mean they followed our planning and designs, but we've never actually had construction workers among us."

"Interesting. I didn't know that," Rolakan answered.

"Is it? Interesting, I mean. Don't you want me to elaborate? Is there nothing you want to ask about? Now I am the one who finds that interesting."

Rolakan said nothing.

Alinda sighed when she realized that Rolakan was only being polite rather than interested in having a conversation with her. She turned her head to the other side and glanced at Cilia, who flew on her pod next to them before shifting her gaze toward Jihave who rode in front.

"So how is our destination decided?" Alinda asked, raising her voice to make sure Jihave could hear her. "How do you know which direction we need to take?"

Cilia's face grew hot as her red seed blinked before she turned toward Alinda with her eyes bulging out. "Alinda enough! You haven't stopped talking since we left. I thought I talk a lot but compared to you, I'm an introvert."

"Do you mean to tell me you are not interested in knowing anything about why we are moving in this direction?"

"If you stopped talking for a minute and noticed your surroundings, you could have seen that we are following an invisible animal. You can't see it, but you could at least notice its movement around us!" Cilia's voice grew louder.

"Her," Jihave clarified.

"What?" Cilia quickly turned her head to him.

"That Majestic is a *her* not an it." Jihave glanced at his invisible deer and muttered to himself, "At least for now. Soon, when she grows accustomed to my body, she will change gender."

Cilia's heart rate increased, and her tone turned into a shout. "This is what you comment on, and all of that naivety she is showing doesn't catch your attention?" She paused, feeling her red seed blink faster and faster before she took a deep breath. "I'm sorry. I shouldn't have talked to you like that."

Jihave slowed his tiger to get closer to Cilia's pod. "It's okay. I understand your frustration. I have to say this though; I don't think you are naive, but you are the one who is showing naivety. Alinda noticed Lafayette early on. She also doesn't say or do anything without calculation. At first, I thought she was just bored and trying to pass the time, but it became more obvious as she spoke. She seems to be testing us. Perhaps it is a combination of boredom and investigation. Or maybe she is just trying to define how much she can trust us."

Jihave pivoted his head and stared directly into Alinda's eyes. "Am I wrong?"

Alinda turned her head the other way while keeping it stuck to Rolakan's back to hide her wide grin.

Cilia closed her eyes and took a deep breath, then shook her head and dipped her chin closer to her chest as her posture slumped.

"Anyway," Jihave continued, pride shining through in his voice, "Lafayette is one of the rarest Majestics in our forest. She is very hard to track since she is invisible, and I can feel her tattoo on my body, even though no one can see it. However, if you tame her after the capture, she can lead you to whatever your heart desires as long as you let her move freely. So, enjoy the journey she is taking us through and trust that we will get there at the end."

23

At the foot of a mountain, in front of a long staircase that led up to a temple, Jihave and his companions stood against an open red gate engraved with the phrase, "Peace is not deserved. It is earned."

"The artifact is in that temple." Jihave kept his eyes fixed on the small building at the peak of the mountain.

"Are you sure?" Cilia asked.

"Um… No, but I can feel it. My intuition has never betrayed me." Jihave scratched the back of his head.

"Okay, guys. Let us climb those million stairs based on that man's intuition." Alinda clapped twice.

Jihave squinted as his eyes met hers. "Do you realize you keep undermining my authority by doing that?"

"I didn't know you had already established one." Alinda laughed out loud.

The relationship they both had was strange. Usually, Jihave wouldn't accept such behavior from anyone he didn't know well, but regardless of Alinda's annoying traits, he couldn't be mad at her. Perhaps it was because she was the youngest among all the companions. Even though he knew that her faction thought highly of her, she was still only seventeen years old. Perhaps he felt she was the younger sister he never had but always wished for.

They took about two hours to climb the stairs. At the top, a monk waited for them in front of the temple's main entrance. His top half exposed, bald except for one braid. He wore long, wide red pants and had a tattoo of an eye in the center of his forehead. He knelt the moment they appeared atop the stairs and gestured with his hand for them to enter.

The four entered the temple's main court without exchanging words. At the main hall, two lines of monks paved the way. They all sat on the floor, cradling a candle that had red flames. At the other end, the head monk sat slightly higher from the rest. The four teammates walked toward the head monk and positioned themselves in front of him. Jihave imitated the way the monks sat, and so did his companions.

Jihave took a deep breath and prepared to address the head monk. He straightened his back, raised his chin, and locked his gaze of determination with the monk's brown eyes. The companions looked at each other in silence, waiting to see what Jihave was up to.

Jihave exhaled loudly and nodded before he said, "Hi."

The monk repeated his greeting.

A moment of silence then filled the air until Alinda broke it with a high-pitched laugh. The others followed her example.

The monk shifted his gaze to the candle in front of him and waited for silence to prevail once more. When it did, he asked, "Why are you here?"

"We are looking for an artifact that—"

"Say no more." The monk raised his palm. "A long time ago, three warriors came with a box that had an artifact. They asked us to hide and protect it until they returned. We have kept it hidden for almost eight centuries. Now you return to claim what is yours, and we shall give you access to the path."

"Great. That was easier than I thought." Jihave stood.

"If you solve my riddle," the monk continued.

"Of course." Jihave returned to his previous position. "Hit me, old man."

"I speak with no mouth, I tell you no lies, the center of your world, my spies are your eyes." The head monk paused. "You have only one chance to answer."

"No," Alinda interrupted Jihave before he could speak.

"What is it, Alinda?" Jihave pivoted his head toward her.

"The answer you were about to give is wrong. Give me a few minutes, and I will find the right one." Alinda sounded serious for the first time since their journey began.

Jihave nodded at her as she closed her eyes. Everyone waited in silence for Alinda to find the correct answer, so devoid of movement that even if an insect had entered the temple at that moment, they would have heard it.

Seven minutes later, Alinda opened her eyes. "The answer is my mind."

Jihave smiled. "That's good. Now tell us what's in your mind. We can't read it."

"No. The answer is *my mind*," she said, putting an emphasis on her last two words.

"Why would the answer be your mind? Did you think the Forbidden Warriors would bother with creating an ancient riddle just so the answer could be your mind?" Jihave kept his expression stoic. "If you need more time to find the true answer, it's okay. You are young and need experience. I understand."

Alinda blinked in surprise. "I looked into the future and saw what you're doing. Quit joking around."

"Looks like you're not as fun as I thought you were." Jihave chuckled before facing the head monk to tell him Alinda's answer.

The monk nodded. "I shall allow you to continue your journey, and seek what you want, we did our job." The monk blew his candle out and rose. The other monks did the same, which prompted Jihave to copy their actions. Even if he had no candle, he imagined one in his head.

The four companions followed the monk as he ambled out of the temple hall.

"I don't know what this artifact does or represents, but I know that it is part of a bigger plan." The monk searched his keychain that carried nearly a hundred keys. "But my job was not to ask or search for the truth. My job was to keep it safe." He opened a door uncovering a dark room. "Through this door, you should be able to find what you seek. Now, leave my temple."

"Won't you finish your story?" Jihave shouted as he watched the monk walk away.

"There was no story to finish," the monk muttered as he returned to the temple hall.

"Can you see what comes next?" Jihave asked Alinda.

"No, I can't. I'm walking into this as blind as all of you are."

"So, we are going in? All of us, together?" Jihave asked.

"We started this mission together, and we will finish it together." Cilia nodded.

"Technically, we didn't start it together."

"Alinda!" Jihave shouted, chastising her remark.

She rolled her eyes. "I was joking."

They all looked at each other for a moment, then together, stepped into the dark room.

24

Once the four entered the room, the large door closed on its own, and with it, the light behind them disappeared.

"Do you know what we didn't think about?" Cilia's voice conquered the darkness as her seeds began to glow. "The monk could have lied, and we are simply in a prison."

"That sounds like fun." Alinda pitched a small laugh.

"What—" Before Jihave could finish his question, the floor disappeared, and they fell onto a large slide. There were many ways for them to stop their rapid descent, but as the light slowly returned, they saw how Alinda was enjoying the slide, which gave them a sense of security, so they decided to experience her happiness.

A pile of soft sand waited for them at the bottom as they fell on top of each other. Cilia grunted as she felt the sand slip into her skintight outfit.

"Wasn't that fun?" Alinda's grin widened.

Rolakan fixed the mess caused to his wide turban. "Our definition of fun is obviously different."

"I enjoyed it too." Jihave placed his palm on Alinda's shoulder and smiled.

Alinda ran slightly ahead and stood in front of three different stone passages. "The artifact is this way," she said, pointing to the path on their right.

"I thought you said you couldn't see the artifact," Rolakan said.

"I can't. However, I should be able to see the end of all the passages, only I can't see this one. So, it's safe to assume that the artifact is this way." She gave them all a grin of triumph.

"That makes sense." Cilia's eyes grew warm as they fell on Alinda.

"See. I told you that the artifact is in this temple," Jihave said playfully.

"Man, we're no longer *in* the temple." Alinda stuck her tongue out.

"Technically, we still are," Jihave quickly stated.

"The monk literally said, 'Now, leave my temple.'" Alinda repeated, imitating the monk's voice.

Rolakan shook his head and patted Jihave's back. "Don't bother. You won't win with her."

As they walked deeper into the cave, carvings appeared on the wall. The language was different from any they spoke.

"Do you think it's a language from this side of the world?" Jihave asked.

Cilia struggled to swallow. "It isn't. It's an ancient language from the first civilization."

Rolakan brushed his fingers over the carvings. "I've never seen it before. It looks beautiful."

"Can you read it?" Jihave turned his head to Cilia.

"A little. I don't understand the entire text, but I can translate words here and there, nothing more. Old world. Immortality. Death. It doesn't make that much sense." Cilia glanced at Alinda.

"Perhaps they were talking about the end of their world," said Jihave.

Cilia shook her head. "If the monks received the artifact less than a millennium ago, then it was after the first civilization, but not too long after that they could have still remembered the language." She looked at Alinda who had said nothing since they began seeing the carvings. "What do you think, Alinda? You learn about the old language in your schools, don't you?"

Alinda avoided meeting Cilia's eyes. "We do, but only if you majored in ancient languages. I didn't." Alinda stopped there. It was the first time she had lied to them. She knew exactly what the writings on the wall meant, and it scared her. She didn't know what to think of it. She kept her mouth shut, as she knew at that moment that there was only one person she could talk to, and that person was Kawan.

"Okay guys, we don't need to worry about this right now. All we need to think about is claiming that artifact." Jihave felt a shudder pass through his skin that forced him to stop and examine his surroundings before he freed his double-headed ape out of its tattoo.

"Is everything okay?" Rolakan brought his thumb to his chest and prepared to open any gate he needed.

"I'm just being cautious," Jihave replied, speaking in a hushed voice. "No need to be afraid but stay alert all the same."

The path ahead appeared dangerous. The light they had gained faded away as images of death began to appear on the walls.

Rolakan noticed that Alinda had put distance between them since her conversation with Cilia. "Alinda. Stay close to us," he said in a commanding tone. Ever since he saw her in the Forbidden City, it annoyed him that she was so young. He didn't like that her faction sent a teen on such a dangerous mission and he felt somewhat responsible for her. "Alinda. I said, stay close to us," he repeated, making his voice louder.

Alinda, who was still several yards ahead, stood still to wait for them before she made sure that Rolakan heard her loud sigh. But before they reached her, a shudder passed through her body and tears accumulated in her eyes.

"What's wrong? Did you see something?" Rolakan held her shoulders with his hands.

Alinda said nothing. She looked as if her mind wasn't there while tears streamed down her cheeks.

Jihave moved closer to her. "Whatever you saw, I don't want you to worry. We will protect you." He reached to grab her, but she quickly pushed her body into Rolakan's arms, hugging him to Jihave's surprise.

"Now, I want to know, Jihave began, speaking with a firm tone. "What did you see?"

"Not now Jihave." Cilia pulled Alinda away from Rolakan and took her into her arms. She brushed Alinda's hair with her fingers and said nothing. At that moment, Cilia didn't see a member of another faction; she saw a kid that needed assurance. She whispered something into Alinda's ear, to which Alinda nodded twice. Cilia then wiped the girl's tears with her fingers and walked with her arm placed around Alinda's shoulder.

"We're not alone," Jihave said as his ape sped forward. "We will wait here."

The four halted with eyes glued on a turn ahead of them that prevented them from seeing the rest of the path. Seconds passed like hours as Jihave and Rolakan stood on guard until they heard a sound. A small explosion followed by a cry for help that escaped the ape.

Jihave and Rolakan immediately ran in the direction Jihave's ape had gone while Jihave freed his tiger and Rolakan opened the fourth gate of magic before materializing a ball of fire in his hand.

They were ready for battle.

25

The two men reached the injured ape to find Kawan and his companions on the other end of the passage with cell or gate-like iron bars to their back, through which the artifact was visible.

Rolakan shifted his gaze toward Ryn—his Kalangou friend who was now a member of Kawan's team—before extinguishing the fireball he previously conjured in his hand. "What did you do?"

"It attacked us first. I acted only in self-defense." Ryn relaxed his fisted hand. With an open palm, the stone fist he had created using the power of the fourth gate made his hand look like he wore a glove made of stone. Ryn stood only five-feet-four-inches tall with a slim body, dark skin, bald head, and dark-green eyes.

"This is my fault." Jihave blinked and spoke slowly. "I sent him straight into battle without investigating if the threat was real or not." Jihave knew, however, that his ape would have never attacked if it didn't feel bad intentions coming from his enemy. He moved toward the Majestic and cradled it before he absorbed it back into his body.

"What are you doing here, though?" Jihave spoke with a strong tone as he turned to face Kawan again.

Kawan smirked, shaking his head. "The same thing you are, searching for the artifact."

"Shouldn't you have gotten it by now? It looks like you were waiting for us." Jihave shifted his eyes to Maringrad—the Averetti on the other team—and ignored Kawan.

When Cilia and Alinda heard the chatter, they caught up with their team members. As soon as Alinda saw Kawan, she locked her eyes with his and shook her head slowly, but he ignored her.

Kawan shifted his gaze between the members of Jihave's team, but avoided meeting their eyes. "We were on our way to get the artifact when we heard you arrive. We waited to tell you we had arrived first. Remember, there are no fights allowed over the artifacts."

"There are no fights over a claimed artifact, but this one is up for grabs. Perhaps you should let us pass, and you go search for another one." Jihave thrust his chest out and took a step closer to Kawan.

Kawan brought his gaze to his feet and shook his head repeatedly. "I don't want to fight you. I really don't. We all have members of our factions on the other side, and I'm sure you became friends as we did. Please take your group and go. We arrived here first." Kawan slowly raised his head and met Alinda's eyes before blinking back a tear.

Alinda saw his face and let out a deep sigh before she took two steps backward. Maringrad looked at Kawan's eyes and took a few steps to the front, leaving his team to his back before he freed his inked elephant.

"So you captured him!" Jihave freed his tiger in the same moment before the Majestic moved up to the elephant with barred teeth.

"I don't want to fight you either." Maringrad brought his feet together as he assumed his battle stance. "But you are leaving him no choice. He beat you here. Accept your defeat and go search for another one. Otherwise, I won't hesitate to fight back."

A single second seemed like an eternity as they all felt a single stream of wind make its way through the artifact room to the narrow stone passage where they all stood. All eyes shifted slowly between faction members who never imagined they would one-day fight against one another until the tiger's roar broke the silence, and everyone moved at once.

Cilia, Jihave, Alinda, and Rolakan, stood facing their old faction members, Naradia, Maringrad, Kawan, and Ryn, respectively.

Once the fight began, Alinda found a small hidden corner and sat on the ground. She used her hands to lock her ears before she squeezed her eyes shut, saiting to see the outcome of the battle.

Naradia brushed her black seed, releasing her body armor and weapon. She pulled out her transparent gun and shot only toward Cilia, who found herself trapped in a corner behind her full body shield. Cilia's eyebrows furrowed as she tried to understand why her friend chose her as a target.

Rolakan threw two balls of fire out of his hand. A large one toward Naradia, and a smaller ball toward Ryn to prevent him from blocking the first one.

Ryn smiled. Seeing the fight as a chance to kindle his old competitive spirit and remind Rolakan that he never lost to him in their friendly brawls. "You will have to do better than that," he said to Rolakan as he materialized a wall of water ten-inches thick across the entire passage to counter both balls simultaneously.

Kawan looked at Ryn's water barrier as it fell to the ground and pressed his key chain before it converted into a sword larger than his height. He ran toward Jihave as the sound of splashing water increased with every step he took. He raised his sword, but before he could swing it forward, he foresaw a kick from the ape Jihave freed again that would send him flying into the wall, so he forced his body to turn around and face the second threat.

Rolakan swirled the wind below his palm into a long thin micro-tornado and manipulated its shape until it resembled a sword before he used it to counter Kawan's fast and repetitive strikes against him. He gasped as he retreated across the passage, managing only to deflect. When Kawan saw that Rolakan had nowhere to back up to, he half smiled and gave the latter a chance to attack. Each time Rolakan advanced, Kawan quickly changed from defense to offense, backing him once again to the same wall.

Jihave stood still with his arms locked behind his back before he pushed his ape back into battle. But when the ape tried to surpass Maringrad's elephant, the inked Majestic rammed it into the wall. The elephant then hammered on the ape, trapping it between itself and the wall until the tiger attacked, sinking its fangs in the elephant's thick skin. The elephant then proceeded to crash its entire body on both sides of the passage to get rid of the tiger, causing the ground beneath them to quake.

Maringrad ignored the traces of dirt falling from the ceiling due to his elephant's rampage. His heart raced when he saw the ape prepare to land a powerful punch on his Majestic, and he ran toward it. Using the wall as a base to push himself toward the ape, Maringrad grabbed the Majestics arms and tensed his body to cage the ape.

Jihave saw Ryn and Naradia move toward him, and he released a small wasp out of his palm tattoo. The wasp multiplied itself into hundreds and thrust toward the two opposing team members.

Naradia pressed her black seed atop the right side of her chest before her armor wrapped her entire body, including her face, a technique that proved effective.

Ryn, however, felt the pain of each of the wasps as if it was a stab deep in his skin. His breathing became thick and heavy, his blood rushing in his veins before he conjured a mud cocoon around his entire body to protect himself against future attacks as well as to numb the pain.

Cilia took multiple quick breaths before she left the comfort of her shield. She pulled her handheld cannon out of her armor and blasted Naradia repeatedly before the latter had a chance to switch her eyes away from the wasp attack.

Naradia's armor remained intact against Cilia's attack, but the pressure was too much, and her body began to fall toward the floor. When she saw Cilia stop firing and move closer to her with a quivering chin, she grabbed her gun once again and fired back at Cilia, forcing her to retreat to the comfort of her shield.

Kawan glanced at Jihave who had stood still the entire time before deflecting an attack from Rolakan. His small smile disappeared from his face as his expression turned more serious before he struck a blow to the handle of Rolakan's sword forcing the wind to rampage. Kawan glared at Rolakan, then retreated and turned toward Jihave with fast steps. When he foresaw the fireball that Rolakan threw nearing him, he forced his body to do a quick turn, but when he faced the right direction again, he found his cheek too close to Jihave's fist.

Kawan quickly threw his body in the opposite direction to avoid the punch, losing his balance in the process. He saw what was coming next, but without control over his body, Kawan braced his arms for impact as Jihave's invisible deer rammed into him, throwing his body to the wall.

Ryn felt his heart race faster and faster inside his self-made prison. He heaved a heavy sigh before he set his cocoon on fire to heat the mud before forcing it to explode, launching the hot debris everywhere.

Both Naradia and Cilia used their shields to protect their team members, but the debris managed to hit the tiger and the elephant. A loud roar filled the entire place as the tiger fell off the elephant's back.

Jihave's eyes widened, and his face froze for a second before he and his ape sped toward Ryn. When Rolakan saw his team leader rush in the direction of his friend, his feet froze in place as his brain failed to process the next step. Cilia, however, fired her cannon randomly around them to provide a layer of cover.

Naradia lifted her feet and quickly jumped in front of Ryn with her shield to protect him, creating a window for both Maringrad and Kawan to attack a distracted Jihave.

Maringrad began his attack but retreated after with a single glance, he noticed his elephant do a half fall. In that split second in which he saw his elephant falling next to Jihave's tiger, Maringrad was reminded how an Averetti felt when their Majestics fell. He placed his hand against his heart and squeezed his skin as he realized that he was about to attack his best friend with an intent to kill. Kawan, however, had already jumped in the air and was about to pierce Jihave's back with his sword.

THE COMPANIONS

Part One

ALINDA

"Alinda."

"I told you I am tired of running. It has been two days. I need to rest."

"Alinda... Alinda... Wake up." Alinda's father, Macro exhaled loudly as he shook his head. "You are talking in your sleep again. Come on, it's time for school." He pulled the bed covers off her.

Alinda tried to open her eyes but gave up before she slowly rolled to the other side of the bed and shoved her head below her pillow. "Can't I sleep a little longer?" She yawned.

"No, you can't." Macro grabbed her pillow and threw it to the other end of the bed. "You are late already. Get up and get ready."

"Fine." Alinda pushed off the bed in slow motion. When her eyes met her father's, she exaggerated her frown before trudging into the bathroom. She knew she needed to prepare quickly to join her teacher and classmates that waited for her on the roof. Until Delphian children reached the age of twelve, their class teachers collected them one by one every morning and showed them how to free-run to school.

When Alinda's teacher saw her step onto the roof with heavy steps, she crossed her arms over her breasts. "You're late again, Alinda. We have a long distance to cover."

"Why can't we have a hovercraft or something like the Lunardis?" Alinda rolled her eyes. "Free-running everywhere is exhausting."

"You are only ten years old, and you're already complaining about sport?" The teacher shook her head before she moved to the front of the group to lead them.

Alinda intentionally mimicked her teacher's sour face while making sounds that meant nothing.

When they arrived at school, Alinda saw her best friend Layan waiting for her at the front entrance.

"Did you make your class arrive late again?" Layan punched Alinda's arm.

"Ouch." Alinda's eyes widened. "It wasn't my fault. Why do you always assume everything is my fault?"

"Because it always is." Alinda opened her mouth to speak, but Layan quickly added, "We have to go. I don't want to be late for gym class. We will start a new practice today."

Both girls ran toward the class, arriving right before the teacher joined them.

The teacher centered the class standing in the school playground. "Today, we will train on the obstacles course. This course will help you develop your saiting skills and teach you how to see more timelines quicker. To pass this class, all you need to do is to start here," the teacher said, pointing at a red line painted across the floor, "and make it to the other end of the field, so don't be hasty or worry about it. You have the entire year to do it, and you will notice progress quickly."

Most children cheered and clapped. Only a few showed signs of stress. Alinda, however, was thinking about her dream from that morning. She saw a terrain she wasn't familiar with and wondered where her brain got these images.

One by one, the students stepped into the obstacles course for their first try.

The course was made of a hundred and fifty feet long and sixty-five-feet wide block of metal that stretched across half the gym's floor. Every fifteen feet into the course, a one-inch thick hole that stretched across the full width of the track was visible. Wooden bars three feet long with different widths surfaced out of the holes at random times before retracting beneath the course within a few seconds.

For a student to complete the course, they needed to march through the entire track with none of the wooden obstacles blocking their path. If an obstacle cut them off, they had to restart the entire track. This device taught the Delphian children to use the power of saiting on the go, as they had to foresee each obstacle before it appeared and then adjusted their movement accordingly.

Everyone noticed how Alinda's eyes wandered away before she started the course. It was clear that she was lost in her mind, neglecting her teacher's pointers before she stepped in. However, she cruised through the entire track as if it wasn't there, prompting everyone to clap for her, but she didn't pay attention to that either. She replayed her dream again and again in her mind and wondered about the people she saw in it; so caught in her dream that she didn't even notice when her teacher ended the class early.

Alinda came back to her senses only when she heard her following class's teacher call for her.

"They need you at the headmaster's office." The teacher said before the principal's assistant knocked on the door.

Alinda dallied her way through the desks and waited for the assistant by the door. She could have saited to see what they wanted from her before she arrived at the headmaster's office, but she hadn't cared enough to worry about it.

When the headmaster saw Alinda join him, he smiled and pointed for her to sit. "How are you feeling today, Alinda?"

"A bit disoriented but rather fine." Alinda took the seat on the other side of the office.

"Quite the description from such a young girl. Do you care to tell me why?"

"I had this dream today, and I don't understand it." Alinda fixed her eyes on her swinging feet.

"You know, dreams usually come from our subconscious. They try to tell us something about ourselves."

"I know that, which is why I'm confused. I saw things that have no connection or meaning to my life."

"To your life?" The headmaster chuckled.

"Are you looking down on me because I'm only ten years old?" Alinda swung her feet faster.

"On the contrary. I think you are an exceptional young woman. That is why I asked to see you. Didn't you see that on your way here?"

"I try not to see things I can't change. You would tell me anyway, there was no reason for me to foresee it."

"That is wise of you." The principal admired the way she spoke so maturely. "I called you here because I think this school is too easy for you. You have portrayed abilities far beyond your age."

"Where will I go?" Alinda stopped swinging her feet and fixed her eyes on the headmaster.

"To the Mandara School for gifted students. What do you think?" The principal smiled when Alinda stood and jumped around, clapping her hands. "I will take that as a yes then."

The principal chuckled. "Go back to your class for now, and I will prepare the transfer papers so you can start there tomorrow."

Alinda ran out the door, skipping steps as her grin widened.

The gym teacher who had waited in the corner the entire time moved closer to the headmaster. "Don't you think this is too big of a move? She is only ten. Gifted students don't normally start there before the age of fifteen."

"How many students do you know that passed that course on their first try, and without paying attention?" asked the headmaster.

"None."

"Exactly... None."

MARINGRAD

The corners of Maringrad's father's eyes lifted as he watched his son prepare for his first hunt. "Once you cross the valley, follow your training. Do your best and try to catch that tiger but know that it will be okay if you don't. You will have other chances." He sat on one knee to match his son's height. "The one thing you need to remember is to go for the young ones. Your tiger will be your best friend, and you want to grow together. Now, off you go." He ruffled his son's hair.

Maringrad felt his heart race but kept a calm face. He nodded to his father before he crossed the valley into the southern forest. When he reached the edge of the forest, he took off his slippers and continued barefoot to avoid making any unnecessary noise.

As he advanced into the forest, he carefully inspected the trees for marks that showed a tiger's nest. He took nearly half a day to find one. Once he confirmed the marking belonged to a Majestic tiger, he climbed a tree to have a wider view of the area. He had learned in school that the tiger's weakness appears only against aerial attacks.

He moved from one tree to another easily while keeping his focus on the ground below until he noticed her. The tigress's stripes glowed white, indicating she was a new mother. He followed her as she strolled across the woods, feared by other creatures. This was ironic, since Majestic tigers were vegetarian by nature, and they only ate one type of plant that grew only next to swamps. When a tigress birthed new cubs, she had to keep them far from water striders until their skin became strong enough to repel the carnivorous insect. To make sure the water striders couldn't reach the newborn, the tigers kept their babies two hours away from any water source.

Maringrad followed the tigress for an hour until she arrived at the swamp. He watched the Majestic as she ate before quietly following her back to the nest.

He lay atop a branch, watching the loving mother feed her newborn cubs before she cradled them to sleep. He stayed awake the entire night watching the baby tigers, trying to decide which would be the coolest, but the tigers were too young, and their stripes were still black. There was no way he could know which color their stripes would change to as a tiger's hide didn't change until they reached three months old and with it the color of their stripes. An adult tiger's stripes differed in shape and color, making each tiger unique. The only similarities they shared was how their stripes glowed in the dark.

The night was long, and the more he observed the cubs, the sadder Maringrad felt. Separating a baby from its parent reminded him of his own mother, and how death had taken her away from him, but then he also remembered how all his friends showed off their captured tigers' tattoos. His father was always away, so he never went on a hunt like the other kids whose mothers' had accompanied. His mother had died when she gave birth to his younger brother Bofrat.

At sunrise, he watched as the tigress left on her journey to gather more food. He waited for her to be far enough before tying an elastic rope around himself. He attached the other end to the branch and jumped toward the five baby tigers grabbing the one he could reach first. When the elastic rope pulled him back up, he freed himself and ran as fast as he could across the trees, trying to find a suitable cave. Once he found it, he blocked the entrance trapping the cub inside with him.

The tiger attacked him several times, but he could easily defend himself against a Majestic that didn't have its claws and fangs yet.

When the tiger got tired, Maringrad chose a spot at the end of the cave and sat. He brought his knees close to his shoulders and rested his arm and head on them while maintaining eye contact with the tiger. Their stare remained unbroken for nearly half an hour. Every five minutes, the tiger moved closer and closer to him until they were nearly touching.

The tiger brushed on Maringrad's legs before climbing on his back without Maringrad moving a muscle. The cub sniffed his neck a few times before sinking its only tooth in it, creating a blood connection between the two. The tiger's body slowly disintegrated into ink and merged with Maringrad's body leaving nothing but a baby-tiger tattoo on his neck. Maringrad felt a burn that passed through his entire body, but he stayed still for a while longer.

◉ 🐟 ⚘ ☯

When Maringrad returned to the edge of the valley, he found his father waiting for him. He ran into his arms and cried. His father understood that he missed his mother and gave him a long hug before congratulating him on a successful hunt.

"I want you to love this tiger as much as you love your brother. You need to take good care of him. Protect him while he's young, so he repays the favor when he grows older."

"Yes, father." Maringrad wiped the tears off his eyes.

"What will you call him?" his father asked.

"Soniac." Maringrad named him after his mother.

His father smiled. "Well then, it's time to return home and feed Soniac."

On their way back, Maringrad jumped up and down.

"Why are you so active all of a sudden? Aren't you tired?"

"I can't wait to show my friends my new tiger. Most of them have two beasts already, and I am finally catching up." Maringrad smiled, showing his teeth.

His father stopped and faced him. "Listen. Your tiger isn't a beast. He is your best friend and will be by your side even when the world turns its back on you. He is you. Engraved in your soul, and you should care about him more than your friends' opinions because tigers are the only Majestic you can't replace if they die, and you lose most of your soul with them."

"But father, everyone calls them beasts and they show them off. Why can't I do the same?"

"It doesn't matter what they say or do. Even if the entire world does something, that doesn't mean you should do the same. What you do and say is what defines you. Remember that always." Maringrad's father believed that if he taught him nothing but this, then he taught his son everything he needed to know.

CILIA

Cilia stood in her room, in front of a wall that she turned into a three-dimensional image display using her purple seed. White wedding dresses centered the wall, and she flipped through them by waving her hand, as she had done countless times before. Once a dress appeared on the wall, she would turn around to face a mirror on the other side and see how it looked on her. Lunardis used the power of the yellow seed allowing them to change the state of any material, the black seed, allowing them to pull metal particles in their bodies out through their skin, and the purple seed allowing them to shapeshift any object to create the clothes they wore. When shopping for clothes, they looked only for the design and used their seeds and imagination to recreate it on their bodies.

Cilia's frown grew larger as she switched from one dress to another. After the sixteenth dress, she sighed and shook her head before she threw her back on her bed.

She stayed there for a few minutes, staring at the ceiling until she felt a burst of energy course through her body. Then she jumped out of her bed and left her apartment.

She walked down the lively streets of Lunar's main city. She passed hundreds of billboards advertising their latest technology until she came to a quiet neighborhood. She waited until the night fell before she walked into an old, abandoned park.

Under a small bridge, she leaned her back against a door and looked in both directions several times. When she felt alone, she passed through the door and climbed down a staircase that centered the dark room into a long passage. She walked for a few minutes before she climbed down another staircase that led to a bigger room. There, she looked around before pressing her black seed twice to activate part of her armor, which only covered her six seeds. She walked out of the room into a grand hall filled with people.

Most of them had no clothes on, and those who did had very little. The one thing they all shared was their white eyes, almost vacant of pupils. Cilia smelled their lack of hygiene as she carefully advanced through the hall. She greeted a lot of them by name and asked if they needed anything, but none answered her question.

Halfway across the room, one of the homeless tried to snatch one of her seeds, but she pushed him away easily. She thought about retaliating with her cannon but chose not to.

Near the end of the room, a black-haired girl with several burn marks on her body sat on the floor. Her flesh appeared as though it was part of her bones, and she wore nothing but a bracelet on her left arm.

"I miss you." Cilia sat next to the girl who appeared half-conscious.

The girl fought to sit correctly before looking toward Cilia with a blank expression. Her eyes, like the others, had a transparent pupil that was hardly visible. She struggled with moving her arm to reach a bracelet on Cilia's hand that looked exactly like hers. She scratched it twice with her fragile fingers before she rested her head on Cilia's shoulder. Cilia cradled the girl's hand with hers and sighed quietly.

"I'm going on a mission far away from here. When I return, it will be time for my wedding. I want you to be there. I can't see myself getting married without you." Cilia tried to blink back her tears but failed.

The girl used all her force to slip her fingers into Cilia's and squeezed her hand.

"I found a black-market dealer. He said he could find me six real seeds of a deceased person. You won't be able to use their power, but they should have enough energy to breathe life back into you so you could come back to the surface and live with us. No one will be able to tell the difference."

"Cost?" The girl spoke with a broken voice that Cilia could hardly hear.

"Don't worry about that. I have already negotiated the price." Cilia's tears grew faster and denser.

The girl pushed her head closer toward Cilia's neck.

"It's okay. I can handle it." Cilia kissed the girl's head. "You know, once I come back from the mission, I will start a career in politics. I have good friends that can back me up. And one day, when I'm in a leadership seat, I will impose a new law to allow everyone here to come back to the surface. Our technology is advanced enough to fix everyone. All we need is the desire. We pretend to be the most righteous, yet we give up on our own people and leave them to rot as life slowly slips out of their bodies." Cilia's sobs became louder as her words began to fail her. She stayed there in silence until she fell asleep, holding her little sister's hand.

When she woke up, she realized it was morning already, and she had to leave for her mission. She kissed her sister's head again and walked out of that place, unable to contain her anger. She knew that it could have been her in that dump instead of her sister. She was almost tempted to try the new drug on the street that gave an immediate and lasting high. The drug came in the shape of a seed which in order to use, one had to replace one of their birth seeds with the drugged one. Seed traffickers took advantage of the addicts and stole their detached seeds, leaving them without birth seeds. The thieves knew the magnitude of power and knowledge those seeds contained.

Lost in thought, Cilia muttered to herself, "Only Lunardis would know how to maintain and use a seed that has been separated from its owner. How low does someone need to be to join such a trade, where they destroy the lives of their own faction members?"

Cilia was determined to not only save the life of her sister and those who shared her fate but to punish anyone who took part in the crime. She knew that the ladder began at the feet of those who invented the drug seed, but she didn't know how high it went. It didn't matter though. She would fight until her last breath.

NARADIA

When Naradia received the letter that informed her she didn't get the job, she didn't waste time crying over it. She placed her purple seed on the table in front of her and browsed other opportunities.

She knew it wouldn't be easy for her to get a job with her family reputation. Her parents and her older brother were drug addicts. They continued their drug habits for a long time after they lost their seeds by helping the drug dealers capture new victims until Lunar guards caught them. However, the story that dominated the news was, "When Will the Little Girl Fill Her Parent's Shoes?"

Her name was everywhere. Even the government marked her so they could track her at all times. According to the law, the government could only mark criminals with a past record of over two offenses, but they threatened her of receiving the same sentence as her parents if she ever told anyone about the marking.

Naradia was a simple girl. She wanted no trouble. All she wanted was for her family's past not to define her life. She never forgot the nights when she had to sleep without food because she couldn't afford it and the shameful looks thrown at her by those who recognized her in the streets.

There were days when she felt that her struggle would never end. That was until she met Cilia. She applied for a janitor's post at Cilia's father's new company building and receiving the usual letter of rejection. They needed a hundred janitors to keep the large office building maintained and received only thirty-nine applications, yet they rejected her. When she saw the number of applicants, her blood boiled, and she felt the need to act before she lost her will to live.

She walked into the building, prepared to fight for her right to have a job for which she was over-qualified. While filling the recruiter's ears with the frustration of a hundred rejections, Cilia stood outside the door listening to her every word about her life and family amidst a wave of anger that left the recruiter speechless.

When Naradia ran out of steam and felt that all hope was lost, she stormed out of the office with tears in her eyes. But Cilia stopped her by grabbing her arm.

"Follow me." Cilia smiled.

Naradia followed, and a few minutes later, she sat frozen in her seat opposite Cilia's desk when Cilia offered her a different job with better pay. "I won't disappoint you, I promise." Naradia's eyes accumulated more tears.

Naradia was grateful for the opportunity and wanted to prove to Cilia that she deserved it. She worked at the company for five years after that, climbing the promotional ladder steadily. In that time, she and Cilia grew closer and became friends. Cilia even introduced her to Evailen, Cilia's best friend.

She had become the head of the Invention and Research Department when Cilia introduced her to Enyo who stole her heart on first sight. Naradia tried to grab his attention for a long time without success until one day she saw him as she walked down the streets of their city.

He was sharing a meal with another woman in a fancy restaurant. She watched him through the restaurant's window as he took a knee and proposed. A fire ignited in her eyes, and revenge consumed her until the woman turned around and was recognizable to her. It was Cilia, the one person who believed in her.

Naradia cried all the way home then all night long. When morning came, she told herself that Cilia made her who she was that day and that her heart was a small price to pay to settle her debt, but time proved that the fire in her heart, though small, could still burn.

Now engaged, Cilia and Enyo were seen in public often. The owner of the largest innovation company marrying the daughter of his only rival was the only thing Naradia saw in the news. Every time she saw them together, she could only think about crushing Cilia's heart with her bare hand.

She would lie awake at night thinking about how to destroy Cilia's life and win the heart of her love at the same time. She believed that if Cilia were out of the picture, then nothing would prevent Enyo from being with her.

Her dark thoughts spoke louder than her gratitude for where she was in life, and finally, she took action.

One day Cilia went to talk with her in confidence. She told Naradia she was looking for a way to return the light to someone who lost all their seeds, and that she hoped Naradia could help her since she knew her parents had also been living for a long time without their birth seeds.

Naradia saw a chance and took it without hesitation. She dug up one of the old contacts she knew through her parents and made a deal with him. The deal was that they drag Cilia to a secret location claiming that he will get her the seeds she needed then drug her and take hers instead.

That day was still far away, and Naradia was losing her patience. She had to keep the appearance of friendship during the mission. When she found out they would be on opposite teams, she pretended to be sad, but secretly she was happy. Maybe, just maybe, she would get the chance to finish the mission sooner and get rid of Cilia once and for all.

ROLAKAN

Rolakan leaned his back against the couch, reading his graduation certificate repeatedly. At seventeen, he was the youngest in his class to have complete mastery over the third gate, but he wasn't the youngest ever to do so.

Rolakan looked in silence at his mother who sat on the other end of the couch knitting a new scarf for him. He closed his eyes and took a deep breath before speaking. "I would like to travel."

"Where to?" She continued her knitting.

"I don't know. I have two years break now before I am required to train for the fourth gate. I thought I could take that time to explore Mastoperia and see what the other factions look like." Rolakan brought his lips to the side, wishing his mother Ayeta would look at him.

"You can go to the information center and see whatever you want in the crystal. I heard they even have a large reflective screen now. Do that instead."

"It isn't the same. I don't want to see something, in particular. I want to *experience* the other factions. I want to see how they live and learn who they are." Rolakan turned his entire body toward his mother and crossed his legs.

Ayeta stopped knitting and finally turned to meet his gaze. "Those are enemy territories. The only reason for you to go there is if you are on a mission."

"All I need is to announce my arrival to the other factions. There is nothing in the law that prevents me from going there, and there are no rules that say I can't travel on my own. Plus, we have been at peace for almost a decade now. Let me go. Please." He locked his hands together in front of his chest.

His mother frowned. "Those two years you get are not for you to waste. You should use them to increase your experience. Just because you have mastered three gates, doesn't mean you know how to use them perfectly. You still have a lot to learn, and you need to invest all your time toward that. You graduated a year younger than all of your peers. If you keep that up, maybe one day you can become one of the strongest magic users. Don't you want to be on the council one day like your grandfather was?" Ayeta restarted her knitting.

"What is the point? We learn things we never use in our daily life. It's only purposed for war. Other factions have technology while we still use centuries-old material. That scarf you have been spending days to knit can probably be made in seconds at Lunar. I need this Mother. I need to make sense of our way of life." Rolakan moved closer to his mother and took hold of her hand.

"There is a lot you still don't know about magic," she argued. "Everything will come to you at the right time, but you need to be patient. Patience is our virtue, my boy. The gods of the gates love us because of it. So stop questioning your birthright and embrace it. You have the potential to become one of the best magic users this faction has ever seen."

"Why? Because I'm a pureblood? What does that even mean? My whole life, everyone has expected me to be great at everything. What if I don't want to be great? What if all I want is to be ordinary?" Rolakan's voice grew higher and louder until his mother had to warn him to watch his tone. He apologized and left to his room.

He looked at his certificate again and wondered, *Why do we even get certificates for each gate we master? It isn't as if I will apply for a job one day and show it to someone as credentials.*

People in his faction received their work assignments at twenty-one. Their only chance to move up was when they excelled at their mastery. Even then, they would still be assigned to a job they didn't choose. Kalangous regarded each other based on how great their magic was, yet no matter how powerful they were, they still couldn't use their magic in daily life.

"What is the point of all of this?" he muttered to himself. "Why shouldn't I run away right now? I mastered three out of the five gates. That's sixty percent done. It's even rare to find gate five masters, and I have a lot of time to learn about the fourth." Believing that he had enough knowledge to survive in the world on his own, he packed a few clothing items and snuck out his window.

He jumped out of his second-floor window, walked to the fence, and threw his backpack over it. When he followed his bag, he noticed a man leaning his back against the fence with his arms crossed over his chest.

He glanced at the man from the corners of his eyes and recognized him at once, So he pushed his mouth to the side before pretending he was sleepwalking.

"Follow me." His father laughed.

Rolakan lowered his head and slouched his shoulders before he followed his father.

"In this world, there are two types of people. Those who lead and those who follow. Leaders have the greatest responsibility but carry the most pain. A great leader always questions his leadership." His father's voice was deep and calm.

"What makes you think I don't want to be a follower?"

"If you did, you wouldn't have come out of this window."

Rolakan kept his head down.

"Your mother told me you wanted to travel to enemy territories."

"It's okay. You don't have to lecture me. I will go back in and find a practice program."

"I didn't expect you to give up so soon. Perhaps I was wrong." His father tilted his head.

Rolakan looked into his father's eyes, waiting to hear his next words.

"Silence is always a wise choice," said the father. "I will allow you to go explore the rest of Mastoperia as you wish if you promise me that no matter what you want to do with the rest of your life, you will be back here no later than one day before your twentieth birthday."

"I Promise," Rolakan quickly answered, his eyes wide.

"I will send a message to the other factions announcing your arrival. Go hug your mother and prepare well for your journey."

Rolakan hugged his father and ran back into the house. He didn't want to waste a minute.

RYN

Ryn left his house after midnight with a clear destination in his mind. Before he entered the city's main graveyard, he looked around to make sure that no one could see him. Once he felt safe enough to sneak in, he quietly jumped the low fence and moved among the scattered shrines, until he reached a statue of his ancestor. He then used second gate magic to shake the floor beneath him. Seconds later, the statue split in half, revealing a secret door guarded by two men.

Ryn shifted his gaze between the guards and spoke in a quiet tone, "Let him in."

"Let who in?" asked one guard as he leaned forward, tilting his head left and right to see if there was someone else with Ryn.

"This is the password, you idiot." The second guard slapped his colleague on the back of his head. "Excuse him, Master Ryn, it's his first day." The second guard held the door open.

"If you have a problem with the password, ask Rolakan to ask me to change it." Ryn chuckled as he passed through the door into an ancient staircase leading toward an underground level.

The lower floor was a shelter that ancient Kalangous built to protect the children from the horrors of war. Carvings of ancient Kalanian covered the yellow-stone-pillars, while statues of mythical creatures decorated the walls.

Ryn walked past the crowd filling the large hall, watching as they gathered in different groups, each focused on a single activity. Some painted, others played music or board games. He shifted his face toward a group that dance-battled one another, smiling before he climbed a few steps to a higher level at the end of the hall. He stood next to Rolakan, who rested his elbows on a wooden fence watching over the crowds.

"That is what I call a crowd." Ryn smiled. "However, if we aren't careful, we might end up with the entire city here." Ryn placed both of his hands on the wooden fence.

"That wouldn't be a bad thing." Rolakan didn't take his gaze from the crowd.

"You and your ideas to free this city. We aren't under siege, you know." Ryn turned his head to face Rolakan.

"But we are. We're imprisoned by our outdated ideas."

"I agree that our rules and regulations need drastic changes, but we still need to be careful. If the situation gets out of our hands, then everything we built could vanish. We need to make sure we have everything under control and be happy with what we accomplished."

"It isn't enough." Rolakan sighed. "We still work in hiding to do something that shouldn't be considered a crime. All we want, all anyone here wants is to practice a hobby they like. It relaxes them and makes the price we all have to pay for using our magic bearable." He clenched his fists.

"Banning hobbies allows us to focus on perfecting our magic." Ryn focused on the crowd, watching how they enjoyed their freedom of choice.

"If I didn't know you so well, I would say you've switched sides." Ryn faced Rolakan.

"There are no sides. This is what I want you to understand. We all want what is best for our people even if our visions differ. Good leaders question their superiors, great ones question themselves."

"Spoken exactly like my late father," said Rolakan.

"He was a great man, and I'm sure he would have approved of all of this." Ryn glanced at Rolakan from his peripheral view.

"I wouldn't know. He didn't even make it to my awakening." Rolakan looked at Ryn as the latter focused his gaze on a person he recognized among the crowds.

"Don't forget he agreed to let you leave the faction and tour Mastoperia. No parent ever does that." Ryn moved down a couple of steps. "Excuse me," he said before heading toward the person who had grabbed his attention.

He stood near a group of rappers and watched as they battled one another with improvised lyrics. His head moved along with the two beatboxers who supplied the beats, but his eyes stayed on the one person standing alone in the back. The man who had his face covered stood in silence, watching but never participating.

"It's an honor to have you here," Ryn whispered near Rondai's ears.

Rondai didn't turn around to look at Ryn. Instead, he moved directly toward the exit.

"Please don't go." Ryn followed him. "Just wait. Please." Ryn grabbed his arm.

"I was just curious when I found out there is a secret community, but it was a mistake to come." Rondai slowly pulled his arm away.

"It's okay to be uncomfortable. Someone of your rank risks a lot to be here, but I know that this is not your first time and that you always hang around the same group. I just—"

"So why did you speak to me today?" Rondai interrupted with a sharp tone.

"The council told me I will go with you on a mission to the outside world. They've nominated you to be a royal guard, didn't they?"

"Didn't they tell you the nature of the mission?"

"They told me what I need to do and that you are the leader of this mission. You know our leadership. They never tell us why and we're not allowed to ask, but I figured since it was time for new royal guards that—"

"It looks like you've figured it all out then. So what do you want from me?" Rondai denied Ryn the chance to finish his words for the second time.

"Are you unhappy with the mission or me?" Ryn took a step closer to him.

"It doesn't matter how I feel. Our faction is our home, and we serve it with our blood." Rondai's eyes narrowed as they stared into Ryn's.

"I know the slogan of our faction. If not for the thousands of times I've said it every school morning, then for the fact that I live by its words. But putting my faction above everything doesn't mean blind obedience." Ryn felt his heart racing.

"Is this why you created this place?" Rondai reverted to his normal tone.

"What makes you think—"

"You always stand next to your partner, watching over everyone from above. Neither of you participates in any of the activities. Though you walk among the crowds from time to time, he never steps down." Rondai smiled. "You are happy with what you have, and want to make sure that everyone else is too, but he wants more. A lot more."

"You—"

"Did you think I wouldn't study this place and learn everything I could about it?"

"I apologize for my ignorance. I wouldn't expect less from someone of your caliber." Ryn lowered his head.

"Tell me about this community. Your motives behind it."

"Perhaps a look from a higher place can paint the picture better." Ryn led him toward the upper level. "A long time ago, I wanted to be a painter, but my parents destroyed all of my creations and suppressed me every time I showed interest in anything other than magic. Each time they denied me of my art, I clung to it even more. Eventually, my mother had to explain how hobbies were against the law, and that they feared the council would ban me from learning magic if I didn't abide by the law. I listened to her for a while, but I couldn't repel my painter spirit. Like everyone you see here, I gave in and continued practicing the thing I loved the most. Only this time, I did it in hiding."

Ryn sighed. "This place used to be a shelter in the early days. The third council saw it as a reminder of our weakness since they used it to hide from the enemy. They wanted to destroy it, but my ancestor converted it into a shrine for his wife before they had the chance. He knew that no one would dare destroy her temple."

"Perks of being a pureblood."

"Exactly." Ryn nodded. "Only my family knows about the secret door he created inside the statue, and since I knew that none of them ever came here, I made it my studio."

Ryn's gaze became distant for a few seconds before he shook his head and returned to reality. "One day, on my way out, I noticed someone on the other side of the graveyard. It was my partner, Rolakan. He had just returned from a trip outside the faction."

Rondai raised his brows and looked at Ryn.

"I know." Ryn smiled. "I told him many times that his father was the coolest for letting him do that. He is probably the only one who visited the other factions in our time. His father had asked him to return one day before his twentieth birthday for his awakening. He did as his father wanted, but when he returned, there was no one to greet him."

"Did they..." Rondai failed to finish his question.

"No one knows. I've heard executed, exiled, imprisoned. Once I even heard someone say they escaped, and that was why they sent Rolakan away first. All we know for sure is that they are nowhere to be found and that the council took their candles away." Ryn turned his gaze to Rolakan, who stood a few feet away from them, watching the crowds in silence. "When he returned from his trip, the guards by the city's gate wanted to strip him of anything he brought back from his travels; a backpack filled with gifts and souvenirs he had collected from other factions, but before they could take it, his awakening started. As soon as they saw his eyes turn black, they told him to go to the temple, and that they would continue searching him later.

"Rolakan didn't understand what was happening to him, but he knew that if he survived, he would lose all his belongings. So, he came to the graveyard to hide it all, ignoring the pain coursing in his veins." Ryn closed his eyes and took a deep breath. "I was on my way out from a painting session when I saw him. I knew that day I wasn't alone. That there were others who cared enough to break the law and look past their misery for a chance to enjoy the simple things they loved.

"We became friends that day, and we created this place for all of those who remind us of who we are." Ryn blinked back a tear and knew that he owed Rolakan an apology.

26

When Delphians saite, they experience time differently. Their mind's eye allows them to live in each timeline as if they were in the present. They can live for weeks in their third eye and return to reality before a fraction of a second passes. The stronger they get, the greater the gap between both times becomes. For some, it feels like they can pause time, but it doesn't come without risk. The longer they remain in a single time, the weaker their brains become, and without discipline, their imagination becomes their reality until they die in both their real life and their fake one. For that, Delphians practice meditation every day.

Kawan saw several timelines within the moment he spent in the air aiming for Jihave's back. In the last moment, before his blade pierced the Averetti, he swung his sword to force his body to turn mid-air before he used the wall to jump over Jihave in an attempt to avoid the one timeline he didn't want to play out.

"*Noooo!*" Rolakan screamed as he ran toward Kawan, shooting fireballs out of his hands, but Kawan deflected them easily.

The others froze in their places, realizing that this fight had gone too far. They all spoke of death easily, but none of them had ever caused it.

Jihave took two steps back and clenched his fists. He braced his weight against the wall before he fell completely into a seated position. Rolakan jumped over him and sprinted to capture the body of his fallen friend before he touched the ground.

At that exact second, Kawan pulled aside Alinda, whom he shielded behind his back, sword poised to defend her while hers disappeared.

When Cilia saw how Alinda was shaking, she tried to approach the little girl, but Kawan glared at Cilia with fierce eyes that forced her to reverse her movements.

"I just wanted to comfort her." Cilia forced her feet to quit retreating.

"No one will approach her." Kawan's voice was calm but firm.

Rolakan cried loudly as he brought Ryn's limp body closer to his chest. Maringrad extended his arm to approach Rolakan, but the latter conjured a circle of fire surrounding both himself and Ryn, separating them from everyone else.

🌀🍃🪷☯

When Alinda hid from the fight, she remembered the dreams she had seven years prior and connected her present to her past. She knew what she had to do but didn't want to do it. Amidst her crying, she sneaked a peek at the fight and saw Kawan launching toward Jihave with his sword. She nervously saited, hoping to find the right action, but none of the timelines she saw allowed her to save Jihave. Only what she had seen in her dreams could save his life.

In her dreams, she saw a monster protect her from his friends that tried to harm her after she had slain one of them. She believed the monster was Kawan, and that she had to take down a member of his team. However, she had to time her kill so Kawan would see how Rolakan would attack her in his mind's eye and have no choice but to interact before he pierced Jihave.

Without thinking, she pushed her ring, making her sword jump out and threw it toward Ryn. She then disappeared and reappeared behind him to grab her sword, and stabbed him from the side upward, piercing his heart immediately. They were all so busy with the fight that no one noticed how she disappeared and reappeared, using an ability that no one else, even in her own faction, could.

Silence filled the place for a few minutes as none dared to talk. Rolakan stared at Alinda with teary eyes before he carried Ryn's body to the entrance.

"You can't get out that way," Kawan spoke in a quiet tone. "The only way out is through the room of the artifact."

Rolakan changed his direction toward the iron bars. He manifested a lighting blade in his right hand while supporting Ryn's body with the other one. After he sliced the gate open with his blade, he noticed a staircase near the back of the room, which he calmly aimed for, passing next to the artifact as if it wasn't even there.

Jihave stared at Kawan as the latter kept his guard up to make sure no one harmed Alinda. Jihave bared his teeth to him even though he understood Kawan's behavior.

When Alinda finally managed to brace herself. She stood up and moved toward artifact.

"Wait, I will protect you." Kawan blocked her way.

"Don't worry. I know what I'm doing." She pushed Kawan's arm and continued toward the staircase.

Kawan sat on the floor and burst into tears.

Jihave paused in front of him. "It isn't your fault alone. This falls on all of us." Then he followed Alinda.

The others followed Jihave leaving Kawan alone on the floor.

Atop the hill above the artifact chamber, the wind swept over the green grass that covered the ground. Alinda approached Rolakan while he placed stones around Ryn's body to form a complete circle.

"Don't. If you come closer, I will kill you." Rolakan continued placing the rocks one after the other.

Alinda pulled out her sword and placed it on the ground. She fell to her knees, extended her open palms backward on the grass, and lowered her head.

"I didn't saite to see what you would do so I don't react to it. I offer you my life, and I forgive you for taking it away."

Rolakan dropped the rock in his hand and stood straight with eyes focused on her before he moved toward the sword and grabbed it. He stared at the blood of his best friend dripping from the blade for a long moment before he shifted his gaze between the sword and Alinda several times. In the end, he threw the sword on the ground and returned to complete the circle of stones, uttering nothing.

When he finished, he sat outside the circle and stared at Ryn's face. "What has become of us, brother? We set out to change the world together, yet, we parted fighting one another." Rolakan's tears streamed down his face. "I hope you forgive me."

He opened the third gate and waved his hand toward Ryn. The entire ground within the circle of stones elevated and moved toward the south. Everyone watched as Rolakan sent Ryn's body home.

Alinda couldn't contain her sobs, the noise rising when Cilia held her.

Kawan waited for Rolakan to calm down before he approached him, hoping to offer some comfort, but Rolakan spoke first. "Keep your words to yourself. I don't need them. We both stuck to our sides and fought one another. Maybe we didn't comprehend it, but there had to be casualties. Otherwise, this would have never ended. He knew the risk as we all did."

Rolakan finally understood why his people portrayed ruthlessness in front of everyone, even though they held the kindest of hearts. Because when others sensed their kindness, they used it against them.

27

Both teams spent the night on the open green field that looked mysteriously far from the temple mountain. The only signs of life they saw were tiny lights of a village down the hill. Those who slept woke up as soon as the birds sang. Rolakan was one of those who couldn't. He sat next to the hole where he had placed Ryn before he sent him home.

Jihave moved to stand behind Rolakan and placed his hand on Rolakan's shoulder. "You can go back to your faction if you want. I understand if you don't wish to continue."

"No." Rolakan shook his head. "I started this mission, and I will see it through until the end. This is my faction's resolve and how I can honor him. We must win. Otherwise, his death was meaningless."

Rolakan stood and slowly blinked back a tear before he moved toward Kawan who sat away from everyone. "I'm taking that artifact for our team. If you have a problem with that, you fight me right now." Rolakan looked down to meet Kawan's eyes.

Kawan raised his head for a second then brought his gaze back to the ground, uttering nothing as he was already saiting what to do next in his mind.

A couple of hours later, Kawan stood and signaled his companions to approach him. "It's time to go," he said quietly.

Maringrad freed his tiger out of his skin and proceeded to ride him. "Where to now?"

"We will head to the western continent of Vetera." Kawan rode behind him. "Ryn gave us the locations of all the artifacts. We will honor him by getting at least one."

"Just the three of us?" Naradia centered her lotus-shaped pod. "We won't be able to survive another fight." Her voice trembled.

Kawan sighed. "There will be no more fighting, not for us, but we have to play it smart from now on."

"What is your plan then?" Maringrad petted his tiger before the Majestic moved south.

"Give me some time, I will figure it out." Kawan placed his arms around Maringrad's waist and closed his eyes.

A few minutes and several timelines later, Kawan opened his eyes again.

"Maringrad, stop here," Kawan said with an urgent tone of voice. Once they stopped, he turned his face to his other companion. "Naradia, can you contact Enyo and connect me with his team leader, please?"

Naradia nodded, trying to hide her faint grin. She brushed her purple seed several times and thought about Enyo before the wind appeared to swirl in front of them and take the shape of Enyo.

When Maringrad saw the clear image of Enyo, his eyes widened. He approached him and moved his hand across the figure to make sure that Enyo wasn't actually there. "This is fascinating,"

"Naradia!" Enyo smiled. "How are you?"

"Not good." Naradia smiled back but quickly donned her poker face when she realized how inappropriate it was.

"What's wrong?" Enyo raised his brows.

"Kawan needs to talk to Rondai. It's important."

Enyo nodded.

Naradia pulled a smaller seed out of her pocket and gave it to Kawan. "Stick this to your brain, and it will allow you to communicate with Rondai through us," Naradia said to Kawan while Enyo did the same with Rondai. The two men could then see each other.

Kawan glanced at Rondai's stance before shifting his eyes away to avoid direct contact. "You don't look as tense as you were at the Forbidden City."

"Having the best team is relaxing." The corners of Rondai's mouth lifted, taunting his competitor.

"So, you connected with your team as well," Kawan spoke quietly. "I wish I could say I'm glad for you. Maybe this mission is meant to bring us together, so we understand that we are all the same and that our factions and powers don't define us." Kawan's eyes imprisoned their tears.

"What do you want Kawan?" Rondai squinted. "What kind of game are you trying to play?"

"No games. There is just something you need to know, and I thought it was best if you hear it from me." Kawan took a deep breath. "Yesterday, my team and I encountered Jihave, and we engaged in a fight over the second artifact."

Rondai's heart raced. He had known someone claimed the second artifact when it disappeared from his device, but he sensed there was something else.

"Unfortunately, we lost Ryn in the battle," Kawan continued. "I'm deeply sorry. He had become a good friend over the last few days. It was a short time but losing him feels like I have lost a brother." Kawan could no longer cage his tears.

Rondai's quietness flipped into a roaring cry. He didn't know Ryn well, but he admired his quest to change their faction. He cried not just because he lost a faction member, but because he believed in the purity of Ryn's heart, and how seeing him manage that secret society gave him hope. He cried and cried then he stopped.

"Where's Jihave right now?" Rondai redirected his gaze to Kawan, his face reverting to the one they saw in the Forbidden City.

"We left when his team was about to claim the artifact, east of the Akiro mountains in the northern continent of Cras." Kawan wiped away his tears.

Rondai's tone grew louder, and his muscles tensed. "He had the nerve to go for the artifact after what he did."

"I am sorry for your loss."

"I have to go now." Rondai took the seed off his forehead, and his figure disappeared.

"I think that's it for this call." Enyo looked at Naradia before she nodded and the two brushed their seeds to drop their connection.

Maringrad stood in front of Kawan with raised brows. "Why did you do that?"

"It wasn't nice, I know, but as Naradia said earlier, we can't handle another fight against any of the other teams. I don't want to lose either of you."

"I still don't understand why you did that." Maringrad shook his head.

"Rondai is angry at Jihave now. He takes great pride in his faction and feels responsible for its members regardless of our current situation. He will now seek Jihave to avenge Ryn, meaning he will be out of the competition for a while. This smooths our way and allows us more time to get the remaining artifacts."

Maringrad heaved a heavy sigh, his heart raced as he thought of Jihave. He didn't approve of Kawan's action, but he couldn't blame him for trying to buy himself some time even if he thought it was a cowardice tactic.

"What about Evailen?" Naradia asked.

"When we were at the Forbidden City, I saw how Yasmina looked at her former team leader, Rondai. She seemed to be the most affected by their separation. I'm sure she has a way to keep tabs on him." He paused regarding his teammates' expressions before continuing. "As soon as she knows that he's going after Jihave, which could be dangerous for Rondai, she will follow him even if she had to break away from Evailen. Also, Evailen won't allow that so she will join her. Even if she agreed to let her go alone, she would be a member short, and that will balance the odds for us."

Maringrad squinted, tilting his head slightly, "Why do I feel you are speculating this time?"

"I can't see a future that isn't mine. Rondai will base his decision on my words so I can see it, but I can't see Evailen. However, perhaps Naradia can shed more light on Evailen's character." Kawan turned his head toward her.

"Knowing her, I agree that she won't allow Yasmina to go on her own, but that depends on Yasmina knowing in the first place and reacting exactly as you expect."

"Then we have to hurry and get to the third artifact as soon as possible," Kawan said before he and Maringrad climbed the tiger again, and headed toward the western continent of Vetera as fast as they could.

28

Rondai felt the death of Ryn deep in his heart. From the start, he believed some would fall along the way, but never thought it would be one of his faction members. They were the elite his council chose for a crucial mission. The purebloods that synchronize perfectly with magic.

He felt the pressure of the gates on his heart as his thoughts faded away. A tear tried to escape but evaporated against his raging sclera. He could only feel his hand move to his heart as he opened the third gate, conjuring a piece of wood that he stood on before steering it toward Jihave's location.

Hearing the news, Rondai forgot about the mission and his companions. Only one thought dominated his mind, the thought of death as he moved as fast as he could.

Salvanra had seen the darkness in his eyes and knew that if he reached Jihave in that state, they might end up killing each other, but she had no time to discuss the situation with her other teammates. She freed her tigress, mounted her, and followed Rondai.

Both Enyo and Terqwan didn't know what to do. Their only option was to follow their companions, but they had no method of transportation other than Enyo's lotus-flower-shaped pod, and it had enough space for one person only.

Enyo looked at Terqwan and moved his hand as if to say, "Well, we have no other option." Terqwan nodded at him before Enyo pulled out his pod, and the two men squeezed themselves awkwardly in the tight space available.

Salvanra got close to Rondai several times, but each time she almost caught up with him, he would increase his speed. The more she failed, the stronger her heart pumped determination in her veins. Her tigress sensed her goal and pushed her own limits until they eventually caught up with him.

"You need to stop; we have to talk about this!" Salvanra shouted so Rondai could hear her.

"There's no stopping until I have his heart." Rondai was already at his maximum speed. The more he pushed, the harder his magic pushed on his heart, and he wanted to save power for the fight. At that instant, only the tactical-gate-five-master was present.

"You are not thinking clearly Rondai. I understand how you feel. You have every right to be angry, but vengeance is not the solution. You need to think rationally."

"You are just saying that because he is your boyfriend. You are the one who isn't thinking properly, Salvanra. You will say anything to protect him. You are the last person I will listen to."

Salvanra knew that he was probably right. If she heard that someone had killed Jihave, she would most likely react the same. However, what Rondai didn't know was that she cared about him too. She felt comfortable around him as if she had known him for years and hoped he felt the same way.

"You are right, but that doesn't mean I don't care about you too. I won't let anyone hurt Jihave, but I don't want to see you hurt either."

Rondai stopped the moment he heard her last phrase and moved down to her level as she brought her tiger to a stop facing him.

"I don't want to kill you too Salvanra, but if you plan to stand with him against me, then know I won't hesitate to eliminate you or anyone who would dare stand in my way." Rondai stared into her eyes.

Before she could utter a word, he flew away to continue on his path.

Salvanra watched as he flew away and realized that he knew exactly what he was doing and that the situation hadn't confused him at all. The darkness that took over him came from within, and this new man was who he really was.

She continued to pursue him as a baby dragon came out of her side. The dragon flew faster than she rode. As it drew closer to Rondai, the dragon accumulated a ball of dark blue fire in front of his mouth and threw it toward Rondai who easily blocked the dragon's attacks using sheets of iron that he materialized behind him.

Rondai didn't bother to slow down to fight the dragon who continued his barrage of fireballs. But Rondai didn't even need to look behind him to dodge the attacks. He could have spiked the dragon several times, but he didn't. He wasn't sure if he was saving his energy for the fight or worried about breaking Salvanra's heart over her dragon. What he was sure of however was that this battle didn't interest him.

The dragon was young and inexperienced in battle. Soon it became tired of flying and fell from exhaustion. Salvanra stopped to cradle her Majestic as it slowly crawled back into her side. She thought about catching up with Rondai again to try a different tactic, but it was too late. Rondai was too far ahead now, she wouldn't be able to catch up with him in time, so she sat on the ground trying to figure out what to do. Shortly after, Enyo and Terqwan caught up with her.

"What happened?" Enyo glanced at the shiny drops of sweat atop Salvanra's skin.

"Nothing. I tried to talk some sense into him but failed. I fear there is nothing stopping him." She sighed.

"Did you give up on him?" Terqwan asked.

"I don't know." She heaved a heavy sigh. "I don't think I can handle seeing either of them dead, though."

"Then why are you sitting here. No matter what, with or without a plan, we have to catch up with Rondai and stop this fight." Terqwan presented his hand to her and pulled her up.

"You are right. I'm sorry I left you back there guys." Salvanra took Terqwan's hand and moved toward her tigress to mount her.

"Don't worry about it, but do you mind if I ride with you on your Majestic? You won't believe how crowded this pod can be with two people." Terqwan brought his hands together in front of his chest to imitate begging.

Salvanra smiled and presented her hand to help him mount the tigress.

29

"No. No. No!" Yasmina shouted.

Evailen jumped out of her sleeping bag, struggling to gain perspective before she saw Yasmina crying by the side of the lake where they camped for the night. She moved toward her with fast steps. "What's going on?" Evailen knelt next to Yasmina before she wrapped her arms around her and brought Yasmina's head closer to her chest.

"Ryn—" she cried, the words struggling through her broken tears and irregular breathing "—is dead."

Evailen tightened her hold to bring Yasmina closer and sat in silence, her own tears trying to escape. She didn't know Ryn, but she could feel Yasmina's pain. Evailen's red seed flashed repeatedly confused by her own feelings. Her red seed translated her emotions based on brain and body functions. However, empathy confused it because it meant dealing with emotions that had no visible effect on Evailen's body.

Malani and Bofrat woke up to Yasmina's loud cry. When Bofrat saw her, he freed his tiger at once to scout the area.

Malani grabbed Bofrat's arm and spoke quietly, "Take it easy. There isn't a physical threat."

Bofrat nodded and resealed his tiger in his tattoo as the two men moved toward the girls.

Malani sat next to Yasmina and took hold of her hand. "I am sorry for your loss."

"What happened?" Bofrat's eyes widened.

Malani stared into Bofrat's eyes and whispered so only he could hear, "Ryn is dead."

Bofrat's face froze, and he stopped breathing for a second before he crossed his legs together on the ground and faced Yasmina. He asked everyone to form a tight circle and connect their heads together before his snake crawled out of his arm and wrapped them all in a hug. Soon after they were much calmer and the crying stopped.

"What do you want to do?" Evailen asked Yasmina.

"Rondai sent me a message."

"What did it say?" Evailen placed her palm on Yasmina's back.

"He is going after Jihave."

"Hold on a second." Bofrat's eyes bulged out. "I don't mean to press on your wound, but I need to know what happened. I'm sorry." Bofrat separated his head from the huddle.

"I don't have a lot of details," Yasmina said separating herself as well, "but apparently Jihave and Kawan engaged in a fight over the second artifact, and Ryn was killed as a result." Yasmina saw the shock on Bofrat's face and felt her heart race again. "He is from your faction. Perhaps if you were there, you would have supported him." Yasmina forced her eyes to narrow.

Bofrat saw her anger rise and glanced at his snake who was back on his arm. He took a deep breath, knowing that his snake retreated after it felt his doubt. When he pushed his snake out again, Yasmina placed both of her hands on the ground and pushed her body backward.

"I won't hurt you, Yasmina. I know that our factions hate each other, and we were at war for many years, but that was the older generation. My generation is trying to be better." Bofrat stayed still hoping to regain her confidence.

"All lies. Your people are masters at deceiving. You just tried to hypnotize me. How do I know you are not trying to do the same with your words?" Yasmina took a battle stance.

"Calm down Yasmina. He isn't your enemy." Evailen moved closer to her.

"It's okay, Evailen." Bofrat pointed with his palm. "Let her take it out on me. I understand. You can shoot whatever you want at me Yasmina. I won't fight back."

Yasmina froze at his words realizing her anger was against the wrong person. She started crying again and placed her head between her knees.

Bofrat moved closer to her and placed his arm on her back before he spoke. "I'm not defending Jihave, but there must be a mistake. He is stubborn and crazy, but he is the most peaceful person I know. I just want to find the truth, and I promise you that if he did kill Ryn for the artifact, then I will stand against him myself."

"Bofrat is right. Jihave didn't kill Ryn." Malani lowered his head.

"What happened then?" Evailen asked.

"It was Alinda who killed him in the battle." Malani had saited far in the future until he saw a conversation with Alinda where she told him what happened.

"Alinda! She's so young for this." Bofrat tilted his head toward Malani with raised his eyebrows.

Malani ignored him and fixed his gaze on Yasmina. "I guess if you want to take your anger out on anyone, it should be me." He was ready to absorb all Yasmina's anger just to make sure she wouldn't try to hurt Alinda.

Yasmina stood. "We need to stop Rondai. If he engages in a fight, he might kill Jihave, and I don't want him to bear this burden." She moved toward her sleeping bag and folded it until it fit in her pocket.

"I agree." Bofrat freed his tiger and prepared for their departure.

Evailen watched them hurry to depart. "Wait. We can't leave without a plan."

"The plan is to stop the fight. What else do we need?" Bofrat mounted his tiger.

Evailen shook her head. "What will you do when each of you sees your faction members in a critical condition? Can you guarantee you won't be worked up and take part in the fight? You are both emotional, and you know it."

"What do you suggest we do, then?" Yasmina crossed her arms against her chest, "Should we let them kill each other?"

"No, that is not what I'm saying. We will all go, but you won't approach the fight. I will head there alone, and you will wait for me at a safe distance."

Malani took a step closer to Evailen. "What if you can't stop the fight alone?"

"Then, and only then, you can join me. If I feel I can't break them apart, then I will send you a signal." Evailen straightened her leather outfit.

"Fine." Yasmina sighed. "I will transport us then." Yasmina opened the third gate and manifested a two-square-meter plank of wood before everyone mounted it as Yasmina steered them in the direction of the location Rondai told her.

Evailen studied Yasmina's reddened face as they flew to the fight and placed her hand on the latter's back. "One day, you will have to explain to me how your magic works."

Yasmina turned her head to her and smiled slightly before she returned her gaze to the road ahead and increased their speed.

30

"Something bad is about to happen. We have to stop!" Alinda shouted in Jihave's ear as she rode with him on the back of his tiger.

"What is it? We hardly even left." Jihave signaled the group to stop.

"Rondai is coming at high speed. He will catch up with us soon." Alinda stepped off the tiger.

Cilia's eyes bulged as she got off her pod and moved closer to Alinda. "Is he coming after you?"

"He's coming to fight Jihave, but I can change that." Alinda glanced at Rolakan, who sat on his wood in silence.

Jihave tilted his head. "How will you do that?"

"Don't worry about it. You guys go ahead, and I will catch up with you later." Alinda's voice hitched.

"I won't let you sacrifice yourself Alinda. You are a member of my team. Stop thinking like you are in this alone."

"I can see the future. I know what to tell Rondai to calm him down. He doesn't know I was the one who killed Ryn. He will listen to me, but if he sees you, he will start his attack immediately."

Rolakan sighed and kept his gaze focused on his feet. "You are such a bad liar."

"I'm not lying!" Alinda shouted.

Rolakan stepped off his wooden piece and dematerialized it before he turned to face Jihave. "If Rondai will listen to anyone, it will be me. I know how he feels, and I can calm him down."

Alinda positioned herself in front of Rolakan to force him to meet her eyes. "That's not true. He's too angry and can't see clearly. He will believe you're a traitor who abandoned his own faction." Rolakan opened his mouth to argue, but Alinda continued, her voice rising. "He will fight you, and you will die too. I saw that timeline already."

Rolakan narrowed his eyes. "Maybe you are lying again."

"I'm not lying!" Alinda screamed her words.

"Enough!" Jihave centered them, his voice as loud as Alinda's. "I'm the leader of this group, and I'm the one who says what will and will not happen."

The other two brought their chins closer to their chests.

"I will wait for him alone. I will try to talk him out of it, but if he needs to get it out of his system by fighting, then we will do so. You go ahead, and I will find you when it's over."

Rolakan chuckled. "It's almost funny that you think we will leave you alone. Rondai is strong, and if he fights with the intent to kill, then he will succeed."

"Don't underestimate me Rolakan. You know nothing of my true power." Jihave took a step closer to Rolakan, using his height to show off his strength.

"And you know nothing of his. He was the youngest ever to master the first three gates of magic. He is only twenty-six and is already one of the strongest magic users in my faction, and don't forget, his father was Rakamai." Rolakan raised his chin to meet Jihave's eyes, his mouth twisted to the side.

Cilia hunched her shoulders. "Rakamai? The man who took out an entire Averetti tribe by himself?"

Jihave crossed his arms. "Rakamai also died in that battle."

"Yes." Rolakan nodded. "He did die that day, but not because of wounds caused in battle."

"Really?" Jihave tilted his head. "What killed him then if it wasn't the Averettis?"

Rolakan looked into Jihave's eyes and said nothing. Silence almost prevailed, but Cilia stepped in.

"What are you guys talking about? It doesn't matter if he died or not. The man still took out an entire tribe on his own. He is a legend everywhere. You can't fight his son Jihave."

"Maybe you are right." Jihave took a step back and paced in a circle, cracking his knuckles. "But we aren't talking about the same person here, and his father was already the head of their faction by that time. He had mastered all of their power."

Rolakan narrowed his eyes. "You find that exciting, don't you?"

Jihave turned his back to everyone and smiled, saying nothing.

"Fine." Rolakan sighed. "I can't fight him, but I can make sure you don't kill each other. I am sorry, but I am not going anywhere."

"You will be disobeying a direct order from your team leader. I thought the chain of command was the most important thing for Kalangous."

Rolakan half-smiled and said nothing. The fact that Jihave said those words reminded him how the leader didn't know him at all.

Rondai jumped off his flying wood the moment he saw Jihave on the horizon, leaving the plank in free fall. When he reached the ground, he closed the third gate and opened the fifth immediately. Transparent, invisible energy surrounded his entire body as he stalked toward Jihave.

Rolakan saw Rondai's fast and confident steps, and ran toward him, hoping to straighten his mind, but Rondai released a charge from his open palm that threw Rolakan off his feet before the latter even got close to him.

Alinda and Cilia didn't see Rondai's attack and moved closer to each other. When Alinda did see Rondai, she tried to step in to talk to him, but Cilia held her back, tightening her hold each time Alinda tried to free herself. Cilia had quickly analyzed the situation, believing that Alinda's interference would lead to her death.

"Listen—" Jihave started as he saw Rondai approach, but Rondai launched two more charges toward him.

Jihave's ape jumped out of his body immediately to protect him, but the charges threw the ape to the ground. Jihave took a step back and freed both his tiger and falcon simultaneously. The two Majestics and their master ran in random movements as Rondai fired repeatedly. Jihave's ogre-faced spider climbed out of his right calf while he fell toward the ground, hit by one of the invisible charges. The spider rested on Jihave's head and pierced his fangs into the edge of his forehead, allowing Jihave to share the spider's ability of sight, which allowed him to see the invisible aura that surrounded Rondai.

With his enhanced sight, Jihave dodged Rondai's charges one after the other and so did his Majestics who all shared the same power as their master. The new power allowed Jihave, his ape, tiger, and falcon to trap Rondai quickly, but the latter stood still, moving only his eyes, watching the tiger and ape approach him from the sides, the same moment the falcon dove toward him.

Rondai looked into Jihave's eyes and saw them clearly, even though they were meters away from him. He understood what Jihave wanted to say, but his own eyes had a response, *I'm not blowing off steam. If you don't want to take this fight seriously, then you will die.*

At that exact second, Rondai exploded all the energy he concentrated while standing still blasting all three Majestics at once.

Only the ape survived with minimal injuries due to its metal-hard skin. The tiger fell unconscious with heavy wounds while the falcon died on the spot.

Jihave screamed in agony as he felt the death of his falcon deep in his soul. He lost a piece of himself as his heart changed. He no longer cared about Rondai's feelings and his only thought was to kill the killer.

Jihave freed his rhinoceros beetle–one of the rarest Majestics in the fantastic forest.

31

The rhinoceros beetle is one of nine rare Majestics that live in the Fantastic Forest. Only members of the elders have succeeded to capture it. The Averettis consider the beetle rare for several reasons. First, the beetle is small. The largest known male beetle was measured at 2cm long and 90mm wide. Second, the beetles don't have a known location where they nest since they don't live in groups. Third, even the youngest beetles will give an elder a hard time in a fight.

When in danger, the beetle enlarges up to a hundred and twenty times its original size. It can carry objects that are eight hundred and fifty times its body weight, and it can ram with the same force. The beetle's two horns are sword-sharp, they can cut through two meters thick silver easily. The material of its armor remains unknown to this day. No one knew that Jihave captured the beetle except for Salvanra.

Jihave's beetle flew out of his ankle and adjusted its size to his body before it flew back toward him. The beetle wrapped Jihave in full body armor, allowing him to multiply his physical strength by eight hundred and fifty times. His armor was theoretically indestructible.

As soon as the merge was complete, he ran toward Rondai, channeling his anger, and threw a punch that sent Rondai flying over fifty feet away.

Rondai wrapped his body with his entire aura to protect himself, which eased his fall, but he still suffered damage.

Rolakan's pulse accelerated when he saw Rondai fall on the ground. He moved closer to the fight and opened the fourth gate before he created an earth barrier ten meters deep around Jihave, but the latter punched through it without a drop of sweat.

When Jihave saw Rolakan prepare to attack again, he rushed toward him and kicked him back to where Cilia and Alinda stood.

Rondai snuck some of his aura into the ground as he used both his hands to stand. Taking a deep breath, he enveloped his body with the remainder of his energy. He then levitated himself using his aura and flew toward Jihave at high speed with a closed right fist that was ready to drop a punch on the Averetti's armored face.

An instant before he could land his attack, the energy he fed into the ground snuck up on Jihave, strangling his movements.

When Rondai's fist met Jihave's face, two of his fingers broke, feeling as if he had hit a metal statue. He took a few steps back contemplating his next move, his gaze, one with Jihave's. Rondai saw his opponent's eyes drop to his hand, and he flexed his fingers, shutting all the pain inside of him before it made it to his face.

Jihave tensed his muscles, feeling the aura strangling him. He narrowed his eyes at Rondai before he pushed his arms out to break free. Even though his face was invisible, his body language spoke loudly of his cold emotions.

When he saw Rondai fly toward him for another punch, Jihave focused his sight on tracking Rondai's aura. Discovering that Rondai focused all his aura around his fist, Jihave released his beetle's wings and flew up into the air just as Rondai was about to reach him. Flying above him, Jihave grabbed Rondai's arms and raised him in the air too. He then brought his feet back to the ground before he hammered the Kalangou into the floor repeatedly from one side to the other.

Jihave threw Rondai upward with all his power but didn't raise his head to calculate when Rondai would fall back to the ground. Instead he started swinging his arm, accumulating all the beetle's brute force into his fist for one final punch.

Rondai didn't have the power of saiting, but anyone could see where things were going. His body lost control over his muscles, and his eyelids gradually closed on their own.

His life flashed in front of him as he believed that his death was imminent. It was an honorable death to die in a fight, he thought.

Just before reaching the point of impact, Rondai gave in to his powerless body, leaving it to whatever came at the end of his free fall. He believed he was ready to accept his fate, but there was this little voice inside of him he couldn't silence. It was the voice of anger. A voice that rather than encourage him emphasized his weakness. A voice that told him that if an Averetti could defeat him so easily, then there was no future for his faction.

Without realizing the movement of his own body, his hand traced a six against his chest. He felt his heart physically change to mimic the shape. The pain was too intense compared to the injuries sustained from the fight, which he believed were insignificant, and the thought had him forgetting he was falling to his death. He sensed the molecules in his body become unstable one by one adding to his agony as he screamed to the peak of his voice, and then there was silence.

He opened his eyes to find himself in an empty white space. He thought he stood on the ground, but there was nothing below his feet.

"You look confused." The voice came from behind him. Rondai turned to find a face he didn't recognize accompanied by another eleven unfamiliar Kalangous.

"Who are you?" Rondai asked.

"My name is Relda. A previous member of the Kalanian council, and so is everyone you see here." She brushed her long hair away from her calla lily-colored cheeks.

"Am I dead already?"

"Not yet, but you opened the sixth gate. The door to the afterworld."

"I thought there were only five gates." Rondai focused his gaze on her green eyes.

"Only the council knows about the sixth and seventh gates," said Relda.

Rondai's eyes widened. "Does this mean there is even more than seven gates?"

"There is no time for this. You are almost at the ground."

"What do I do? I can't escape the hit." Rondai took a deep breath, thinking that he was hallucinating and that his death had already occurred.

"Open your eyes!" everyone shouted at the same time.

When Rondai opened his eyes, he was inches away from Jihave's punch. He regained control over his body, but there was no time to avoid the hit. At that exact second, a large dark, muscular man-shaped body with a jackal head pulled him away, evading Jihave's fist in the nick of time.

Rondai stood across the field from Jihave as other jackal-headed figures fell out of the sky, surrounding him like bodyguards protecting their employer. There was twelve of them, and they all used gate five magic.

Jihave threw punches at them one after the other, but they were more experienced in the art of war, managing to quickly focus their auras to where the attacks would land. The Jackals waited until they sensed the signs of fatigue appear on Jihave before they shifted their auras to their fists and defensive stances to attacking. Once they landed the first punch, they tossed him among themselves as easily as passing a ball.

To the untrained eye, this fight had no magical powers. It looked like a bunch of people all dressed in costume, beating a man in a different one.

Rondai took advantage of the time his guards granted him and closed his eyes to rebuild his power. He concentrated all his energy into a bullet-sized aura. It became visible to everyone for the first time after the heavy concentration forced his energy to transform into dark matter. Rondai himself didn't see that he created a micro-wormhole until he opened his eyes, ready to throw it toward Jihave's heart and shatter it to pieces.

32

Evailen and Salvanra arrived at the same time. They came across one another atop a hill over a hundred and fifty feet away from the fight. Their eyes widened, and their mouths fell open when they saw the intensity of the fight going on before them.

Rondai, badly wounded, sat on one knee cradling a wormhole that despite its miniature size radiated danger. On the other side of the field, they saw the jackal-headed figures passing Jihave in his beetle armor among themselves using only punches and kicks.

In the beginning, no one except Salvanra and Bofrat realized that Jihave was the one in different armor; however, no one understood who the Jackals were or where they came from.

Bofrat forced a blink, as his palms began to sweat and his pulse accelerated. When he saw his friend wearing the beetle's armor, he recalled all the times he told Jihave that he wanted to capture the Majestic beetle, and wondered, for how long Jihave had lied to him about having already captured it. However, when he saw how the Jackals easily dominated Jihave and his armor, his brain short-circuited. Bofrat had always regarded the beetle as undefeatable. For a second, he thought the Jackals were Majestics.

"When did Kalangous develop the power to control Majestics?" he muttered to himself.

Salvanra felt her heart contract at the sight of the battle and freed her tigress, bear, and red-tailed-spider, but when she tried to move toward Jihave, Terqwan and Enyo quickly restrained her.

"Let go," she shouted, but none listened to her so she turned her Majestics toward the two men. "Let go or they will attack you."

"Stop it Salvanra!" Bofrat shouted to overtake the Majestics' roaring. "Look at the situation before you rush in."

"You want me to take time to analyze while these things are killing Jihave?" Salvanra shouted as her tigress and bear rammed into her captors who held their positions by tightening their grasp on her. "Let go or I will allow them to sink their teeth in you!" she demanded, her voice turning into a scream.

"He deserves it!" Bofrat shouted, matching her tone of voice before he freed his tiger, snake, and eagle to restrain Salvanra's Majestics.

"How dare you say this about your best friend? How many times did he save your life?" Salvanra's Majestics sensed her anger against Bofrat and engaged in a fight with his. "How many times—"

"Enough!" Bofrat turned to face her and pointed at the battle. "Look at Rondai and how wounded he is. Or did he inflict this upon himself?"

"I have had enough of this." Salvanra freed only the arms of her ape, giving herself an extra set of arms that she used to liberate herself from her teammate's hold.

Enyo brushed his black seed to armor himself as he prepared to grab Salvanra again, but before he could, Terqwan placed his hand on Enyo's shoulder.

"Don't," said Terqwan, tilting his head toward the fight.

Enyo looked at the situation below and quickly ran toward the battlefield.

🌀 🐦 ✾ ☾

When Salvanra took her first step toward Jihave, Bofrat held her wrist and pulled her to him before he placed his forehead on hers. Salvanra understood the sign; Averettis connected their foreheads with their Majestics to show respect and offer peace.

Bofrat whispered, "Ryn was a close friend of mine. He was my secret contact in Kala. The one I did all our off the record trade with. He believed in our values and wanted to make this world a better place, and now I have to pretend that I am not affected by the death of my friend to keep his secret safe." Bofrat blinked back his tears.

"Jihave is your friend too." Salvanra let one tear slip. "I don't want to fight Rondai either, but Jihave is my boyfriend. I will keep what happened here between us so you don't lose Jihave's friendship too, but you and I will always know that you gave up on him when he needed you." Salvanra separated their foreheads and mounted her tigress, but it was too late. Rondai had already released his attack.

🌀 🐦 ✾ ☾

Evailen knew the moment she saw the fight that there was no talking to either of them. Seeing Rondai and his wounds forced her heart into a frenzy of irregular beats, but seeing his attack on Jihave sent a quick shiver through her body. She didn't feel comfortable seeing the Jackals torture Jihave either. Her blue and red seeds blinked simultaneously. Her blue seed wanted to analyze the situation and understand the power Rondai was using, but her red one wanted her to wrap her arms around Rondai to calm him down if that would work.

Evailen shook her head quickly and pressed both seeds to calm herself. "This is not the time for feelings," she muttered. When Evailen heard the argument between Bofrat and Salvanra, she realized there was no one but her to stop the fight, so she released her armor before she launched into battle.

Yasmina's feet froze at the sight of the battle. She had heard about the twelve-guard technique, but for her, it was a myth, and Kala had many. She couldn't process how the technique could be part of their power or which of the five gates she knew of, it correlated to. She also feared that her involvement in the fight would make the situation worse than it already was. Rolakan, Cilia, and Alinda felt the same way. No matter what they did, their contribution would be insignificant.

🟤 🦎 🪷 🌀

As Rondai accumulated his entire aura into a bullet-size wormhole, he thought about Voradium—the strongest metal in all of Mastoperia known to date—as he focused on his power. He thought if he created a bullet strong enough to pierce Voradium then he would have no problem reaching Jihave's heart regardless of the power of his armor. He waited until Jihave fell to the ground, struggling to get back up on his feet, and moved his Jackals away before he aimed directly for the Averetti's heart.

The moment he sent his bullet away, he saw Evailen jump in front of Jihave to defend him. She had a Voradium armor and shield and believed two layers of such metal would surely stop the attack, unaware Rondai had prepared for such level of resistance. Evailen, however, didn't have time to calculate and think of the possibilities. Instead, she thought more about Rondai. She didn't want him to regret hurting Jihave and live with the pain for the rest of his life.

Rondai didn't understand why his heart beat so violently as soon as he saw Evailen intercepting his shot. He never felt that scared before. He tried to control his wormhole bullet but failed. In that split second, he realized he could control something else though. He moved his twelve guards faster than his bullet and lined them in front of Evailen.

The bullet passed through all twelve guards, pierced Evailen's shield and moved toward her chest, but Enyo and Cilia placed their shields in front of her.

The bullet still pierced Enyo's shield and didn't stop until it hit Cilia's. The bodies of twelve Jackals and a Voradium shield slowed it enough to allow the two to be there in time. Had they not thought fast enough, Evailen would have died.

The bodies of Jackals fell toward the ground and vanished in black smoke. When Rondai saw that his bullet didn't reach Evailen, he collapsed into unconsciousness the same time Jihave's fatigue forced him to fall to the ground as his beetle separated itself and returned as a tattoo on his body.

Salvanra made it to Jihave as he fell and began treating him immediately.

"I'm sorry." Jihave struggled to make his voice heard.

"Just rest now. I will take care of you." Salvanra continued treating Jihave's wound while he slept from exhaustion. Her eyes, however, kept wandering toward Rondai who looked in much worse shape.

Evailen and Yasmina ran toward Rondai and tried to wake him up without success. Yasmina separated Rondai's garment from his body and moved her fingers among his scars to see if he had inner damage. The sight of the battle wounds froze Evailen for a minute. She had never seen that many scars on one body before. When Yasmina couldn't find any internal wounds, she held Rondai's hand and spoke in the original Kalanian language.

"What are you doing?" Evailen asked.

"I am praying for the gatekeepers to keep him with us." Yasmina continued her prayers.

"This is the time for actions, not prayers." Evailen took a small rectangle device out of her pocket and placed it on Rondai's chest. The device covered his entire body with a green energy field and scanned it but couldn't pinpoint the reason for his critical condition.

33

Jihave woke up to find himself surrounded by Salvanra and his companions. Most of his wounds healed within the thirteen hours he slept as his body gained his Majestics' healing powers. The moment he opened his eyes, Salvanra hugged, and kissed him.

"How do you feel?" Alinda sat next to Jihave.

"Never better." He smiled at her, coughing as he tried to sit up.

"Take it easy," said Salvanra as she cradled his hand.

Jihave smiled and said nothing.

Alinda playfully pushed on his shoulder. "You know that this temper of yours will be the death of you one day."

"I'm not sure you can only see your future. You keep seeing things that prove otherwise."

"It's called intuition, and it has nothing to do with seeing the future." She teased him with her tongue.

Salvanra felt her face heat up watching them downplay the situation. She had been so worried about Jihave, and he woke up to act as if nothing happened.

"I will go check on Rondai." Salvanra stressed her words to remind everyone that there was another man still in danger.

When Salvanra bent over Rondai, Yasmina was sitting next to him holding his hand. Evailen sat on the other side, her eyes red, clearly deprived of sleep.

"How is he?" Salvanra dropped to her knees next to Evailen.

"He's stable but still unconscious." Evailen kept her gaze on Rondai.

"Do you at least know why he is like this?" Salvanra placed the back of her hand on his forehead to check for fever.

"I think Yasmina knows but she won't or can't tell me."

"Maybe we should ask Rolakan."

Evailen sighed. "He doesn't want to talk about it either. He said if Rondai is meant to wake up, then he will, other than that, he had nothing to say."

Jihave came up behind Salvanra and placed his hands on her shoulders. "Are you okay?"

"Shouldn't you be asking about him first? Salvanra instantly countered.

"I spoke to Cilia, and she explained the situation to me, but I sense you are mad at me." Jihave kneeled to place his arms around her.

"I'm mad at you. There's no doubt about that. You took things too far. You should have understood his anger and tried to calm him down instead of trying to kill him."

"I did try to calm him down. I allowed him to take it out on me and I didn't fight back seriously until he killed my falcon, Molanga. I was angry then, and I couldn't hold it back."

"I'm sorry. I really am." Salvanra turned to face him. "I know how it must've felt, but this is exactly why you should have understood him. This is why he started the fight; because he lost someone important to him too." She sighed. "We promised each other to change the world and not do things the way our ancestors did. I expected better from you."

"You're right. I took things too far. I'm sorry." Jihave lowered his head.

"I'm not the one you need to apologize to." Salvanra tilted her head toward Rondai.

Yasmina shrugged, her gaze focused on Rondai. "Can you please take this somewhere else? I don't want to hear any more."

Jihave stood to leave when he heard a voice.

"I'm sorry," Rondai said, his eyes still closed. "I listened to my emotions and behaved horribly."

Jihave sighed and left while the three girls moved closer to Rondai.

Rondai opened his eyes and looked at Evailen. "Do you accept my apology?"

"Were you talking to me?" Evailen raised her eyebrows.

"I would have never forgiven myself if I hurt you."

"Don't worry about it. What matters is that you are still here." Evailen placed her hand on his chest.

Yasmina lightly pressed on his hand with both of hers. "I was worried about you."

Rondai turned his head toward Yasmina. "I have to apologize to you too."

"There's nothing you need to apologize for."

"I've been mean to you the last few years and didn't give you the attention you deserved. I shouldn't have shut you out like I did."

"You were always there for me when I needed you the most. This is what matters." Yasmina smiled.

Salvanra stood, eyes on his face. "Are you okay boss?"

Rondai turned to meet her gaze. "It looks like you will be stuck with me a while longer."

"I'm just glad I didn't have to kill you." She placed her palms on her sides and winked.

"You wish you could." He coughed twice.

Yasmina narrowed her eyes, shifting her gaze between the two. She never saw Rondai that comfortable around other faction members before.

"In all fairness, though, I'm glad you're okay." Salvanra took a deep breath. "Well, now that I know you are better, it's time for me to teach the other baby what it means to evolve, and when you are back on your feet, we will have that talk too."

When Salvanra left, Rondai turned back to Yasmina. "Can you leave me alone with Evailen for a few minutes, please?"

"Now?" Her eyes widened, but she complied when she saw his nod.

Rondai pushed himself into a sitting position, grunting as he felt the pain of his wounds.

Evailen helped him up. "Would you tell me why you were unconscious? You had a lot of wounds and broken bones before I fixed your body, but nothing internal that would cause you to sleep for so long.

Rondai looked into her eyes, the corners of his mouth slightly lifted. "It doesn't matter now. I just want to know if you forgive me."

"There is nothing to forgive. I told you." Evailen placed her hand on his forehead to check for fever.

"Will you give me a chance then?" He kept his gaze focused on her.

"For what?" Evailen drew her brows together.

"To lock your heart with mine for eternity."

"For eternity?" Evailen laughed loudly until she'd nearly ran out of breath.

"I—"

"Wait, wait," she interrupted, continuing her laughter. "I have to admit. This is your best joke yet. I will give you that you know how to choose the right moments to tell your jokes."

"I'm serious."

She covered her mouth with her hand, pausing as her laughter vanished. "Oh. Where did this come from?"

"When I saw you on the other end of my attack, I knew I would never forgive myself if something had happened to you. I'm just acknowledging what my heart wants."

Evailen tilted her head, and she said nothing.

"So?" he asked.

"Um…" She took a deep breath. "I guess I'm not opposed to the possibility of something." Her heart raced, and her red seed blinked. "But what you are asking is strange. You skipped like thirty steps or something. If the circumstances were different, I would have just walked away, yet I'm still blabbing." Evailen blocked her mouth with both of her hands.

"I'm sorry if I offended you. This is how people in my faction act when they choose someone." Rondai slowly blinked, feeling his irregular heartbeats, and absence of words. "I know nothing of the Lunardis customs so do you mind telling me how people ask to partner up in your faction?"

Evailen smiled. "People in my faction ask for first dates. They go on one after the other, and if everything works out between them for a good period, they get married if they want to."

"And what do people do on those dates?" Rondai asked, the corners of his mouth lifting.

"I don't know. They talk and get to know each other, I guess."

"I see." Rondai paused. "Will you go on a first date with me then?" He met her eyes.

"I suppose." Evailen cleared her throat. "As long as you know that it's only to know each other more, and there are to be no magic locking hearts or anything else." She turned her head away from him to hide her blush. The fact that she was the first thing he thought about after he regained his consciousness tickled her heart.

The two followed their impulses, forgetting that inter-faction relations are widely frowned upon.

34

While Rondai was unconscious, he was present in his mind, reflecting on how his anger could've hurt an innocent person. He wondered if he reacted quickly because she was innocent or because she confused his feelings.

When he woke up, he felt her presence even before he opened his eyes. Her scent sent his cells into a frenzy, forcing his heart to race. It was then that he knew what he wanted, and that a lot needed to change.

For his entire life, he had been goal-oriented. He was raised to be a leader and a protector taught that weakness is for no one but himself and that people follow only the strong. He was exactly everything he was meant to be, everything that Evailen wasn't. She made him question his upbringing and morality, wonder if his path was the only one to follow. Evailen and before her Salvanra with her easy-going attitude, and Ryn and Rolakan with their secret society opened a door in his mind to make a new resolve. It was time he let go of his anger and saw everyone as people, regardless of their origins.

After talking with Evailen, Rondai chose to sleep a bit more to help his body heal. When he next woke up, he looked around him and watched how all three teams gathered around a fire, ignoring a past filled with nothing but conflict. He wondered if he had it in him to change, for the sake of himself, for Ryn and for the future of their world.

"Let's take it down a notch, Alinda." Salvanra stood next to the fire, centering the group after Alinda joked about how Rondai played pass the ball using Jihave as his ball. "I think this is a good time for us to acknowledge the errors in our ways. We need to understand that death doesn't choose favorites." She gradually raised her voice. "Death sees no color, no race, and no faction. Words such as pain and grief mean the same to you as they do us. The world is changing. Everything is changing, but us. It's time that *we* means all of us and not just our own factions."

Salvanra shifted her eyes between Jihave and Rondai. "You need to apologize to each other."

Jihave quickly stood and moved toward the center. When he passed Salvanra, he whispered in her ear, "I told you, you'd make a great elder."

Salvanra smiled before she resumed her seat.

Jihave said, "I admit I gave up to my pain after my Molanga died. I lose sight of everything when a Majestic of mine dies, and I need to work on controlling myself. I need to teach myself that the answer to violence is not always violence."

"It's never violence!" Salvanra shouted.

"Is never violence." Jihave chuckled before he turned his gaze to Rondai. "I'm sorry. I shouldn't have fought you from the beginning. Though I think if I didn't put up a fight, I would have died."

"You would have died anyway if it wasn't for Evailen!" Alinda shouted.

Rondai stood and extended his hand to shake Jihave's. "I accept your apology."

"Rondai," Salvanra spit out, eyeing him.

"It's okay, Salvanra." Jihave nodded and moved back to sit next to his girlfriend, leaving Rondai alone in the center.

"I know that you all expect me to apologize, and I probably should," Rondai began. "Part of me wants to, but I can't, and that is what I am sorry for." He paused. "I love the idea of a future that meets Salvanra's imagination. I wish we could all be one and let go of our need for tribalism, but do you know who else wanted that? Ryn." He took a deep breath. "Ryn did everything he could and more to achieve real change. Yet, he found himself stuck in a mission I'm sure he didn't want, dying for something that didn't even matter to him." He blinked back his tears.

"I forgive you because forgiveness is mine to give." He looked at Alinda and Jihave. "But I can't apologize. If I do, then his death was for nothing. Our fight was for nothing. Our—" Rondai shook his head before he moved away from the group. Yasmina stood to follow him, but Salvanra grabbed her arm, asking if she could be the one who talks to him.

🌀 🍃 🪷 🜛

"Are you okay?" Salvanra sat next to him on the grass atop the hill. The fire, small in the background.

"I don't know. I stood up to say something different, but that's what came out instead. I didn't want to apologize, but I wanted to tell them I understand. I would have probably done the same as Alinda had I been in her shoes. I would have done worse than Jihave as a leader."

"Don't beat yourself up. It takes time to get there, and we don't all have the same pace, but you are a good leader." She placed her hand on his back.

"Am I?" He turned his head toward her. "All I did was follow a lead we didn't earn, abandon my team, forget about my mission and start a fight that could have killed not only the two of us but Evailen as well."

"Evailen and her team would have been dead if it wasn't for you chasing after that lead, and you didn't abandon us or your mission. You were hurt and acted irrationally. It was wrong, but none of us is perfect. You just need to work on yourself. I know you have it in you because you couldn't stand to see yourself hurting Evailen and saved her."

Rondai smiled, his face reddening.

"You are so cute when you blush." Salvanra pushed his shoulder with hers. "I heard you are taking her out tomorrow."

"I am. It feels kind of weird."

"Honestly, I didn't expect that you would find a girl from another faction interesting, but here we are. If you can be open to this idea, then there's hope for the world after all."

"That sounds more mean-spirited than it is a compliment, though I didn't expect it either." Rondai threw his back on the glass."

Salvanra turned to face him. "So I wanted to ask you if you would allow me to leave here tonight. I want to track Afakan and find his location while you are still here."

"How will I contact you?" Rondai raised his back off the ground.

"I will leave my eagle with you. When you decide on your next destination, she will find me, and I will meet you there."

Rondai looked at her.

"Don't worry, she will be invisible."

"Okay, but you need to hurry. We leave after tomorrow morning at the latest. I still need to catch the last two artifacts.

"I had better leave then." Salvanra stood. "And good luck with your date tomorrow."

35

Rondai asked Enyo and Cilia about what happens on a date. They both found it amusing to advise the coldest person they knew about dating, while Rondai felt embarrassed by the whole situation, but he could not help his need to impress Evailen.

Evailen appeared at their meeting point in a red dress that complimented her body shape. The dress revealed most of her back and cut into a deep V shape that trailed along her breasts. The colors of her seeds shined, complementing her look and revealing her stardom.

Rondai waited for her wearing the same wide creamy garment he had worn since the mission began.

Rondai smiled to hide how nervous he was. "Did you pack this with you when you prepared for this mission?"

"Is that the first thing you want to say to me on our date?" Evailen teased, the corners of her mouth lifting.

"Right. I'm sorry." Rondai straightened his posture, trying to look serious. "You look beautiful."

"I do, don't I?" Evailen twirled half a turn in both directions showing off her dress.

"You are also full of yourself."

"Again, not what you want to say on your first date." She shook her head.

He lowered his chin.

"So, what will we do?"

"There is a village down that hill. I thought we could try their food together. Yasmina told me how excited you are for exploring this part of the world and anything related to it. What do you think?"

"Sounds like a good plan. I like the idea." Her eyes shined like a newborn star in the dark skies.

Rondai opened gate three and was about to create a plank of wood to use as transportation, but Evailen took hold of his hand.

"What are you doing?" she asked.

"I will take us there."

"No. No magic today. We can walk. It's not that far."

"You want to walk there with those heels?" He pointed at her feet.

Evailen laughed and clicked her heels together as she touched her purple seed. The heels disappeared, leaving her with flat shoes.

"I see. So, this is how you came up with that dress."

"There's no limit to what you can do when it's up to your imagination." Evailen winked, the corners of her eyes lifting.

The two walked down the hill, side by side.

"Why?" Rondai asked.

"Why what?"

"Why did you accept to go on a date with me?"

"Because I wanted to."

"Why did you want to?"

"Do you know what your problem is?" Evailen turned her face toward his.

"Obviously, you will tell me." Rondai continued to face forward.

"That's it. You have no filter. You say the first thing that comes to your mind regardless of the effect."

Rondai paused, considering her words. "Would you rather I choose my words and tell you what you want to hear?"

"No, but you don't need to spell out everything that passes through your mind either."

"Perhaps you are right, but I don't think I would like that. I don't want to feel that I have to censor myself around you as I constantly do in my life. I want to know who you are, and in return, I owe you the same. To tell you what I think at every moment."

He paused, taking a deep breath. "I don't intend to hurt or downgrade you. I only seek to show you who I am by allowing you to know my impulses. I believe when you hide nothing from your partner, you become unbreakable."

"That sounds interesting, but does this mean you would never compliment your partner?"

"Of course, I would. Do I look like someone who doesn't know how to compliment?"

Evailen stared into his eyes with a blank face.

"Okay. I don't ordinarily give compliments, but that doesn't mean I never do it. At least this way you will know it's honest."

Evailen giggled before she spoke. "I guess I should be honest as well. You can say I'm curious. You're contradictory. Your actions and your words don't always match, but they seem to be from the heart no matter what. If I'm honest with myself, I will say you have piqued my interest, and I have no idea what to expect."

When they arrived in the village, they walked around to explore it until they found a restaurant with calm music and tiny lights scattered on the trees. They found themselves a wooden table by the lake.

"You want the truth?" Evailen paused. "You are the last person I thought would be okay with inter-faction relations." She took a seat opposite him.

"Is it because of my personality or my faction?" He placed his elbows on the table.

"Both. Kala doesn't have the best reputation when it comes to being friendly with other factions."

"That is partly true. We don't like the factions, but that doesn't mean we hate everyone."

"Meaning?" She leaned forward and rested her chin on her hands.

"Do you know the story of Metraka and his three children?" Rondai asked.

"No, I never heard that name before."

"Metraka was the great-grandson of Katin—the founder of my faction. He was Katin's favorite and the closest to him. Metraka saw what the war did to his beloved great-grandfather. He understood that even when you win a war, you would still end up with permanent scars. When he became the faction master, he banned magic and sent three of his children to the other factions as scholars. He thought he could bring all factions together, but he was wrong. Years later, the factions asked him for the secret of magic, but he refused. He received the heads of his children as a response to his refusal. Metraka started the second war out of anger, but without magic, our losses were severe. Since then, my faction swore to never give up magic again. As long as other factions have powers, we must keep ours too." He heaved a heavy sigh.

"That was almost a thousand years ago. The world has changed a lot since then."

"Only the appearance of the world has changed, but it's still ruled by power."

"What I don't understand is why do you hate magic so much if it gives you all that power?"

"Because power comes with a price we can't escape."

"Which is?" Evailen leaned closer to him.

Rondai looked into her eyes and felt joy riding the waves of his irregular pulse. He wondered if he should reveal the one secret no Kalangou ever broke. The words rushed to his mouth as he wanted to tell her everything, but they crashed on the tip of his tongue. "Tonight is going well. Let's not ruin it by sadness."

36

The moment Kawan, Naradia and Maringrad set their foot in the city of Kemet, they realized it differed from any they had visited so far. The city appeared as old as their home continent, perhaps older. Ancient ruins were visible at every corner, integrating with a semi-modern city, and surrounded by beggars. Street merchants filled the roads in a chaotic scene defending their prices against any who dare ask for a bargain.

The clothes, tattoos, and overall clean look of Kawan and his companions made them not only the center of attention but also a target for those who fed on ignorant tourists. Every now and then, they saw the edge of craziness. A man or a woman in torn clothing mouthing a prophecy to all who would listen. The locals ignored them and went about their business as if the weirdos didn't exist.

"That is a sight you don't see every day." Naradia looked at one of the crazed speakers through her peripheral vision.

"I think it gives the city a different taste," said Maringrad.

Kawan however, listened to all of them, solving the puzzle of their unfinished sentences. Only one grabbed his attention. He repeated the same prophecy, but unlike the others, his words were clear.

"When the hundred moons unite together, and the sun falls into the ground. When the half-man fights, the angels already drowned. The light will go, and darkness will shine."

"Is any of that nonsense possible?" Maringrad asked Kawan.

"I can't tell, but it's interesting." Kawan stepped away from the man and continued walking.

Naradia followed Kawan. "I see nothing interesting about half a man or a hundred moons. Those are the words of a madman."

Kawan locked his hands behind his back. "All prophecies come from madmen."

"All nonsense comes from madmen, prophecies come from wise elders." Naradia increased her speed to catch up to her companions.

"Agree to disagree." Kawan stopped in the middle of a square and looked up to see the top of an obelisk opposite them. The obelisk had carvings and paintings similar to those they saw on the walls of the tunnel leading up to the second artifact.

"Is it inside?" Maringrad asked.

"It's under it," Kawan replied

Naradia pulled up a pen-like device and flashed it toward the ground. Her scan showed there was a large room under the obelisk.

"We are in the middle of a square full of people. How are we going to get in there?" Maringrad looked around him.

"We will open the obelisk. There is a staircase that goes directly into the room." Kawan fixed his eyes on the ruin.

"How are you planning to do that? I see no doors." Maringrad asked.

Naradia reached into one of her many pockets. "We can bomb it. I have bombs I believe are strong enough."

Maringrad chuckled. "Why do you have bombs? What were you expecting to explode?"

"I just wanted to be ready for any scenario."

"There will be no bombing. As I said, we will open the obelisk. The whole thing is a gate."

Naradia crossed her arms over her breasts. "How do you know all of that? I thought you couldn't see anything related to the artifact."

"It is written right there on the obelisk. All you need to do is read."

Both Maringrad and Naradia looked at each other and asked simultaneously. "You can read that?"

"Not entirely, but it's one of our ancestors' dead languages."

Maringrad patted Kawan on the shoulder. "They call them dead for a reason you know."

Kawan glanced at him with a fake smile before shifting his gaze around the square. "We need to clear the square of people. It says the condition for opening the obelisk is that only one person can be here."

"How do you suggest we do that?" Naradia asked.

"The people in this part of the world seem to believe in a lot of nonsense. It should be easy to distract them with things that appear to be godlike."

It didn't take much to avert all eyes in the square to them. Following Kawan's plan, Naradia rode her pod and flew above the ground the same time Maringrad freed his tiger.

"My children." Naradia flapped her arms wide as she hovered above them. "Today is your lucky day. Your gods have returned. If you want our blessing, follow us."

Most of the people followed them out of the square, leaving it nearly empty. Only Kawan and six others stayed there. The remaining six moved slowly toward Kawan as he stood still.

"Why didn't you follow the others?" Kawan asked.

"Gods don't exist," said the largest of the six.

"Didn't you see what they did? At least, they are not ordinary. Aren't you interested to know more?"

"A trick. Perhaps they are using technology from the continent of Profectus." A long-haired, tall woman eyed Kawan.

"What are you trying to do?" asked a half-naked man with braids. "You are after something, and you're trying to distract everyone."

Kawan heaved a loud sigh. The clock was ticking, and the others could return at any time.

"You are right. I'm looking for something, and I need everyone out of here." Kawan took his sword out of his key chain. "You can either leave now or die here. You have one minute."

The largest of the six grabbed a long pipe off the ground and ran toward Kawan, who sliced the man in half with one blow. The others then ran from the scene as quickly as they could.

The second he was alone, Kawan began the ritual to open the obelisk as he knew they planned to return with reinforcements. He cut his palm open and placed it on the obelisk, watching as his blood moved around the details of the monument. The obelisk opened in half, revealing a staircase that led toward an underground chamber. He stepped inside to grab the artifact and rushed out of the square to meet his companions at the predestined location.

◉ ❦ ✿ ◐

"That was easy." Maringrad walked toward Kawan, who looked bored from the wait.

"Those artifacts were placed here hundreds of years ago if not more. Perhaps they were once heavily guarded or considered to be well hidden." Kawan answered.

Naradia stepped off her pod. "Well, we have one artifact now. This is all that matters."

"Yes, and now it's time to go for the last one," said Kawan.

37

"Are you sure you don't want to tell me the price of your magic?" Evailen moved her chair closer to his.

"Trust me, it will make you sad, and I'm enjoying this evening. Instead, I would rather know more about you."

"Only if you tell me what you see in me." Evailen eyes lit as she fished for a compliment.

Rondai gazed into her eyes for a few seconds. "I see nothing," he said, his voice entirely serious.

"What?" Evailen dropped her jaw, her frown creeping up on her face.

Rondai ignored the outrage in her facial expressions and continued. "The world is always on the move. Everyone has something to say, and a million things they want to prove. People are always trying to demonstrate their power whichever way they can. They don't want you to forget who they are. Even I am guilty of that."

He paused, unsure of whether he said that right, but she gave him a look that encouraged him to continue.

"You are the only one I have met so far that isn't like that. At first, I thought you were naïve and weak. Maybe even a coward. Then, you pulled the craziest, most courageous plan anyone could come up with. Now, I look at you, and I see nothing of our madness—I see only you."

Evailen's face almost matched her red seed. "Huh," she said, raising her eyebrows. "Better than I expected."

She didn't know what else to say, so she opted to answer his question about her instead. "I don't know what to tell you about me exactly. I love video games. I love them so much that I studied game development. I was working as a developer before they sent me to the Forbidden City, which, if I'm honest, I'm not thrilled about. Most people at Lunar find it honorable to serve the peace. I just miss my games so much."

"You can still play them at the Forbidden City, you know."

"I know, but I will no longer be a developer. Anyway, it's too early to talk about that. Oh, and I love storytelling and different cultures. More like story showing. I think this is why I love video games so much. I can tell the stories I want and take part in them as well."

"Do you know how many times you said the words video and games?"

Evailen pinched his shoulder, making him laugh. "I also dance. A lot. I dance a lot and sing. I am a terrible singer, but I do well in a chorus." She paused. "What are your hobbies?"

"Mine?"

"I don't know. Maybe there is someone else here." Evailen looked around pretending to search for a third person.

"Hobbies are not allowed in Kala. We have to focus on our training and assigned tasks."

"That wasn't my question. I asked about your hobbies, not the rules of practice?"

Rondai knew that he couldn't fool her. "I love to write."

"Yay! What do you write? Novels?"

"I write poems. Mmm... on a beat."

"What? No way! You rap?"

"I didn't say that." He turned his face away from her.

"I would have never imagined you as a rapper. Even in Lunar, rapping is considered the art of the non-serious."

"Words can have great power if they are chosen carefully, you know?"

"Oh man, I can see you in a music video with your serious face in this wide-robe-thing you are wearing as women move their butts around you. I would watch that a million times." Evailen couldn't hold her laughter any longer.

For a split second, Rondai felt insulted, but the image she painted soon made its way into his mind, and he laughed even louder than she did. It was the first time Evailen saw him laugh like that. Perhaps it was the first time anyone saw him laugh like that.

When the pair left the restaurant to walk back, they made sure they were side by side, brushing their shoulders against one another repeatedly. They shared stories about themselves and untangled wrong beliefs about their factions. It was almost the perfect night— until a familiar sound brought them back to reality.

Their gadgets beeped several times, announcing a new artifact had been acquired. Rondai was the only one to pull up his gadget. His eyes widened, and mouth opened as he saw the third artifact disappear from the list.

He felt he failed his entire faction by focusing on himself and ignoring the mission. Evailen saw the panic on his face and told him she would make sure the last artifact is his, but her voice didn't make it through to him. In his mind's eye, all he could see was the look of disappointment on the faces of his faction peers. Before a single tear escaped his eyes, he opened the third gate and flew himself on a piece of wood he materialized, leaving Evailen alone.

She watched him as he disappeared into the distance and wondered if they had a beautiful enough night to forgive his behavior, but as she walked back alone, she thought their first date should as well be their last.

Rondai woke his companions, the adrenaline forcing his body to shake. "Pack your things, we are leaving right now."

He couldn't let the final artifact escape his hands, and that was absolute.

38

As Evailen walked back to the hilltop, she reflected upon her romantic life. She hadn't had many relationships, not as much as girls her age usually had. She thought about the three relations she had and realized that she never broke up with any of her exes. Her red and blue seed blinked rapidly as her thoughts caused her heart to tremble. She wondered if there was something wrong with her, but she quickly brushed the thought away. All ex-partners broke up with her for the same reason, because she prioritized her love for video games and programming over everything. "If it means I have to be forever alone, so be it," she muttered to herself.

Evailen believed that if she couldn't be true to herself, she would be miserable, and those who chose to be with her would have a taste of that misery. But that was the dilemma she had with Rondai. When he left, he was true to himself. *He followed what mattered to him the most, but should his behavior negate the rest of the evening by default?* she wondered.

She asked herself if she had the right to be mad at him for leaving her like that. She knew this was only their first date, but it was the most important one for them, too. First impressions are always important because they last for a good deal of time, and can rarely change, if ever.

She understood they were on a mission and he had to place his faction first, but did that attraction between them mean nothing? Was he unable to bring her back with him? Or at least excuse himself before he left?

The questions kept piling on top of each other in her mind. The sun was peeking upon the world by the time she realized the mission would be over soon. Even if Rondai was the one to get the last artifact and there would be one more mission, it would still end. After that, they would become part of the Forbidden City. *Was it possible for royal guards to be involved in a romantic relationship or any relationships for that matter?*

Evailen was a master of getting distracted. Her train of thought was always her worst enemy. She knew that, yet she always gave in to it.

But when she saw Jihave, all the questions in her mind disappeared, allowing her feelings to take over.

"What are you doing?" Evailen moved toward Jihave who was packing.

"What does it look like? We are getting ready to leave." Jihave raised his eyebrows.

"And where are you going?" she crossed her arms in front of her chest.

"I'm not required to answer that," Jihave replied as he resumed packing.

"No, you are not, but I would like an answer."

"Perhaps you got this wrong Evailen. We are still on a mission that requires us to work against each other. Maybe after all of this is over, we can be friends, but don't forget, I owe you nothing." Jihave met her eyes.

"I think you are the one who misunderstood. I wasn't asking."

Jihave realized she was serious as he saw her armor crawl out of her skin and slowly wrap her body.

"I didn't know I was your prisoner." Jihave smirked.

"Only for a short period." Evailen separated her sword-gun from her armor after it completely materialized.

"That is a nice sword you have. I've seen nothing like it before, but are you sure you can defeat me?" Jihave narrowed his eyes.

Cilia saw Evailen pull out her weapon and approached her. "Cut this out Evailen. What are you trying to do?"

"Stay out of this Cilia. It's between me and him."

"You must be mad or something. Since when do we fight for nothing?" Cilia asked, raising her voice.

Jihave sat on the ground and crossed his legs, the corners of his mouth lifting as he watched the two Lunardis argue.

"It isn't for nothing. None of us will go after the final artifact today. We will all stay here, and I will make sure of it." Evailen's face turned red when she saw Jihave was paying no attention to her, but her plan was working as she didn't really want to fight.

"Don't tell me you are doing this for Rondai. You were only on a single date with him. Which was last night!" Cilia shouted before she leaned closer to her friend and half-covered her mouth with her hand, lowering her voice as she said, "How did that go by the way?"

"It was amazing, but it didn't end well. I will tell you all about it later, now is not the time." Evailen whispered from a distance.

"Right." Cilia adjusted her posture, raising her voice again, fighting to cage her smile. "You can't be seriously trying to stall us to allow him to get the last artifact."

"We owe him that much."

Jihave stood up and freed his tiger. "I told you I owe no one nothing."

"You mean you owe no one, full stop," Cilia argued, turning to face Jihave. "Because what you said means you owe someone something."

"I know. Right?" Evailen said with a pitched voice.

"Enough is enough." Jihave sent his tiger to attack Evailen, but the Majestic was slow and moved with a limp. Jihave realized his tiger had not yet completely recovered from his injuries from the previous battle. So he retracted the tiger into his tattoo and laid back on the grass as soon as their bodies combined. "Looks like I'm going nowhere, anyway," Jihave muttered to himself.

"How long is it going to take for him to heal?" Evailen asked.

"Probably another day or so." Jihave placed his arms beneath his head and stared into the sky.

"Then there is no need for me to bother you any longer." Evailen brushed her black seed to remove her armor.

Cilia walked toward Evailen and grabbed her arm before she pulled her away from Jihave's location. "Now tell me everything that happened and don't leave out any detail," she whispered into her ear.

"Later Cilia, we are on a mission now."

"Really? Were you putting your mission first a few seconds ago?" Cilia eyed her.

"You're right. We have time. I will tell you everything that happened. I can't wait to hear what you think, actually."

Both girls laughed the situation off.

39

"What is going on?" Enyo struggled to keep his eyes open after Rondai woke him.

"We have to leave right now." Rondai continued speed packing.

"Did something go wrong between you and Evailen? Is she okay?" Enyo jumped out of his air-conditioned sleeping bag.

"She is fine. Now is not the time to worry about anything other than the mission. Only one artifact remains, and we are the only team without one." Rondai sighed heavily.

"Do we have a plan?" Terqwan sat up.

Rondai stood and turned to face Enyo. "I need you to show me the map of the possible locations for the artifacts one more time."

Enyo yawned before using his seed to create a hologram of the world's map.

Terqwan rubbed his eyes. "Why does it only show six locations? Didn't you say the satellites couldn't see nine points the last time?"

Enyo nodded. "It seems that when other teams removed the artifacts from their place, the satellites were able to scan the location and update the map."

"Based on your analysis, this was the location of the third artifact." Rondai pointed toward the third continent, west of Mastoperia. "I think I know where the last one is. Let's go."

Terqwan raised his brows, meeting Enyo's eyes. "I don't get it. Which location is it?"

"Evailen acquired the first artifact in the first continent, east of Mastoperia. We are on the northern continent, where Jihave claimed the second one. If Kawan found the third in the western continent, then the last will logically be to the south. There is only one location on the southern continent of Eleftheria, and that is where we are going," Enyo explained as they stepped on the block of wood Rondai materialized for their departure.

"I see." Terqwan looked at the wooden piece below his feet, shifting his eyes to Rondai. "Don't you think this plank is smaller than the others you created before?" He stood too close to his team leader as the latter created a small barrier for them to hold onto.

"The smaller it is, the more power I can put into it. This will allow us to move much faster than before.

All three held tight as Rondai flew them toward the southern continent at top speed.

🌀🍃🪷🌑

"Are we crossing the ocean?" Enyo asked the moment they reached the water's surface.

"It's the only direct route." Rondai focused his eyes on his destination.

"I'm almost sure you can't pass on top of Mastoperia, there is a reason our continent remained hidden to this day or did you forget about the tornado wall." Enyo's red seed blinked rapidly.

Terqwan placed his hand on Enyo's shoulder. "Are you afraid of what might happen?"

"A little. Were you able to see something?"

"I did. Not all the way, but we will have to change our route at some point. We won't be able to make it directly across."

"Why don't you tell him that? It would save us a lot of time."

"He is drowning in his own mind right now. I experimented with several possible speeches, but he won't listen to any of them. He has to see it for himself."

Enyo wiped the drops of sweat that began to cover his forehead.

Terqwan patted Enyo's back, smiling at him. "Don't worry. We won't face any danger. He will make his decision relatively quickly."

After half a day, Rondai noticed a huge wall of waves mounted by an enormous tornado in the middle of the ocean. He wanted to create an opening for them to pass through, but he couldn't use the power of the second gate since he was already using the third to control the wood they stood on. He realized he would have to sacrifice his companions if he wanted to make it through the storm, so he reluctantly chose to take the long way by going around their home continent.

Enyo finally relaxed after Rondai altered their course and regained his trust in Rondai's decision-making.

Rondai took a second to breathe as he realized that nothing was going to happen until he reached his destination. It was then that he remembered Salvanra. He called the invisible eagle to show itself by making a sound Salvanra taught him. The eagle materialized as it flew down toward him. She rested on his arm without any movement as if she was a statue. Rondai whispered a message that contained the destination into the eagle's ear and sent it away to find Salvanra.

"Do you control animals now?" Enyo's eyes widened.

"It's Salvanra's. She left her with me so we could tell her where to meet us." Rondai answered.

"And here I thought she abandoned us after your battle with Jihave." Enyo smiled alone as the other two didn't understand it was a joke.

Silence was their fourth companion for most of the remaining journey, leaving only when the continent of Eleftheria appeared in the horizon almost a day and a half later.

Throughout the journey, Rondai played the scenario of him losing in his mind repeatedly. He knew how much his faction relied on him winning the leader's seat. He didn't know the exact reasons behind it, but he thought perhaps they wanted to make sure a member of Kala ruled the Forbidden City, hoping it would give them a chance to double down on their use of magic and allow the people to relax. He didn't care much about the seat, but he wanted to help his people. He imagined the council would strip him of his rank and leave him powerless in one of their hidden villages where they put those who refused or failed to access gate magic. For him, that would be the worst price to pay.

"Perhaps I appeared lenient," Rondai said in a calm tone. "Perhaps I was. I blame none of you, but I have allowed myself to be distracted from my mission more than once. I can't lose the last artifact. I will get it, or I will die trying."

He paused, then said, "I trust both of you, but if you don't plan to see this mission through to the end, then please don't stand in my way because you will die."

Enyo and Terqwan nodded in silence. They weighed his words and felt for him. Even though he used a similar threatening tone to the one he just spoke with after they landed on the first continent, his emotions came through more caring than cold. What they heard was *This is really important to me, and I don't want to hurt anyone for it.*

"I am with you Rondai." Terqwan patted his back.

"Me too. You deserve to get this one." Enyo nodded.

40

Even though Rondai was moving at top speed over the continent of Eleftheria, they could still smell freedom in the air. The absence of civilization piqued both Enyo's and Terqwan's interest, but neither of them dared to ask Rondai to stop for a chance to explore. After another half-day atop the continent, they arrived at the location of the final artifact in the center of the desert.

To their surprise, the artifact was out in the open, visible on top of a simple pillar centering a star-shaped meadow.

Terqwan took off his shoes to feel the sand upon his feet. "This must be the easiest mission ever."

Enyo's eyes widened. "Don't you find it strange that the artifact stayed untouched for perhaps centuries while it stood unguarded?"

"I find it stranger to see well-tended grass in the middle of the desert," Terqwan muttered.

"Really?" Enyo raised his brows.

Rondai stood at the edge of the star listening to his heart tune its beat into an original melody. His stare didn't break its connection with the artifact once, but he needed a moment to move closer. He slowly took his first step toward his goal. His right foot touched the grass first. His hand slightly trembled, knowing that when his other foot touched the grass, the artifact would be one-step away. When his left foot abandoned the ground, so did his perception. Reality altered around him as if moving in slow motion. He smelled the freshness of the leaves before trees grew into adulthood instantly. He heard the singing of birds filling the peaceful forest he now centered. The artifact and the pillar were the only unchanged objects, but none of that mattered to him. He took his final step toward his goal.

"Don't!" Salvanra shouted.

"Good, you are already here. We can finish this together." Rondai pivoted his body, turning his face to see her.

"Don't take the artifact. Leave it in peace." Salvanra took a step closer to him.

"What are you talking about? This is the last one." He raised his brows.

"And the most dangerous."

"Would something happen to me if I touch it? Do you know something?"

"Not to you, but to every other creature that lives here," Salvanra said stressing each word.

"I don't understand. This forest and everything is clearly an illusion. Are you saying you are worried about some imaginary creatures?"

"It's not an illusion. This place is real. Everything around you is real. This star on the ground is a gateway between this world and ours."

"You are wrong. There are no other worlds. It's impossible. This is just the artifact's defense system. It's trying to make me lose my mind. In fact, I don't think you are real either." Rondai doubted his own words, but the absence of both Enyo and Terqwan pushed him to believe. "Yes, I'm sure now. You are just another part of the illusion. There is no way you could have made it here before us."

"Listen to yourself. You are questioning the world when you come from an impossible one. You have magic, and I control animals. Why would it be impossible that there are other worlds?" Salvanra took another step toward him.

"Because outside of Mastoperia, the world is ordinary. Only we are the exceptions." Rondai raised his voice.

"That's not even remotely true, and you know it. Nothing in our world is ordinary."

"Enough!" Rondai shouted. "You are not real. None of this is real. I'm not destroying any creatures by claiming this artifact." Rondai placed his hand on the artifact, but before he picked it up, he heard a familiar voice that he had longed to hear for years.

"Listen to her, son."

Rondai slowly moved his head to the side before his eyes accumulated tears while he stood in silence, looking at his father standing a few feet away.

"I miss you," he muttered, keeping his eyes focused on his father. Rakamai looked the same; dressed in the same clothes as the day he said goodbye to his son before he went on the mission that took his life.

"I miss you too, my son."

"I have so much to tell you." Rondai's tears streamed down his cheeks,

"You can tell me everything. We can live here together. You can tell me about how you became the youngest gate five master, and the new girl you like. We can talk for hours, days, or forever if you want. All you need to do is leave the artifact alone, and I will be here as long as you want me to be."

"I would love that a lot, but what about my faction?" Rondai's voice trembled.

"Forget about your faction. Stay here, and they won't be able to reach you. No one would be able to strip you of your magic or look down on you. All you need to do is come into my arms." Rakamai opened his arms.

"There is only one problem," Rondai said. "My father would never ask me to abandon my faction."

Rondai pulled the artifact away from the pillar and watched as the world around him collapsed and disappeared. When he saw his companions Enyo and Terqwan standing at the edge of the meadow, he quickly wiped away his tears before taking a deep breath to regain control over his feelings. He was good at hiding them.

Rondai painted a fake smile on his face as he stepped off the star. "I would say next time feel free to help, but that was the last artifact so… Thank you."

Terqwan's grin widened. "Help with what? You walked toward the artifact and picked it up. Is it heavy? Do you need help to carry it?"

"So, you didn't see me disappear or teleport out of here or something. I must've been gone for some time," Rondai spoke quietly.

"I hate to break it to you, but you went nowhere. It took you two seconds to get that artifact." Enyo placed his hand on Rondai's forehead. "You don't have a fever, but maybe you should allow me to do a full check."

"No, it's okay." He pushed Enyo's hand away. "We will set camp here until Salvanra arrives, then we will plan our next move."

Terqwan deepened his voice. "Good idea. We can light a fire and share horror stories. Perhaps you can tell us what happened when you disappeared."

Enyo and Terqwan laughed, failing to see the sorrow hidden in Rondai's eyes.

41

Salvanra arrived halfway into the night to a quiet atmosphere. Both Enyo and Terqwan were asleep while Rondai sat in a meditative position with closed eyes, embracing the silence. Salvanra saw the artifact resting in front of him as she dismounted her tigress.

"I'm sorry. I got here as fast as I could." Salvanra sat next to him.

"Don't worry about it. There was nothing you could have done, anyway." Rondai opened his eyes.

"What happened?" Salvanra asked.

Rondai told her everything that happened since he got inside the star.

"I see. So, I was present after all, at least my spirit was here." She smiled.

Rondai looked at her and smiled, grateful that she didn't mention his father or ask him about how he felt. "Did you find the location of the beast?" He stood and picked a few branches off the star meadow to revive the dying fire.

"I did." Salvanra netted her brows in confusion. "Isn't it easier to use your magic to reignite the fire?"

"Maybe." Rondai smiled without a follow-up. "So, did you capture it?"

"Not yet. I only found its location, but I received your message before I reached him."

"So where is it?" Rondai reclaimed his setting position.

"At the edge of the continent, a day's ride to the southwest. It's hiding in a star world like the one you have here." Salvanra's heart pounded faster than usual.

"Okay. We will move when the sun is up. You can rest a little."

"I see that you don't want to talk about it since you changed the subject so quickly, but how do you feel about seeing your father?" Salvanra pushed herself closer to him.

Rondai shook his head, regretting his earlier judgment. "You guessed correctly. I don't want to talk about this."

Salvanra sighed. "Fine. Maybe tell me about what happened on your date with Evailen then?"

Rondai squinted, slowly turning his face to hers. "I didn't think you would be interested in that."

"What are you talking about? We're friends now, aren't we?" Salvanra gave him a little nudge.

"I guess we are."

"So? Spill the beans. Don't make me wait." She gave him another nudge.

Rondai squinted at her again. "I don't know what to tell you. It was good. Fantastic actually. It felt easy to talk to her."

"Oh yeah? What did you talk about?" Salvanra placed her chin on her hand while holding a smile on her face.

"That is private, you know?" Rondai's turned his face away to hide his blush.

"Come on!" Salvanra shouted. "Don't leave me hanging."

"Why are you interested in this?"

"Because this is what friends do, they talk to each other about stuff."

Rondai turned his head back to her. "Are we that kind of friends already?"

"Why not? What's wrong with it?"

"We are from different factions."

"So?" She paused. "Didn't you agree we are friends? What difference does it make if we were this or that kind of friends?"

Rondai said nothing in return.

"Just say whatever is on your mind. I will listen," she added.

"I don't know Salvanra. I'm confused. I never viewed other faction members as worthy of living, and now I like one and call others my friends." He took a deep breath. "I feel like I have two enemies at war inside of me. One wants to open up and accept that I was wrong about the world, and the other keeps reminding me of my faction and my duties." He placed his elbows on his knees and looked down.

"I understand where you are coming from. My mother told me stories about how Kala is a strict faction, but you need to trust your instincts. You don't need to betray your faction, all you need to do is open up a little." She pointed at his heart.

"It's not that easy." He shook his head. "I understand why my faction behaves like that, and now I understand even more why they are strict about us not mingling with other factions."

"Why did you ask Evailen out then if this is what you are thinking about?"

"Because when I see her, I forget about all of this and all I see is her. When she is around, I feel no pain." He looked at Salvanra's face and saw that she gave him all of her attention and found the courage to continue. "I feel something similar with you too. I'm not used to talking like this, not even with my faction members. Literally, except for Yasmina, I have never opened up to anyone. I don't know why, but with you, I can talk. I'm not afraid of being judged, I guess." He saw her face light up a little and smiled before he continued. "I do want to be that kind of friend to you. The one who tells you about everything. Maybe it will happen one day, but I need time."

Salvanra put her hand on his back and smiled. "It's okay. Take all the time you need, because the truth is, I really want you to be my friend. Now let us sleep. I want to rest before we fight Afakan."

The following morning the four companions left to battle Afakan armed with their excitement.

After a day's ride, they stepped together into the star dimension watching as another forest appeared around them. Rondai realized it was identical to the one he saw before and felt comfort in knowing that by taking the artifact, he destroyed only the gate and not the entire dimension, or so he chose to believe.

Salvanra freed her eagle and talked to her in a language that none understood.

"We will follow Lina. She will take us to Afakan, but I don't want us to use any of our powers yet. I don't know what Afakan can or can't sense," said Salvanra.

After four hours of running, Enyo pointed out that the sun hadn't moved. "I am sure it's night in the real world, but it feels like time is standing still here."

Terqwan nodded. "It does feel like this world isn't real. Do you think someone created it?"

"Why would someone create such a place?" Rondai asked.

"Perhaps it once was a prison?" Enyo wondered.

Terqwan said, "It makes sense. If that beast was indeed a remnant of the old civilization, then they had to contain it somehow."

Enyo sighed. "I have a lot of questions right now."

"I know. Me too. It's so exciting."

"Focus." Salvanra cut their speech. "Afakan could appear at any minute."

They followed the eagle for another hour and a half before it stopped at the edge of the forest. They found themselves atop a steep rocky edge with an ocean hundreds of feet below them.

"This can't be possible." Salvanra tapped her chin.

Rondai tried to comfort her. "I'm sure the beast is somewhere around here."

"We are not looking for a tiny animal. Afakan is the largest Majestic we know of." She ran her fingers through her braids and left them there.

Salvanra looked around the place, trying to figure out what she had done wrong until Enyo tapped her on the shoulder. She didn't pay attention to him until he did it again.

"What?" she shouted as she looked toward Enyo who uttered nothing. She followed his terrified gaze to the edge of the forest, where she saw black smoke rising.

At that instant, a huge three-fingered hand made of stone grabbed onto the edge of the cliff.

42

The four companions took battle stances as they saw the dragon-like-beast climb up the edge of the mountain. The beast breathed fire at them the moment he fully mounted the cliff. Rondai opened the fourth gate and fought back with water coming out of his hands. Both elements battled in failure to gain ground over each other.

"This is—" Enyo enlarged his shield and placed it in front to protect everyone from the heat.

"Afakan. I know." Salvanra smiled. "He kind of looks like the father of my baby dragon." Her grin grew even wider as she launched her tigress and ape into battle. The tigress went directly toward the beast's left leg as both Salvanra and the ape climbed opposite trees. Afakan stopped firing at Rondai after the ape jumped in the air and punched his face. Salvanra landed on the neck of the beast as Rondai's water attack accidentally hit the ape, bringing it to the ground.

Afakan flew toward the sky with abnormal movement. Salvanra's heart beat faster as she freed her snake atop Afakan. The snake tried to place its fangs into the beast, breaking apart of their composition each time she tried.

"Should we go after them?" Enyo looked toward the battle in the middle of the sky.

"No. We have to prepare for what is coming." Terqwan pulled his sword out of his bracelet.

"What's coming?" Enyo's eyes bulged out as his armor wrapped him.

"That." Terqwan pointed toward the heart of the forest as the ground began to shake below them. A herd of massive lions approached them at top speed. Enyo's hand shook as he fired his double-barrel automatic gun, still covered in blood from its previous use. His energy bullets forced the herd to separate into two lines but didn't deal significant damage. Rondai materialized rock walls in front of them, but the lions knocked them down easily.

"Go high Enyo. Shoot toward the back of their bodies. It's their weakest part." Terqwan saited the future before he looked at Rondai. "Lighting will work against them, but we need a smokescreen." Terqwan pressed the handle of his sword generating electricity around the blade.

Rondai created a mini-tornado that provided them with protection as well as raising the dust to blind the lions while Terqwan pierced any that made it close to them.

Enyo saw the magnitude of the herd while he shot at their backs. His shots brought some of them down, but there were too many to handle. The herd was closing in on the two men on the ground, and their tactic wouldn't work for much longer.

All the while, Salvanra's plan to hypnotize Afakan proved its failure, and she needed to come up with a new one while she struggled to hold on to the beast. She tried to restrain it by enlarging her snake to wrap its body around Afakan, but even at its maximum length of seventy feet, the snake was nowhere close to enveloping all of its body.

Her skin shivered as she felt the heat increase around her, and she knew what was about to come. She retrieved her snake into her body and let go of the beast moments before Afakan blasted out a stream of fire, causing a massive explosion that caught up with Salvanra rendering her unconscious on the spot.

She could no longer free any of her Majestics to break her fall. A fall from that height would bring her to immediate death.

Rondai doubled the power of his tornado to push back the herd, but he noticed how it weighed heavily in Terqwan. He mixed fire into the tornado to burn the lions but quickly regretted that decision after his fire raged out of control, trapping Rondai between two choices: to either let Terqwan burn to death, or to break all his creations leaving them defenseless.

"Fly us out!" Terqwan's words struggled through his coughing.

"I can't. I am almost at my limit. I can conjure something to carry us out, but I won't be able to control everything at the same time!" Rondai shouted.

"Don't worry. It will work." Terqwan's face started to turn blue.

Rondai created a thin layer of earth below their feet and shot it out the second he let go of both wind and fire. The plan was a success, and they escaped to higher ground.

"I thought you could see the future. Fighting with elements from the ground was a stupid plan. We could have died." Rondai looked at the herd below them in anger.

"The plan worked."

"We barely survived. How do you consider this a success?"

"First, get us out of here. We need to be far from this place. Trust me." Terqwan still struggled with his coughing.

Rondai signaled Enyo to follow them, and a moment later they heard an explosion in the sky. Rain followed immediately with a lightning storm that hit the herd repeatedly taking out most. The few remaining lions escaped the battlefield.

While Salvanra fell from the sky, Afakan flew away, fearing the lightning storm. The others were too busy avoiding the random strikes to notice her falling in the distance.

The land was approaching fast, with no sign of her gaining consciousness. Seven hundred feet to the ground and her speed was still rising, four hundred feet to her crash, her ape and tigress noticed her but the distance was not enough for them to get to her in time. Both Majestics rushed toward their master. The ape jumped on the back of the tigress as it sped across the forest.

Twenty feet to the ground and time slowed as the ape used the tigress's force to launch itself into the air, grabbing hold of Salvanra in the last moment before they both rolled for a great deal of time.

When they eventually stopped, the ape joined the tigress. Both Majestics brushed in awe against a still body before they returned to their places as part of their master's tattoo collection.

43

Rondai ran toward where Salvanra fell, worried that the explosion injured her. He looked at her still body and placed both hands on his waist before he leaned down.

"Salvanra… Salvanra…" He shook her shoulders. "Salvanra!" Rondai screamed directly into her ear, violently shaking her body.

"Alright, Alright… Just stop. You're killing me." Salvanra pushed her body away from him.

"Next time you want to scare us, make sure the Delphian isn't around. He saw through your entire act." Rondai extended his arms to pull her up.

"I almost died for real, you know, and none of you did a thing." Salvanra pushed his hand away.

"Those 'none of you' were making sure you were dealing with only one enemy instead of hundreds." Rondai's smile vanished.

"Okay, okay. Don't be so serious. I was joking with you."

"Are you two done with your bickering yet?" Terqwan interrupted. "Because you know that the beast is coming back, right?"

"No. I didn't. How would I know Afakan's next move? Not all of us can see the future like you." Salvanra kicked Terqwan in the leg as she brushed by him to avenge the joke he previously sabotaged with his knowledge.

The four rested near the edge of a cliff where the fight had started to gather their thoughts and rebuild their energy as they waited for the beast to resurface, but someone else appeared instead.

"No, no, no!" Salvanra shouted. "This will not happen." With quickened steps, she stomped toward Jihave who had just appeared atop his tiger.

"What? I thought you would be happy to see me, love." Jihave approached her for a kiss.

"I'm not." She pushed his face away with her palm. "You are disturbing my hunt. I need you to leave." She crossed her arms against her breasts.

"You mean *my* hunt. Clearly, you fought and lost, and now it's my turn."

"I will have lost when I have died, Jihave. Other than that, I made it here and engaged with the beast first. I have the right to see this through until the end. When I die, you can try all you want." Salvanra turned her back to him and walked toward the edge.

"You of all people know that we follow no rules, and—" His loud voice broke at the view of Afakan.

The beast rocket-launched itself into the sky before it descended at top speed setting everything in his path on fire. Rondai created an earth barrier around them, shielding everyone.

"What's the plan?" Rondai didn't breathe between his words.

"The plan is that you guys stay out of this fight." Jihave launched his beetle and pulled out a silver dagger that enlarged into a sword. "It's time to end this. Let's go." He looked at Salvanra.

Salvanra nodded as she freed her bear, then absorbed it like a soul returning to the body. When their merge was complete, she took off her whip-shaped silver necklace and held it as it grew larger.

"Can you let us out please?" Salvanra turned her face to Rondai.

Rondai turned the barrier into water to put out any remaining fire. The two Averettis ran toward the tree line, climbing quickly to get as close as possible to the beast hovering above. Jihave followed the beast from one tree to the other until he was finally close enough to jump atop its back. He stabbed the back of Afakan's head with his sword several times, bringing the beast closer to the ground with each blow.

Salvanra captured Afakan's right foot with her whip before she jumped off the tree using her bear's added weight to bring it down. Her bear allowed her to manipulate her weight at will, increasing it a hundredfold if she wanted. Afakan struggled to fly but managed to remain off the ground, preparing to blast another explosion out of his entire body.

Jihave felt the heat rising as he saw the fire through the cracks on the beast's stony body, he raised his sword and pushed it down into the beast's neck through the expanding cracks with all of his power, bringing both of them to the ground at once.

Jihave jumped in front of the beast's head as Salvanra wrapped her whip around Afakan's neck. They both struggled to stand still against Afakan's roar. A roar that gradually lowered until it sounded more like a cry.

"You see, we work better together." Jihave smiled.

"I could have—"

"I know you were going easy on him," Jihave interrupted. "But we can't always be lenient in our hunts. Powerful Majestics need to know they will have powerful masters. Stop pretend—"

"Now is not the time for a lesson. Don't you see how he is trying to escape my whip." Salvanra struggled to hold her position.

"What do you think would happen if the two of us captured him simultaneously?" Jihave grabbed the whip to help her stabilize the beast.

"I don't know, but it's worth a shot. Maybe we can share him or something."

"Joint custody. I like the sound of that."

They both moved closer to Afakan to stab him in the heart with their silver weapons for the final claim.

Jihave and Salvanra believed that Afakan was the only Majestic beast that survived its master's death. Captured only by the founder of their faction, Averettis believed the beast's survival was no more than a legend. It would have died with the death of his master like all Majestics did.

Jihave and Salvanra felt the adrenaline run through their bodies as they prepared to pierce Afakan. The two smiled, realizing that their ultimate dream was finally within their grasp.

Jihave was so immersed in the moment that he didn't feel the punch that sent him flying back into the heart of the forest. Salvanra felt her whip break the same time she moved her head to see Jihave flying through the air. Before she had the chance to turn her head back, a second punch sent her in the same direction.

They both stood to find a short, long-haired man who looked like he was in his fifties standing in front of the beast. The man who had his face covered from his nose down by a scarf stared at them with fiery eyes without uttering a word.

Afakan struggled to get up, falling twice as it approached the stranger's back until he succeeded to place his right hand on the man's shoulder. The beast turned into ashes and flew into the stranger's body through the scarf before the stranger turned around and walked toward the edge of the forest.

"Who are you?" Salvanra shouted as she moved closer to him.

The stranger paid no attention to her. He reached the edge of a cliff and jumped. Salvanra ran behind him, but when she reached the side of the cliff, there was no sign of the man.

She stood there for a minute before she returned to her team who witnessed the entire fight.

"It's time to go." Salvanra kept her eyes fixed on the ground.

"Is that it? You won't go after the beast?" Rondai raised his brows.

"He is already claimed. We can't capture a claimed beast. Even if we stabbed him, he would simply die."

"It's time to return to Mastoperia." Jihave threw himself onto the grass. He didn't capture the beast but found it satisfying enough that he succeeded to bring Afakan down. He didn't wonder about the strange man because he knew exactly who he was.

THE COMPANIONS

Part Two

YASMINA

The smell of dry roses filled the sandy playing field as Yasmina's father approached her. The Kalanian symbol shone down on the top of his dark, bald head. His eyes widened, appearing even bigger than usual when he noticed Yasmina running toward him from across the field. She almost fell onto the ground before his large hands caught her. He carried the five-year-old child and brought her closer to his chest as they smiled at one another.

"How is my favorite flower doing today?" Maydon tapped his pointy nose against Yasmina's.

"What did you bring me this time?" Yasmina brushed his face with her tiny fingers.

"I brought you something different. Something that requires responsibility and compassion."

"A pet? Did you get me a pet?" Yasmina kissed his cheeks repeatedly.

Maydon laughed loudly. "No. It's not a pet. You are getting a new brother."

"What?" Yasmina's face turned blank for a second before she began to cry.

"Don't cry, darling. You will always be my favorite flower. Nothing will ever change that." Maydon kissed her forehead. "Do you want to meet him?"

Yasmina nodded as she forced her tears to stop. Maydon turned around and pointed at a nine-year-old boy that stood as far as the playground's entrance.

"He is not a baby. Wasn't he a baby like me?"

"He was, but he is a different kind of brother. We are adopting him." Maydon moved toward the boy.

"What does that mean?"

"It means he had other parents, but now he has no one, so we are taking him in to be one of us. It's important he feels welcomed and loved." Maydon put Yasmina down.

"He has no parents?" Yasmina looked up at her father, grabbing his hands.

"Promise me you will be nice to him."

"I promise Papa." Yasmina ran toward the child and hugged him, but he didn't return the hug.

"What's your name?" Yasmina leaned forward, lifting her gaze up to intercept the child's gaze.

"Rondai." His gaze remained focused on the sand.

"What happened to your parents?"

Rondai didn't utter a word, but his eyes grew watery.

"It doesn't matter because my parents will be yours too." Yasmina hugged him again before she spontaneously started a game of tag and ran back to her family's house. Rondai stood frozen for a second longer before he followed her.

🌀🍥🪷☯

Ten years of brotherhood

"Yasmina… Yasmina!" Rondai shouted as he slammed the house door on his way in.

"Did you pass it?" Yasmina ran down the stairs skipping several steps at a time.

"I did. You are now looking at the youngest graduate." Rondai turned in a circle, flashing his accomplishment.

"I'm so excited. My brother is a gate four master, even though he is only nineteen." Yasmina held him by the shoulders while jumping up and down. "We have to celebrate properly."

"Yes. That we must do, and I can think of no one better than you to prepare such a celebration." Rondai hugged her.

"All right. I know what I will do, but first tell me, what is your plan now?" Yasmina finally calmed down.

"Now, I will practice more. I want to learn the secrets of the fifth gate as soon as possible."

"Don't you think you should take a break and teach your little sister what you know to help her?" Yasmina smiled while holding both her hands together behind her back.

"Now is not the time for a break, but for you, I will do anything. If you want me to teach you, then I will do it. We will be the strongest brother and sister our faction has ever seen. One day we will both be part of the council as the mightiest masters." Rondai cupped her cheeks before planting a kiss on her forehead.

"I knew I could count on you, but first I have to go prepare your party. It will be the best ever." Yasmina jumped up and down again as she climbed the stairs.

Thirteen Years of Brotherhood

Rondai came into the house to find a chaotic scene. Groups of teenagers high on drugs occupied the living room and cluttered the staircase. There was no music, but some seemed to be enjoying some tune inside their heads as they danced around the room.

"What is this?" Rondai grabbed a slightly aware Yasmina by her arms.

"What? It's a party. Do you hate parties too now?" Yasmina gathered her power to pull herself out of Rondai's grasp.

"Since when do you party like this?"

"Since I am eighteen now and I can do whatever I want."

"You may be eighteen, but none of us is allowed to do whatever we want." Rondai centered the room. "Everyone leave now, or I will report you to the council!" he shouted.

Yasmina forced her voice to surpass his. "Who are you to say what happens or doesn't happen in this house? I'm the master here."

"I'm your older brother, your best friend. The one who trained you and helped you master the third gate at seventeen. I won't stand here and watch you throw all that work away for a group of misfits." Rondai's voice broke several times.

"No, you're not. You were a mission that my parents received. They had no choice but to take care of their pureblood master. The mission is over now. Go find someone else to serve your needs." Yasmina kept the same high tone of voice.

"Do you think I don't care that they died? They took care of me when I had no one. They gave up their lives so you and I could have the best future. Is this how you honor them? By disgracing your faction. I won't let that happen." Rondai grabbed her hand, but she snatched it away.

"I said, go away. You lost your parents when you were much younger. You don't understand how it feels to be alone." Now that everyone had left, Yasmina moved toward the stairs.

"Fine. I will go," Rondai spoke in a broken tone. "But not until you have returned to your true self. If you really want to get rid of me, then you have to snap out of this morose state, and I promise you that once you do that, I will keep my distance."

Yasmina ignored what he said and headed back to her room.

ENYO

Enyo sped back into the house as soon as he noticed the time. He crossed the lavish gate into the main garden. He stomped his feet, trying to shake the mud from his shoes and off his clothes.

The lotus flowers that filled the artificial lake seemed to observe him trying to wipe the haunting image of fear from his face. He struggled to push the front door of the house open but managed to do it on his own. He sprinted toward the stairs, intent on hiding in his room, but when he recognized a voice he hadn't heard for a long time, he stopped in his tracks.

His frozen brain followed his automatic movements toward the half-closed door at the end of the main hall. He stood behind the door in silence, waiting for his brain to confirm his thoughts.

"That is not acceptable. I gave you clear orders, and you ignored them and did what you wanted." The shouting voice felt different from the previous one.

"I told you many times before, I won't experiment on anyone. Our goal is to help not to hurt," said the first voice.

Enyo reconfigured the voice in his mind. It was his father, Mora. His heart pounded out of its cage, trying to reach Mora's arms, but his feet remained still. He snuck a peek around the door but couldn't see anyone's face, only a tall, long-haired figure was visible from the rear, but he couldn't see his father at all.

Enyo's parents didn't allow him to go in that room so he couldn't imagine what it looked like inside. Through the tiny crack, he could only spot half of a large portrait that rested on a dark wall of wood. The figure in the picture resembled his grandfather. The back of the stranger blocked the rest. He continued to listen in silence.

"Sometimes you have to hurt a few to help many, or did you forget about our history? How many sacrifices did our ancestors make for us to be who we are today?" the voice calmly asked.

"I'm well aware of our history, and as you said, sacrifices. It was a matter of survival, but what you want me to do is nothing short of craziness. You want me to conduct dangerous experiments on our people for results that aren't even five percent certain. I can't do that. I'm sorry Nacin, but I'm taking you off the project."

"Taking me off the project!" Nacin cracked a loud laugh. "You haven't been in the faction for the last two years. What do you think the leadership will do when they know you left Ma—"

"There you are." Enyo's mother, Lyami, placed her hand on his shoulder, startling him and making him jump.

"I didn't mean to listen." Enyo's voice broke and came out unclear.

"You are covered in mud again." She touched his clothes to check if they were wet. "How many times have I told you not to play in the dirt? Do you want to disgrace your family?" she spoke firmly.

Enyo lowered his chin to his chest.

"Go take a shower and put something clean on. I will come to tuck you in bed in half an hour."

Enyo nodded and moved toward the central stairs of his family's mansion.

"Is everything okay?" Nacin asked as he held the door with his hand.

"Yes, yes. Kids these days like to mess themselves up, you know?" Enyo's mother painted an artificial smile on her face.

Nacin nodded, displaying no emotions as he closed the door.

Enyo sat on his bed, waiting for his mother to arrive. His heart struggled to escape its cage, but the thoughts swirling in his mind contained it.

"You look more troubled than excited. I thought you would be happy to know that your father is back." Lyami said cutting Enyo's train of thoughts when she stepped into the room.

"Who was that man with him?" Enyo stared into her eyes.

"Why are you more worried about the stranger?" Lyami smiled.

"He must be very important if my father met with him before seeing me."

"Oh, my boy. No one is more important to your father and me than you, but your father has very important duties. He runs the largest company in our faction, and that forces him to do things he doesn't want to do sometimes. One day, this company will be yours, and you will understand." Lyami kissed his forehead.

"I don't want it then. If the company will take me away from my family, then I never want to have it." Enyo frowned and crossed his arms over his chest.

Lyami laughed out loud and hugged him. "Go to sleep now, and your father promised me he will spend the entire day with us tomorrow."

Enyo kissed his mother goodnight and slid under the covers waiting for the morning to arrive.

○○○○

Enyo jumped out of his bed as soon as he awoke and ran toward his parents' room. He stood in front of the door and knocked several times with no answer. He thought perhaps they woke up before him and ran to the living room, but there was no sign of either of them.

He searched the kitchen and the gardens, moving from one room to the other in a house that had no sign of life but his, even the servants were nowhere to be found. He sat on the steps leading up to the house door, sure they would return for him.

He watched as the sun-centered the sky but had no doubt they would still come to pick him up. He didn't shed a tear until the night conquered the day.

MALANI

Malani stood against the beast alone, with nothing but his sword in his hand and the power of predicting what unfolds in front of him. It was up to him to save the entire universe from destruction. Armed with his courage, he moved toward the beast with steady, solid steps. He prepared to strike the first blow at the—

"Malani."

"What?" Malani's face turned red.

"This is the third time I called for you."

"I was busy." Malani's voice reached a higher tone.

"Fine. Your father is waiting for you in the main hall. The principal cleared you to go."

Malani uttered nothing. He placed his pen and notebook in their designated spot in his backpack and rushed to meet his father.

"Slow down. We still have time." Malani's father pulled his son's backpack off him as they moved toward the exit.

"I'm sorry. I thought I lost time again." Malani took hold of his father's hand.

"Did anyone notice anything?"

"I don't think so, but I drifted away again."

Malani and his father free-ran across the rooftops until they arrived at a building without a roof entrance.

"Where is the door? How do we get in?" Malani asked.

"The entrance is down there." The father pointed at the street.

"We will go down there? I thought it was forbidden." Malani's eyes widened, and a shiver passed through his body.

"For you, I will break any rule, son."

The father and his eight-year-old boy climbed down an old ladder and landed next to a pitch-black revolving door. Malani squeezed his father's hand as they crossed the threshold into a large main hall.

Huge animal statues decorated the walls. A round desk centered the room, and behind it, a woman sat with her eyes focusing on a book in her hands. She was bald and fully tattooed. At first glance, her black bra would have gone unnoticed, appearing as if it was part of her body art collection.

"We have an appointment with the doctor," said Malani's father.

"Name?" The woman's gaze didn't stray away from her book.

"Mayka."

"Through the second door in the passage behind me, you will find a staircase. Follow the stairs to the top floor. This is where you will find the doctor."

Mayka and Malani climbed back up twenty-stories until they arrived at an open floor with nothing but a wooden desk, three chairs, and a lounge chair. There were no walls around them.

They approached the doctor, who pointed at the two chairs in silence. Mayka tried to start the conversation as he sat down, but the doctor signaled him to keep his mouth shut.

The doctor stared into Malani's eyes. Malani stared back, but his focus fell upon the line of circular earrings that started at the end of the doctor's left eye running over and around his ear before it disappeared where his neck met his shoulder. The stare lasted for a few minutes before the doctor finally spoke.

"What is his problem?"

"He sees things that aren't real, and he can't differentiate it from his view of the future," Mayka answered.

"Do those visions come to you on their own or when you focus on possible timelines?" the doctor asked Malani.

"They come in both cases. Sometimes they take over me on their own. Other times they appear when I focus on the future, but in both cases, I can't tell the difference between the real future and fiction," Malani responded.

"All that we see is fiction until it becomes reality. Therefore, we consider it possible and not a concrete answer," said the doctor.

Mayka leaned forward. "However, its possibility depends on our own actions. Our power lies in our ability to write the future the way we see fit. The things he sees seem to be impossible to happen."

"I see." The doctor smiled. "Tell me an example of the things you see." He locked his fingers together.

"Sometimes, I see myself standing in a land of fire. I mean flying slightly above it. My sword is shining like the sun, and I'm preparing to defend myself against strange-looking flying monsters. All I know in these visions is that if I lose, then the entire world will be destroyed." Malani clenched his fist.

"Is this the only unrealistic vision you have, or are there others?"

"It's the most common one. The location and atmosphere changes. The shape of the monsters changes, too, but I am always ready to fight, and I am always alone. I don't like it."

The doctor turned to Mayka. "How is he doing in school?"

"It's his second year, so there is no grading yet, but no one has noticed anything strange so far. I'm afraid if they do, they will take him to the lab for tests. I don't want to lose my son, doctor." Mayka ended his speech lost in his son's face.

"I will have to run some tests, but I'm confident we will find a solution." The doctor rose from his seat and extended his arm to Malani, who followed him to a corner of the space. They sat near the edge in a meditative pose. The doctor placed Malani's palm above his, leaving a small space for the air to pass between their hands. Neither moved a muscle for nearly ten minutes until the doctor opened his eyes and released the pose. They returned to the office together.

"I believe your son's cerebral cortex lobes are mashed together. Usually, we have four lobes that carry different functions. What he has is one united lobe that carries out all the functions together. That is why his brain can't tell the difference between possibilities, reality, imagination, and inner emotions. You could say, it deals with all the different inputs through a single software that is not equipped to deal with everything. This is why it gives out a distorted image."

"So, what do we do? Can it be fixed?"

"There is nothing to fix. Perhaps your son is the first step of our evolution yet again. His brain can probably have the potential to deal with problems faster and more efficiently, maybe even develop a different power. What I will do, however, is train him to tell the difference through other senses. This way, when he sees an image, he can isolate the layers he believes irrelevant while focusing on what is reality."

"Will that help him fit in?"

"It will help him become who he is." The doctor locked eyes with Malani again. "I will need him to visit me twice a week for our sessions. Now your time is over. My assistant will give you all the remaining information." The doctor pointed at the door.

The doctor spoke loudly to Malani as he was leaving. "Next time, you come alone."

TERQWAN

My dearest Meriaka,

I am writing not for you but for me. A letter that your shiny golden eyes will never see. Words that your ears will never dance to its music.

I love you. I loved you from the minute I saw your shadow dancing with the leaves at Handur Park. I loved you the moment you smiled awkwardly when you realized that I saw you move your body to the sounds of nature. When you used your wavy hair to cover your face, trying to shield yourself from the world, you captivated me. Your soul captured mine, and I never wanted to escape.

The details of your face when we watched our first movie together made me want to stay in that theatre forever. The way you stood for yourself against those who questioned your views on our politics forced me to notice how I was always in the presence of a goddess and no ordinary person. Nothing about you was ordinary, and I mean nothing. Even the simplest touch of your fingers would trigger every little ounce of blood in my body to jump out of excitement. I love you, and I struggle to find the words to express how I really feel.

Terqwan folded the unfinished letter and placed it in his pocket as the music conquered the sound of nature surrounding the open-air venue where he stood among many others. He adjusted his suit before all eyes fell upon the gorgeous dress that complimented Meriaka. A long white dress embroidered by the green lotus flower with a cut slightly higher than her breasts and an invisible back.

The bride to be walked down a grassy aisle, capturing the hearts of those who surrounded her from both sides. She gazed into her future husband's eyes as she took hold of his hands. The wedding was simple and beautiful.

"There you are. I have been looking for you everywhere." Meriaka pulled Terqwan by his hand to the dance floor. He froze for a second until she grasped his arm and placed it around her waist.

They slow-danced to their favorite song without uttering a word. Terqwan felt that the world paused just for the two of them to enjoy that eternal moment. He saw a future where they both lived alone, away from their faction and any sign of society. He saw himself waking up every day to her angelic smile, but soon he had to return to reality. The song had to end, and her husband waited near them to dance with her again.

Terqwan congratulated her and left. He thought he was only leaving the dance floor, but his feet carried him outside of the wedding venue, and all the way through the park to the other end, where they first met. He looked down at the few clouds that surrounded the building within the park. He leaned toward the glass edge, uniting his forehead with it and let go of his tears.

"It was beautiful."

Terqwan raised his head and quickly wiped his tears as her voice pierced his hearing. "What are you talking about?" he slowly turned around, keeping his gaze toward the ground.

"The letter you didn't want me to see." She moved closer to him. "Before you ask, I saw you holding it as I walked down the aisle, and I examined several timelines until I found one where I succeeded in stealing it from you." She smiled as she moved even closer to him. "I told you, you can see other people's secrets even if they hide it. You just have to make their life cross yours, and they will become an open book for you to saite around."

Terqwan's face turned red as she tried taking his hands in hers.

"I love you," she said. "I always have, but we live in a society with rules. There's a reason they match us instead of leaving us to our own desires. Love can be unpredictable and beautiful, but it isn't always the best thing for us. Maybe we will hurt each other, and maybe we would be dangerous for the future. I don't know. I can't see that far, but they can, which is why I'm sure I will have my best chance with my husband and that I will fall in love with him as we get to know each other. You too will find your match one day, and all of those feelings will be nothing but a memory." She caressed his hands.

"Why do you think they didn't match us together? We were happy, right?"

"You are a brilliant man. You excel at everything, and everyone thinks you will have a great future and will be a member in the Skeptic Room one day, but you question many things in our faction and even the entire world. I believe in our reality and our values. Maybe for that, we would fail as a couple. I don't know."

She looked at her digital feather thin wristwatch. "I have to go back before they look for me. I said I wouldn't be late."

Terqwan planted a kiss on her cheek and exited the park. He free-ran aimlessly across the city roofs until he saw a building he recognized. He wandered the floors until he found the apartment he was looking for. He knocked twice and waited for the tenant to open the door.

When the door opened, Terqwan immediately started, "I know I said I don't want to go on your mission, but I have changed my mind. I didn't want to do something that benefits the politicians, but I don't think I should deny myself a chance to see the prohibited world because I couldn't be a little lenient with my values. So, if the offer still stands, I would like to take the chance, please."

"I think after what you said, I would have no better companion than you. You just became my favorite of all the candidates." Kawan shook Terqwan's hands.

BOFRAT

Bofrat moved quietly around their treehouse, trying to sneak out without waking up his younger brother. The moment his feet touched the ground, he ran as fast as he could until he reached two large pine trees where he hid a box of crocodile milk vials. He placed the box in his backpack and moved toward the edge of the Fantastic Forest.

He freed his tiger once he crossed the forest borders, riding the tiger through the land of no man—a land where the desert meets grass and both live side by side in harmony.

They followed the tiny river stream toward the west of Mastoperia. The sun was almost gone by the time he arrived at the great hole where the river falls. He sat on the ground staring at the chasm that seemed to have no bottom, watching as the speeding water disappeared into the belly of the beast.

When night fell, he rested his head on the tiger's legs and placed the rest of his body next to his tiger's as if they were cuddling. He looked up at the stars wondering about his plan and its possible consequences, but he couldn't fight the urge to sleep and soon lost his soul to the world of dreams.

"Hey, you... Hey... Wake up!"

Bofrat felt a foot tap him several times from his side. He jumped up and so did his tiger, roaring.

"Calm your Majestic. I'm not here to hurt you," said the Forbidden Warrior who carried a large tattoo of the Forbidden City carved on his entire chest."

"I'm sorry. It was just a reflex." Bofrat petted his tiger as he smiled, awkwardly.

"What are you doing here? You are far from your faction."

"I just wanted to take my tiger for a walk away from the forest for a change of scenery. We followed the river for a bit, and when we ended here, we were too tired to go back, so we decided to sleep. Did we go too far?" Bofrat scratched the back of his head as he continued to carry his awkward smile.

"Luckily you are still in the neutral zone, but you are not far from the edge of Kala. I hope you know that you are not allowed to go there without being previously announced." The warrior stared at him with a fiery eye.

"Yes, yes. Don't worry. We are not planning to go any further. We will just rest here for a bit, then we will head back home."

The warrior nodded but looked back at him several times as he walked away. Bofrat realized his heart was racing unsteadily, but he didn't feel it until the fear was lifted. He looked at the sky to tell the time before he sat, waiting for the others to arrive.

It was noon before the first showed up.

"So, you are Bofrat," the stranger stated, saying what he already knew.

"Yes, and you?"

"My name is Gabrin. I'm the Delphian who intercepted your message."

"Are you here to investigate or participate?" Bofrat asked.

"I'm here to hear your offer. Let's say I'm here to discuss, but first, tell me how it went with the warrior?"

"He suspects nothing. Don't worry."

Two others arrived at that moment; the Kalangous, Ryn and Rolakan.

"Are you the one who sent the message?" Ryn held his hand behind his back, preparing to attack.

"Yes, but I'm not here to fight anyone. I just want to talk. I have a proposition, and I was hoping that you would hear me out." Bofrat held out both of his hands with the palms facing the Kalangous showing his peaceful intentions.

"How did you know who to deliver the message to?" Ryn asked.

"I didn't. The eagle that delivered the message to you is equipped with a special kind of sense. He can read my intention and the type of personality I'm looking for, and it will search and deliver the message to those who are willing to accept it."

Bofrat noticed how the three men became wary when they realized that such a method could be used to create spies and quickly added, "However, it can be easily countered if the receivers knew of its possibility, and I'm not here to flip any of you against your factions."

"Aren't you all a little bit young to be gathered for negotiations?"

Rolakan and Ryn were the first to take defensive positions, but the old Lunardis eased them by telling them he was there for the same reason they all were before Bofrat urged everyone to sit down so they could discuss the matter further.

"A few weeks ago, I discovered that our elders allow the Lunardis to reach certain creatures in our forests and conduct experiments on them. I realized that they convince us we are all enemies while they collaborate and do unspeakable things. That was when I thought, why shouldn't we do the same? Why don't we trade among ourselves away from the elders and all their political drama?" He paused, studying the expressions on their faces. "I'm sure each of our factions needs something that the other could provide. We will finally do something for the people and by the people. What do you say?"

"How old are you?" the Lunardis asked Bofrat.

"I'm nineteen."

"You two look young as well," the old man said, addressing the Kalangous.

"Perhaps you are the one who is too old for this meeting." Ryn stared the Lunardis in the eye.

"So, what do you all think?" Bofrat tapped his knees repeatedly, changing the subject to calm everyone.

"We are going to do that anyway. So, I'm in," Gabrin quickly answered after he saw the trade happening in the future.

Rolakan looked at Ryn, who nodded back at him. "We need time to think about it, but we like the idea."

"I'm in too. That should be interesting," said the Lunardis.

Ryn sighed. "I suggest that we all go back to our factions to think about this project or find out what our people need that we could provide to each other."

"I agree." Bofrat nodded. "But during this time. Here are some bottles of crocodile milk. It's our strongest alcoholic drink. I wanted to offer it to you as a gift for our first meeting."

Gabrin and the Lunardis accepted the gift with a smile, but the Kalangous politely declined, as they didn't drink alcohol.

They planned to meet at the same place within a week's time to begin the first free secret trade between the four factions.

SALVANRA

The cries of a little girl chasing her small tiger interrupted the morning singing of the Fantastic Forest birds. She jumped from one tree to the other, trying to corner the escaping Majestic. She seized the only chance she had to jump on the back of the tiger before they rolled together a few times while she kept her grip unbroken. She locked two legs with her arm as she pushed the Majestic closer to her chest, and they lay together on the ground with their cries mixing into one.

"Grab this!"

The little girl recognized the voice approaching from behind as her eyes gravitated toward the silver dagger that fell next to her.

"What should I do with it?" She snatched the dagger from the ground with her right hand.

"Gently stab the tiger under the heart." The speaker was calm.

The eight-year-old did as instructed. She didn't unhook her grip even as she saw the tiger's skin change color from dark blue to snow white. She waited until the tiger was calm and slowly removed her arm. The little Majestic brushed its face against hers as it climbed on her shoulder and took its place as a tattoo on her right shoulder.

"Thank you, Daria." The little girl stood and faced her older sister, turning her face up to meet the latter's eyes.

"It's okay, Salvanra. Don't be ashamed. This was going to happen, eventually." Daria patted her head.

"I don't understand what happened. I didn't mistreat him. He was my best friend, and we always played together. I don't know why he tried to escape." Salvanra turned her gaze to her feet.

"First, you never have to defend yourself. Your actions and relationships with your Majestics are yours alone. No one should prompt you to behave in a certain way. Only you know what's best for them. Second, it didn't happen because you mistreated him. It happened because it is a *him*."

Salvanra raised her head to look into her sister's eyes as her brows drew together.

Daria sat on her knees and took hold of Salvanra's hands. "You captured a male tiger. Male tigers are not compatible with our biology as women, so they change genders. The final step of that change is very painful for them, so they try to escape."

"So, what does the dagger do? Is it an enchanted dagger? Is it a secret one?" Salvanra's eyes widened.

"Neither." Daria stood up and prompted Salvanra to move without letting go of her right hand. "The secret isn't in the dagger. It's in the material and the process of making it. The dagger is pure silver laced with water from Elders Lake. When you pierce it inside a Majestic's body, it will calm down and fall back under your control."

"When do I get mine?" Salvanra's tone exposed her excitement.

"By the time you finish school, you should know which weapon you like. You can then get that weapon forged."

"I still have two more years before I finish school. What happens if I lose control again?"

"Silver isn't the only way to control Majestics. There are many others, and you should only resolve to use them in specific cases, but don't worry, I will always be next to you." Daria smiled when she saw Salvanra assume her true child spirit and jump around as they walked back home.

Salvanra may have been jumping as a child, but her thoughts weren't that of one. She was excited because she realized her world offered more than she thought existed. She thought about mastering all those skills and surpassing her older sister whom she always looked up to. Salvanra had a dream, and she was determined to reach it.

"Salvanra?"

"What?" Salvanra turned to face her sister.

"Where were you? I have been talking to you for a few minutes." Daria tilted her head to look at her.

"I was thinking about how awesome it would be if I could beat you one day." Salvanra forced her muscles to smile.

Daria laughed. "Then answer me, so I know if you can do it or not."

"What was your question?" Salvanra brought her eyebrows closer to each other.

"I asked, what did you learn in class today?"

"We learned how to determine a Majestic's mood from the color of their body."

"That is a fun class." Daria adjusted their hands to interlock their fingers. "What color did you study today?"

"The color blood-red." Salvanra waited for the next question.

"And what does that mean?"

"It means the Majestic is enraged by your own behavior. It usually appears when you are mistreating your own Majestic or another from the same kind, which differs from bright-red. That one appears when another Majestic of the same kind is trying to attack you." Salvanra wanted to show off.

"Did you learn how to react in both cases?"

"Yes." Salvanra jumped on the question. "When the blood-red appears, I have to stop anything I'm doing and comfort the Majestic by placing one hand on the back of its neck and the other on the top of the chest and stroke simultaneously and gently. When the bright-red appears, I have to get the Majestic back in my body quickly and choose a different one if I have to fight. I should never let two Majestics of the same kind fight one another unless I really have to because it breaks their heart."

"I'm so proud of you Salvanra. I know you will grow up to be one of the strongest in our tribe, if not in the entire forest."

Salvanra placed her arms around her sister's waist and leaned her head against it. She felt she received the highest praise anyone could ever receive.

44

Evailen and her companions were the first to return to the city of departure, even though they used none of their powers. Instead, they followed the transportation system that connected the outside world together. They took a flight, a train, and a bus before they found themselves walking atop a bridge that followed the edge of the ocean.

Evailen smiled as she danced her steps to the sound of the ocean waves. Bofrat watched her closely to learn her uncoordinated moves before he joined by creating his own dance. Malani however, opted to add melody to their dance using his mouth. Only Yasmina followed them in silence, but her face mirrored her heart's joy.

"Come on, Yasmina. Join us." Evailen grabbed hold of her hands and danced in front of her.

"Sorry Evailen, but I'm not much of a dancer." Yasmina blushed, pulling her hands away.

"What do you do when you're happy then?" Bofrat spoke as he awkwardly moved his body without rhythm.

"Yes, Yasmina. What is your style?" Evailen moved a few steps forward.

Yasmina smiled while looking at her feet for a few seconds before she placed both her hands in front of her mouth. She started to beatbox a melody that made Malani feel ashamed of his earlier tries to do the same. Yasmina drowned in her music while Evailen covered her mouth with both hands, and the other two froze with their eyes widened to their maximum. She stopped a few minutes later when she finally noticed them.

"I'm sorry I destroyed your fun. I'm not that good." Yasmina lowered her head.

"Are you kidding? This was the best beatbox I've ever heard in my entire life," Evailen smiled.

"How did you do that? It sounded like real instruments." Malani stepped closer to her.

Yasmina tucked her hair behind her ears. "Do you want the technique behind it?"

"No. I mean when or where did you learn that?"

"Nowhere in particular. It's just something Rondai, and I used to play with growing up. I'd make the beats, and he would add lyrics to it."

"Wait. You rapped with Rondai?" Evailen placed her hand on her heart. "Oh man, what I would do to see that."

"Well, we don't do that anymore." Yasmina's lip quivered.

"What? Why? It must be so much fun." Evailen shook her head.

"You know how it is. Brothers and sisters grow apart as they grow up." Yasmina started to walk again, failing to notice the dropped jaws on her mates' faces.

"Rondai is your brother?" Malani caught up to her.

"Yes. Well, he's my adopted brother, but that changes nothing about the fact for me."

Yasmina didn't realize that she opened a gate of questions as they kept firing requests for information at her, but she was reluctant to discuss details of her past. She only answered general questions.

"Fine. If you don't want to give us details, then I will ask him instead." Evailen paused, realizing she wasn't sure if she wanted to talk to him again but chose to ignore her thoughts. "What do you want to do until the others arrive?" She saw that they were at the port, but none of the other teams were there yet.

Yasmina pointed at a beach close to the port. "I would like to rest if you don't mind. You can find me on that beach when you return."

Bofrat went with Evailen on a last adventure to explore the world while Malani stayed with Yasmina.

"You don't have to stay with me. I won't run away." Yasmina smiled.

"Actually, there was something I wanted to talk to you about." Malani walked by her side toward the beach.

"No more Rondai questions please."

"I will try." Malani smiled. "Are you okay?"

"Yes, I am." Yasmina narrowed her eyes. "Why?"

"It's just that you haven't talked about Ryn since we left. I mean I'm glad you look okay, but I wanted to be sure you aren't holding anything in. There's no need to suffer alone."

Yasmina looked at Malani with warm eyes.

"I guess what I'm trying to say is we're friends now, and friends reach out to each other for support." Malani placed his hand on Yasmina's shoulder.

"I truly appreciate you saying this. I too consider you as a friend, but this mission is almost over, and we will go back to our factions and readjust to the mutual hate we share for each other's factions."

"Why does it have to be like that? You met us, and we all risked our lives together. Why would I hate the faction of someone I like...someone I admire?"

The awkward silence tried to manifest between them, but Yasmina conquered it with her words. "I admire you too, and Bofrat, and Evailen. I'm grateful to have met you all and to have learned so much about your factions, but our lives are different. You wondered if I was okay because losing a faction member is a big thing for you. I've lost enough people in my life that it has become ordinary for me to bury my sadness and move on."

"That sounds sad."

"Exactly. For you, but not for me. I have a different perspective. One that only my faction members can understand. You will never understand what it means to—"

"Help me understand," Malani interrupted.

"I can't. It's not something I can explain with words, but a feeling you get when you experience life within our culture."

"Try me. Just give me a chance. What have you got to lose?"

Yasmina sighed. "Okay… When we turn twenty, we learn that our magic has a price. We find out about it when our hearts literally break in half. Then, we spend the entire day screaming our lungs out as we feel the cells reattach themselves. However, before that happens, each half of our heart is stamped with the seal of magic. A seal that collects payment each time we use our powers."

"What kind of payment?" Malani raised his eyebrows.

"You see… this is what your brain went to, information."

"I'm sorry, I just wanted to know more about what happens so I can see the full picture."

"The full picture is: you are born with your powers while we have to work hard to learn ours. Then we have to pay a price for our hard work. This is why we don't like other factions. Because as long as you have powers, we can't give up ours." Yasmina stormed off, leaving Malani frozen in his place.

45

"What is going on?" Rondai tapped Malani's shoulder.

"I think I upset her, though it wasn't my intention." Malani focused his eyes on his feet.

"Don't worry about it. I will talk to her." Rondai started toward the beach.

Rondai saw Yasmina sitting on the beach, a few feet away from the ocean.

"Do you mind if I join you?" Rondai smiled.

"Come on, you know I don't." Yasmina sank her bare feet deeper in the sand.

"What's going on with you?"

"I don't know. Each time I try to be happy and light like them, I end up feeling sad instead."

Rondai took off his slippers and sat next to her. "Are you afraid to open up?"

"Are you really talking about opening up?" Yasmina turned her head toward Rondai.

"What is that supposed to mean?"

"It means that you've been shutting me out for a few years now. We barely had a conversation until this mission." Yasmina kept her face tilted toward him, despite the sun's rays bright in her eyes.

"I only did that after you shut me out of your life. Or did you forget?" He crossed his arms on top of his raised knees.

"I apologized for doing that many times, but you of all people should know how it feels when you lose both of your parents. I acted out. I know that I hurt you badly, but did you ever think maybe the reason it came out on you was because I trusted you the most?"

"Trusted?" Rondai looked into her eyes.

"Trust. I still trust you. You know that." Yasmina looked back into his eyes with a frown he recognized.

Rondai moved closer to her touching his shoulder with hers, nodding. "I know, but I was in bad shape as well. They were my parents too. They took me in and raised me as their own. It was hard to lose my parents twice, and I felt like I was a cursed to those who were closest to me. This is why I put distance between us. Because I didn't want you to get hurt too."

Yasmina faced Rondai, copying his posture before she placed her head on top of her arms. "Yes, you are cursed, but so am I, and so is everyone in Kala. My parents didn't die because of you, they died because their time ran out. It's the price we all pay, the more we use magic, the sooner we die."

"Yasmina, the master of arguments." He teasingly pinched her cheeks.

Yasmina's eyes grew watery even though her face smiled.

"What is wrong now?"

"Nothing." Yasmina wiped away the tear. "I miss this. You and I talking like old times."

"Well, we are talking now." He ruffled her hair. "So, tell me, what did Malani say to upset you?"

Yasmina chuckled. "I think he was trying to tell me he likes me."

"And that upset you?" Rondai raised his eyebrows.

"He doesn't really know me. We only spent a few short weeks together."

"So?" Rondai frowned.

"I'm sorry. I didn't mean to undermine whatever you feel for Evailen."

Rondai stared into her eyes with a blank face.

"Actually, unlike everyone else, I'm not surprised you like her," Yasmina continued, staring back into Rondai's unchanged face. "I mean, she is clearly your type."

"My type? I didn't realize I had one."

"Are you kidding me? Lakara, Dora, and Manya?"

"You can say as many names as you want. That still proves nothing."

Yasmina imitated his hand movement before pretending to speak in his teenage voice. "Oh, Yasmina, how my heart jumps out of my chest each time Lakara comes into the classroom."

"I was twelve. Plus, I dated none of them."

"You dated no one, I know, but you liked them."

Rondai raised one eyebrow, staring at her.

"My point is they all shared similar qualities. Cute on the surface, unafraid to speak their minds and spontaneous. All are qualities that Evailen has."

"Since when did you become an expert on relationships?" Rondai narrowed his eyes.

"Since I outmatch you by six to zero."

"You didn't have six relationships."

Yasmina ignored his remark. "What did surprise me, though was that you made a move on her and asked her out." Yasmina laughed. "Though it was funny how you did it."

"What was funny about that?" Rondai spoke in a pitched tone.

"Will you lock your heart with mine forever?" She imitated his voice again. "What was that? We don't talk like this anymore; you are so outdated." Yasmina pitched another laugh. "I had to pretend this is how it worked in our faction when she told me about it, so you didn't come out as weird."

"Okay, enough. I get the point. My relationship skills are nonexistent, but I learned that from your father."

Yasmina squinted. "It's a little mean to bring my father into this. He was handsome, stylish, and captured my mother's heart. You know she was a beauty in her prime."

"I'm sorry, but it's true, and now it's your turn to advise me." Rondai smiled. "What do you think I should do?"

"Speak to her from the heart, like you are doing now. You and I can't help but show our tough masks to the world. Maybe it's just us, or maybe it's a faction thing. I don't know, but if you really like her, then open up to her."

"I did that, but then I blew it all up when I rushed after the last artifact. I'm afraid she might not want to talk to me anymore." Rondai sighed.

"She doesn't shut up about you when we are alone, so trust me, she still wants something. But even though she didn't tell me, I could see she was mad because of what you did, so I can't really judge. Just apologize to her, and I think she will understand. I mean she stopped Jihave from going after the last artifact for you. That's something."

"She did?" Rondai raised his eyebrows, and Yasmina nodded. "I will do that then. Thank you." Rondai kissed her cheek. "And you? Will you give Malani a chance?"

"I have a boyfriend Rondai, for eight months now. Something you would have known about if you talked to your little sister."

"Okay, okay… I was an ass. I feel like I'm getting cornered a lot in this conversation." He raised his arms up in a playful show of defeat.

Yasmina smiled.

"I'm sorry for shutting you out all this time, and I promise to be a better brother and do my best to rebuild our old relationship."

"Don't worry about that. You will always be my favorite brother." She teased with their childhood catch-phrase before she playfully punched him.

Rondai put his slippers back on and stood. "Do you mind?"

"No. Go find her." Yasmina smiled as she laid back on the sand. She told herself that the best outcome of this mission was reconnecting with her brother.

46

Rondai stood in front of the entrance to the port of departure, adjusting his garment several times.

"So, Yasmina is your sister. Did it not occur to you to mention such detail on our date? I guess you say only what you want to say." Evailen moved toward the entrance without stopping.

"I'm sorry." Rondai grabbed her wrist as she brushed by him. "I know I behaved stupidly, and that I should have at least taken a moment to excuse myself."

"Exactly, a moment. That was all it would have taken you." Evailen stared directly into his eyes.

"I wouldn't have been able to forgive myself if I didn't get the last artifact. I thought I had time, and it hit me hard when I found out there was only one remaining. I stopped thinking rationally, and I behaved badly. Please forgive me." Rondai closed his eyes. "I am sorry."

"Apologies are nice. They convey one's respect to the other person, but I'm not sure they are enough. I understand the importance of the mission, and that it means much more to you than it does me, but how can I ignore that you forgot about me so easily? I felt like I didn't exist, and it was you who gave me high expectations when you used big words to ask me out."

Rondai stood in silence, feeling the words freeze on the tip of his tongue until he decided to give his words control over him. "You're right. I'm no expert, but I think no relationship should start with an apology. If you don't mind, I will tell you everything in my mind, then you can decide on what you want to do. Is that okay?"

She nodded. "But can we walk while you talk? I would like to hear what you have to say, and I don't want any of the other teams to arrive here and interrupt us."

Rondai followed her back into the city. "First, according to Yasmina, people in my faction don't talk the way I did when I asked you out. She told you we did to save me the embarrassment. The truth is, I have never been in a relationship. There were girls I liked in the past, but whenever I was alone, I convinced myself that focusing on my magic was more important than any relationships. The result is that I became the youngest gate five master in the history of my faction. I'm ranked sixth among the top ten non-council-magic-users. The youngest of the other nine is twelve years older than me. I have been on more missions than anyone my age ever has or would. In fact, this mission we are on would be child's play next to some of the things I did. Yet, I almost lost, and I blame you."

"You're not off to a good start Rondai," she quietly stated.

"I told you, I won't sugarcoat it. I will just tell you the truth." He paused in case she wanted to add something, but her silence encouraged him to continue. "You are the only one who has piqued my interest enough that I was willing to side the mission, which I did when I stayed the extra time for our date, and I don't regret that one bit." He sighed. "I like you. I have no doubt about that. I want to be with you even though I know it entails a lot of complications. So, when it comes to my feelings, they are clear as the sun above us. However, this is but one side of the coin."

"What is the other side?" she asked.

"My faction. Unlike most in Kala, I wasn't raised to follow, but to lead. I'm a pureblood, a direct descendent from Katin himself. I have a duty toward my people, and I will be a member of the council one day, even if it is after serving the Forbidden City for two centuries and a half. My job is to take care of my people. This is what I've known my entire life. To put myself first is to put everyone else last. I was okay with ignoring myself. I never even needed to question it until you came along."

"So, it's all my fault." Evailen blinked slowly. "We can just forget about this, then, and you won't have to be torn apart."

"Then you weren't listening. I don't want you to leave. If I did, then I wouldn't have bothered telling you all of this. I want you to understand how I feel. I don't always have the luxury of choice." He sighed. "But I choose you. I want to be with you and see things through but being with me is a gamble. You need to understand that sometimes I will relapse. It won't be because I don't want to be with you, but because of everything I told you. So, I understand if you don't want to be with me anymore, and I understand that it would be entirely my fault. If I'm completely honest, I would've probably called it quits too if the situation was reversed. I don't know if I should appeal to your logic or your heart, but I'm hoping for another chance either way. It's up to you to decide if I deserve it or not."

"Fine."

"Does that mean—"

"But," she interrupted, "since you have been honest with me, then I will also do the same. I told you from the beginning I'm curious. At first, my curiosity was unguarded, but now I will be cautious. I will give us a chance, but only one because I think the timing wasn't perfect for our first date, and I won't ignore that I enjoyed most of that evening with you. However, if you let me down again, then there will be no more conversations, no appeals, and no other chances." She stopped and looked into his eyes.

Rondai nodded. "And I want nothing more."

"As for your entrapment between me and your faction, you can talk to me all you want about it, but I'm not the one who will deal with this. This is up to you to figure out. The way I see it is that our being together shouldn't contradict your duty to your faction. So, figure it out however you want, but you can no longer use that in any future argument. Am I clear?"

Rondai chuckled.

"What's funny?" She crossed her arms in front of her chest.

"I like how you speak your mind. It's like seeing a beauty and a beast." He smiled.

"And which one am I? The beauty or the beast?" She narrowed her eyes.

"You are both the beauty and the beast."

"I feel like—"

"It's a compliment. Just leave it at that," he interrupted.

She smiled and continued to walk. "So. Yasmina is your sister."

"Yes, I thought I answered that question already." He caught up to her.

"And you were in a band together."

"No, who said that?" His eyes widened. "Did she tell you that?"

"She said you used to rap to her beatbox. Is that true?"

"Yes, but—"

"Then you were in a band together," she interrupted with a smile. "Next time you piss me off, I will tell everyone that."

He smiled, thinking Yasmina was right. Evailen checks all the boxes of what he likes.

47

A small ship approached the dock shortly after the four teams arrived at the port. Fifteen Mastoperians boarded the boat. They spent a little less than a month in a world they thought they would never visit and may never see again. They all knew that their lives had changed. Friendships made, and new enemies surfaced. The lines between factions blurred, and it all happened in the subtlest way possible.

"What do you think will happen now?" Jihave leaned his back against the bowsprit of the ship.

"I don't know." Evailen rested her arms on the ledge, centering both Jihave and Rondai. "They said if each of us claimed a single artifact, there would be another task to decide who the leader is."

"Maybe it will be a display of power. I will win that for sure." Jihave chuckled.

"I think we all know I beat you in our fight." Rondai imitated Evailen's position allowing their arms to brush against one another.

"As I remember, it was you who fell unconscious." Jihave slightly raised his tone.

"Trust me, that had nothing to do with you." He recalled his encounter with his ancestors and shivered.

All three of them laughed out loud, they had no idea what was coming next.

Kawan watched them from afar with a face empty of expressions. He took a deep breath before he moved toward the end of the ship where he found Yasmina sitting alone with her legs crossed and eyes closed.

"Do you mind if I sit next to you?" he asked her.

Yasmina pointed with her hand at the empty space around her without uttering a word. Kawan, however, sat in front of her with his eyes focusing on her face.

"How can I help you?" Yasmina opened her eyes when she felt him facing her.

"How close are you to Rondai?" he asked.

"That's none of your business. Anything else?" Yasmina looked him straight in the eyes.

"I know you don't know me, and I'm not here to invade your privacy."

"Well—"

Kawan interrupted her, "I'm not interested in gossip, nor did I talk to Malani about you and Rondai."

"If you know what I will say, then why ask me? You could sit a few meters away and have all your answers without us talking." Yasmina crossed her arms.

"I want to show you something. I was hoping I could steer the conversation in a direction that will help you understand."

"Obviously you are failing, so why don't you jump into the subject."

"Fine." Kawan parted his lips slightly. "Do you know that Delphians and Kalangous are connected?"

"In what way?" Her eyes widened.

"I can, for example, enable you to see the future if you allow me to."

"Can't you do this with anyone?" She leaned closer toward him.

"No, only with Kalangous."

"And why is that?"

"A long time ago, before there were factions, Delphia, the founder of my faction, visited her brother Katin to see the pool of magic that gave him his powers."

"Pool of magic? Is this what you call it?" Yasmina chuckled.

"Anyway, when she saw it, she wanted to jump into it. She wanted to have the same powers as him, but he didn't allow it. The two fought in front of the pool, and Katin won the battle."

"So backstabbing runs in your faction since the beginning of the new age." Yasmina shook her head. "However, she failed, so how could we be connected then?" She narrowed her eyes.

"Because Delphia was injured in the battle and a drop of her blood fell inside the pool, allowing a part of her genes to remain there forever. Now each time one of your people uses the pool, they gain a connection with us."

"With your logic, we should be able to use your powers, but we can't."

"I told you I can make it possible for you to see what I see. You can't access our power on your own, but you can temporarily access our minds as long as both sides agree on it."

"So, what do you want to show me? And if it is that important, why don't you show it to Rondai? He is more powerful than I am and can help you with whatever you truly want."

"You will understand once you see. I just need you to accept that I bring you into my mind. Otherwise, it won't work."

"Fine." Yasmina sighed. "This better be as important as you say."

"I thought you would be curious about having the ability to experience the power of Delphians." Kawan's eyes widened.

"I'm not. Let's finish this please."

"Okay. Give me your hand." Kawan extended his hands with open palms.

Yasmina placed her hands on top of his, but Kawan adjusted them, so the back of her hands were touching his palms.

"Now close your eyes and focus on my breathing. Match yours with mine."

Yasmina did as instructed. She listened to his breathing until she aligned hers with his. Once their synchronization was perfect, the blackness disappeared, and she felt as if she left her body. She could see an image as if she was watching a movie play in front of her.

A minute felt like a lifetime for Yasmina, before she had to gasp for air as she opened her eyes again.

"That was… I thought your power… Why did you show this to me? Is this a trick?" Yasmina's hands were shaking.

"I guess you can say I am special when it comes to power, and you know why I showed you this."

"How do I know you are not tricking me?" Yasmina let a single tear slip out.

"I think you know the answer to this too. Now you know the truth, and you know what you need to do. The rest is up to you." Kawan stood to leave.

"Will you do your part?" She looked up to him.

"The truth is, I don't know what I will or won't do." He turned around and took a couple of steps before pausing. "It's funny. In my faction, they teach us that if we can look far enough, we can have all the answers. I saw further than anyone could see, and all I found was more questions."

48

Enyo rested his hand on the side of the ship, watching the continent of Mastoperia draw closer as they slowly moved toward port.

"Hmm... How I missed that smell." Enyo took a deep breath.

"What smell is that? I smell nothing." Alinda sniffed the air several times.

"The smell of Mastoperia. What else would it be?" he answered.

"I didn't know that our continent had a smell. What does it smell like? Because obviously, something is wrong with my nose."

"It smells ancient." Enyo took another deep breath.

"Okay, you're just saying nonsense now. I will let you enjoy your smelling fantasies while I go say goodbye to the others before we get off the ship." Alinda tapped his shoulder twice before she walked away.

She found Rolakan standing close to the ship's exit door.

"I thought you should be the first I say goodbye too." She stood behind him.

"I thought you became closer to Jihave. Wouldn't he be the one you want to spend the last moments with?"

"You are eager to leave this ship, so I wanted to make sure I catch you before you leave."

"What do you really want Alinda?" Rolakan turned around to face her.

"You have been quiet since—" She paused, lowering her chin. "For a moment after I thought you were okay, but you quickly went back to your silence."

"I hope you're not here to tell me how I was behaving through this journey." He crossed his arms in front of his chest.

"No. I want to apologize again, though I'm not sure if you can forgive me." She rubbed her arm.

"What's done is done. There's no need to dig it up."

"Would you be able to forgive me one day at least?" she asked.

"It's not me you need to ask for forgiveness. You need to ask yourself for that."

"Perhaps one day I can, but not today."

"Then there is nothing left for us to talk about. I would like to be alone, please."

Alinda nodded and started to move away.

"Alinda," Rolakan called for her, bringing her to a stop. "You knew it was going to happen, right? This is why you hugged me in the passage before the fight when you cried."

Alinda took a deep breath. "If you're asking if I could have changed it, the answer is I don't know, but I really tried to find another way out. No matter what, someone was going to die in that fight. The question was how many, and I chose the timeline where most of us lived." She stood in her place for a few seconds after she saw Rolakan turn his head back to the ocean before she made her way to the upper deck where she found most of the group engaged in what appeared to be an amusing conversation as everyone was laughing.

"If someone told me that one day I will see members of the four factions laughing out loud together like old friends, I would have considered them crazy for sure." Alinda interrupted their laughter.

"Come on, Alinda, join us." Jihave pointed at the empty seat next to him, but the ship's horn sounded at the same time announcing their arrival at the port.

The group said their goodbyes to each other and made promises to meet again before they stepped off the ship.

Rondai and Evailen were the last to step down. Their time on the ship brought them even closer to each other.

"I hate that this journey had to end," Evailen said as she descended the stairs.

"It's not over for us. There is still another mission, then after that, we will serve at the Forbidden City together." Rondai smiled.

"I know. I'm now looking forward to that." Evailen smiled back as she placed her feet on her continent once again.

Yasmina waited for them at the bottom. She asked Evailen to talk to her in private.

"Of course." Evailen smiled at her.

The two girls moved away from the crowd.

"I need you to promise me something." Yasmina lowered her head.

"I will if I can."

"Promise me you will take care of Rondai."

"I'm sorry?" Evailen drew her brows together.

"He can be arrogant and hot-headed sometimes, but he has a pure heart."

Evailen stared into her face. "I will do my best not to break his heart if this is what worries you."

"Our hearts are much tougher than you think, but this is not what I'm worried about. I just want you to promise me you will take care of him." Yasmina looked down.

"I don't understand. What—"

"Evailen stop. Don't argue. All you need to do is promise me that even if you drift apart, you will still look after him."

"Fine, I promise. Now tell me what is going on?"

"Thank you, and I want you to know that I'm really happy to have met you. Under different circumstance, we would have been best friends, but life is what it is." She hugged Evailen. The latter hugged her back, her eyes narrowed. "Now, I need to talk to him." Yasmina moved toward Rondai, leaving Evailen frozen in confusion.

Rondai smiled at Yasmina as she moved closer to him. "I hope you didn't want to talk to her about me. I think I'm doing pretty well on my own."

"Do you love me?" Yasmina locked her eyes with his.

"What?"

She kept her stare unbroken.

Rondai stood in silence for a second, focusing on her eyes before he held both of her hands. "What is about to happen Yasmina?"

"First tell me, do you love me?"

"Of course, I do. You are my favorite sister in the whole world."

"Then hold me in your arms." She moved closer to him.

Rondai didn't hesitate before hugging her. He could feel the tears running down her cheeks, so he asked her one more time what was going on.

"I'm afraid," she muttered.

"Of what?"

She pushed him away and dried her eyes with her hands. "In about a minute, two of the royal guards will arrive. I have a mission that involves them. You can't interfere. These are the orders of the council. You have to only focus on your own mission."

"Okay." Rondai paused. "Okay… Whatever the mission is, you can do it. You are the strongest person I know."

As the two guards walked into the port, Yasmina quickly planted a kiss on Rondai's cheek before she turned around to walk toward the guards. A few steps later and she couldn't help but turn around again and run back into Rondai's arms. "I love you." She whispered in his ear. "It's all for you." She whispered again before she faced the guards and ran toward them.

When she was a few feet away, she opened the fourth gate by performing the hand signal and manifested a lightning rod in her hand.

"No!" Rondai screamed, seeing what she was about to do. His feet left the ground, running toward his sister as he opened the fifth gate of magic.

When he saw her jump in the air, aiming to land a strike on one of the guards, he extended his arm forward before his entire aura sped toward her, taking the shape of a giant arm. But before his aura could grab her, a sharp blade surfaced out of the earth below Yasmina.

Rondai released another loud scream. His voice, combined with Evailen's and Malani's cries echoed through the mountains behind them. The rest of the companions froze in their places, eyes wide, and hands shaking. Only Kawan, and next to him, Naradia stood in silence, unshaken by the view, even when they saw Rondai run toward her.

Rondai grabbed Yasmina's body as it fell to the ground. Split in half from the earth blade, Yasmina bled everywhere, even though the two halves of her body remained connected.

The Royal guards approached Rondai whose tears streamed down his cheeks as his cry grew louder and louder. They looked at the group as they slowly moved toward Rondai and Yasmina, with fire in their eyes.

Radaman, one of the royal guards, conjured a fire that spiraled around his arm. "I don't know what happened to you in the outside world, but don't think that we will tolerate any attack on us."

Radaman shifted his gaze between the team leaders. "You have three days to rest at your factions. Then the four candidates must appear at the Forbidden City. Fail to come, and you will die."

Rondai raised his face to look at the royal guard as he stood, anger taking control of him. With his face turning red and his body heating up, he prepared to attack, but before he fully stood, the guards vanished in front of him, and all his tears rushed back to his skin as he screamed louder and louder.

49

Rondai carried Yasmina's body, which he wrapped in his garment into the main hall of the holy temple at the center of his faction. The masters gathered in the council room, waiting for Rondai the moment he entered Kala.

The oldest master moved toward Rondai as he burst into the room. "You have no business bringing her here."

Rondai placed her on the temple floor and assumed his battle stance. "You gave her this mission. It's time you pay for—"

"Don't be hasty again." Rolakan placed his hand on Rondai's shoulder. "We should give them a chance to explain first."

"Do you still want to listen to them after everything that happened? They gave her a mission to attack a royal guard."

The elder quickly added, his voice calm, "We gave no such mission. She lied to you and betrayed her faction. Now we have to prove her attack was a singular act before the entire faction faces the Forbidden Warriors' wrath."

"Lies. These are all lies!" Rondai shouted, tears streaming down his face. "She told me herself that she received a mission."

He reached to his heart with his thumb to open the fifth gate, but the gate didn't open.

"Your magic won't work in here," said the elder.

"I don't need it, anyway." Rondai charged toward the elder with darkness in his eyes, but other council members held him back by grabbing both his arms, blocking his movement before he reached the elder.

The elder took a step closer to Rondai, staring him in the eyes. "I understand you are angry but don't think we will tolerate such behavior."

Rondai ignored the elder and tried to break free once again with no success. After a few tries, the blood in his arm veins shone in fire-yellow through his skin. When one of the masters blocking Rondai saw his arm, he knocked him out with a single chop on the back of his neck.

The elder turned to Rolakan. "Get out of here. Your mission is complete. This is now a council only matter."

Rolakan nodded and left the temple, uttering nothing. He saw traces of shock on their faces and believed that he needed to leave the temple before his life became threatened.

"Is it possible?" asked one of the council members.

The elder shook his head. "Now is not the time for questions, we need to deal with this, and then we can figure out how it happened."

The council members moved quickly, carrying Rondai to a hidden room below the temple, and placed him in a pit of water that centered a six-headed star. Each of the members sat at one edge and closed their eyes.

Shortly after, Rondai regained his consciousness. When he opened his eyes, he found himself in a bubble of water levitating above the pit, only it contained fire instead of water. Above him, he saw a red portal marked with symbols he had never seen before, yet, he felt at peace.

"Did you see them?"

Rondai heard the voice but couldn't tell which of the members surrounding the pit spoke the words. However, he knew whom they spoke of. They meant the twelve Jackals who helped him in his battle against Jihave.

"Yes, I did," he answered.

The six members immediately chanted in ancient Kalanian. He wasn't familiar with the language, but he could grab a few words that crossed to their modern language. The bubble swirled around him, and gradually boiled as they chanted. He felt the heat take over his body as every ounce of it burned. His cloth melted away, and he screamed in agony, but all he could hear was the sound of their chanting getting higher and higher. Eventually, he lost his consciousness once again.

He woke up later on the floor of the council chamber naked. He tried to open his mouth to speak but couldn't, as if he lost the connection between his brain and the rest of his body.

The elder squatted in front of Rondai who lay on the floor, his eyes open. "In a few hours, you will regain full control over your body. Once you do, you will have complete control over the sixth gate to open and close it as you please. This is the first time we have seen someone who isn't within the council open the sixth gate." The elder paused. "You are indeed special. I guess it's time for you to know the truth."

The elder moved closer to Rondai and spoke just inches from his ear. "There are seven magical gates. We keep the last two hidden from the world, including our faction members. Revealing that secret is punishable by death."

The elder then stood and walked back before he continued to speak in his normal tone. "Mastery of the sixth gate gives you access to the power of your ancestors, deceased pure-blood Kalangous who also mastered the sixth gate. With their strength, only those who mastered the same number of gates or higher could surpass your power."

Rondai couldn't speak, but in his mind, he asked hundreds of questions. To the others, he didn't move a muscle.

"You will have an army of your own, but that power is limited," the elder continued. "You can use only twelve ancestors at a time. When one of them dies during your own battles, another will replace him. When you summon them, only you will be able to see them as who they were, everyone else will see them in the form of the sixth gatekeeper, regular body with hardened skin under a Jackal's head. For now, you can summon fifty-seven ancestors. That number might seem high to you but trust me when I tell you it's not enough when you are at war." The elder paused once again contemplating his next words. "Use them carefully because the price of this gate is your own heart. When the last of your Jackals die, so will you."

Another council member approached Rondai. "During your time here, I will teach you how to gain full control over your Jackals individually and collectively rather than letting them fight on their own for you. However, you will have to practice on your own since you will become the new leader of the Forbidden City, but don't worry, you can always summon your ancestors at any time to ask them for help with your training. However, don't let the appeal of learning from strong masters make you forget that in addition to the individual price you have to pay for each gate, there's another that collects the ticks of your heart each time you open a gate, regardless of which one it was. The more magic you use, the shorter your life becomes."

Rondai felt a quick kick in his elbow and gathered all of his force to push on it, but with it being the only part of his body—other than his eyes—he could control, he failed to move.

"Don't try to force your body and focus on my words," said the council member, seeing the signs of struggle on Rondai's face.

The council member crossed his legs on the floor next to Rondai and told him everything he needed to know about the sixth gate while the latter remained still. He told him everything except the truth about them wiping parts of his memory. Rondai left the holy temple, not remembering that Yasmina ever existed.

50

Evailen ran toward Rondai as soon as she saw him step into the Forbidden City.

"I'm so sorry. I don't know what to say." Evailen held him tight, hiding her face in his body as she struggled to cage her silent tears.

"Whoa…" Rondai chuckled. "It was only three days. I thought we were taking this slow."

Evailen stared into his eyes and slightly shook her head. "Oh my dear, are you still in shock?"

"What are you talking abo—"

Before Rondai could finish his sentence, Jihave grabbed the two of them and tightened his arm, trapping Rondai between him and Evailen.

"No no no, what is going on?" Rondai pushed the two of them away.

"Don't bother, he remembers nothing about her," Kawan spoke quietly as he casually passed by them on his way to the main hall.

"What do you mean?" Jihave shouted.

"His faction wiped his memories of her so he can finish his mission. He doesn't even know she existed." Kawan didn't bother to look back at Jihave.

Evailen and Jihave froze in place, their faces pale and eyes wide.

"What's going on?" Rondai repeated.

"Um… nothing." Evailen fought hard to force her face to smile but failed. "It's just we missed you." She grabbed his hand and led him toward the Forbidden City palace.

"So, we are holding hands now." Rondai smiled at her.

Evailen looked in his eyes and blinked back a tear. "Do you think they will send us back to the outside world?" She tried to keep a calm tone as her heart stammered in her chest.

"I doubt it. I think they will have to result to the ordinary selection method now."

Kawan stopped by the main gate and turned his head to the couple, staring at their connected hands. "Do you really need to bring your romance in here with you?"

"Leave them alone." Jihave intentionally put force into his shoulders before bumping it into Kawan's. "I think it's cute. Two competitors from two factions notorious for their mutual hatred found love together." Jihave smiled slightly. "That would make a good book."

"That is if the leaders of this place let them continue their relationship. They are stepping on dangerous ground here." Kawan kept his eyes low as he shook his head, following Jihave into the palace.

"They shouldn't have a say in who should be with whom." Jihave clenched his fists.

"I agree with you." Kawan kept his gaze at his feet. "But we know nothing of the Forbidden City and its inner rules, and they don't strike me as the type who would have relationships with anyone. All I'm saying is they should be careful."

Jihave ended the conversation. He didn't want to be part of something that felt destructive.

Shortly after the four centered the main hall, the forty warriors joined them, and the royal guards appeared before Kalita, their leader assumed her place on her throne.

"Congratulations! I honestly thought you would take much longer than you have, but you proved to be worthy of our succession." Kalita's grin widened.

Kawan straightened his posture. "We had, as predicted, got one artifact each. What's the second mission that will decide the leader once and for all?"

"Oh, the Delphian." Kalita half-smiled. "You have changed a lot since the last time you were here. What happened to the shy, silent old you?"

"You and your agenda. Now stop wasting our time and tell us what we have to do now?"

One Tap.

Two Taps.

"Respect," said Radaman, the third guard.

"That's fine," said Kalita. "They went through a lot on their journey. We can tolerate a little anger." She turned her head to meet Kawan's eyes. "But don't mistake my forgiveness for weakness Kawan." It was the first time the leader called any of them by name.

Kawan took a deep breath and uttered nothing, throwing a quick glance at the other candidates who stood in silence.

Kalita rested her back against her throne. "Each of you has returned with a single artifact, but only the leader can have all four. The only way to make that happen will be through arena fights."

"What are you talking about?" Jihave took a step forward, shouting his question. "You will actually make us fight each other for it?"

"Calm down Jihave. Arena fights have rules and regulations. They won't be death fights." Rondai half-smiled. "I will go easy on you."

Jihave quickly turned his face to Rondai, eyes narrowed. "The point is not whether they would be death fights or not. According to the law, arena fights must be public and accompanied with free entry. All our factions will be there, cheering for their fighter. This is cruelty against us. It would divide our people further. The warriors of this city should bring us together, not pit us against one another." Jihave's veins popped out on his forehead.

"I agree with Jihave." Evailen nodded. "There's a reason the arena was closed for decades. It has always fueled wars."

"Are you done with your analysis?" Kalita tapped the edge of her throne armrest with her finger. "Being a peacekeeper is not a fun game. You need to be harsh, sometimes ruthless and know that the law comes first. You can't be afraid of punishing those who stand in your way and challenge your authority." She paused regarding their faces. "Without power, this world will fall into chaos. The new generation needs to remember the power of the warriors before one of you becomes the leader."

Kalita sighed. "After hearing your comments, I have decided the fights will be to the death. I won't accept that weaklings lead my city."

"What if I don't want to join this fight?" Jihave raised his voice.

"Then you will forfeit your right to be in the Forbidden Force and must hand your artifact to your designated opponent."

"I will do just that then. I have no intention in continuing this joke any longer." Jihave turned around to leave.

"I wasn't finished Averetti." Kalita raised her tone, bringing him to a stop. "After you approve your forfeit, you will have to wear the Anubis bracelet for the rest of your life."

Jihave's neck muscles tensed as he turned to face the leader. "You want me to wear the Anubis bracelet for not wanting to kill someone?"

Evailen raised her eyebrows. "What in the lotus's name is the Anubis bracelet?"

"The Anubis bracelet is a device that takes away the power of Averettis, denying them the ability to merge with and control Majestics." Kalita turned her head to Evailen. "It's similar to you losing your six seeds. Which is what would happen to you if you forfeited as well."

"That's not right." Evailen felt her body heat as her red seed blinked fast. "You are taking away our free-will."

"You lost your free-will the moment you accepted this mission, and I will argue with you no longer." The leader raised her head. "We have already decided the order of the fight. The Averetti will fight the Delphian in a week's time at the golden arena in a broadcasted public event. Then the Lunardis will fight the Kalangou four days after. The winners of both fights will meet in a final event to decide the new leader. If you wish to forfeit then do it now, otherwise I expect you to appear for your fight."

Rondai felt his chest compresses against his heart. He slowly turned his face to Evailen whose gaze fell to her feet as she stood in silence.

"I thought we would be leader and guards." Rondai's voice slightly trembled. "All four of us were meant to be part of this."

"Drastic moments require drastic measures and your factions could always send new guard candidates. Now do any of you wish to forfeit?" Kalita stood, her throne to her back.

None of the four answered.

"All right then. May the best of you win." Kalita left the room, followed by her guards before the forty warriors exited the hall leaving the four competitors standing in silence.

None of them dared to utter a word.

51

Salvanra sat on the edge of a lake, dipping her feet in the water. Sunrays penetrated her naked body while she used her arms to support her back. She leaned her head backward and closed her eyes, listening to the sound of peace generating from the feet of her Majestics playing around the lake.

"I knew I would find you here." Jihave came out of the forest that surrounded the entire lake.

"Come join me." Salvanra leaned her head backward to look at him from an upside-down view.

Jihave crossed his feet on the ground next to her. "We need to talk."

"What is it?" Salvanra adjusted her pose to face him.

"I know we have been distant lately, and that we were spending less time together. I don't know if something happened to you during the mission or if you were still mad at me because of my fight with—"

"Are you breaking up with me?" Salvanra slowly leaned forward as she held both her hands together and placed them on her legs.

"No, no. That is not what I'm here for. Quite the opposite actually." Jihave took a deep breath. "I need you. I know I can be arrogant and pushy sometimes, but for the first time in my life, I feel trapped, and I don't know what to do." Jihave lowered his head.

"What's going on? Tell me." Salvanra reached for Jihave's hands and cradled them. "I was mad at you because of the fight. We agreed to make ourselves an example of a new united world and change how our ancestors did things. It surprised me when you let your negative emotions take over you." Salvanra exhaled. "I never expected you to be the one who would fall for that, but that doesn't mean I will abandon you or give up on you. We are a team, always." She pushed on his hands and pulled them closer to her.

Jihave didn't hold his tears back. He cried silently while Salvanra moved closer to him and placed his head on her shoulder. He wrapped her waist with his arms and uttered nothing for a few minutes. When he calmed down a little, he told her everything that happened at the Forbidden City. Salvanra dropped her jaw when she heard about the death fights.

"It's a show of power. This is what that is." Salvanra calmly stated.

"They are the keepers of peace. Their job is to bring us closer together, not force us to kill each other."

"Well, when you think about it, they are only there to enforce the law. They don't care about us getting closer together. Otherwise, there wouldn't be so many laws about trespassing on other faction grounds. They see our unity as a threat and don't want us to become a united front."

"What do you mean?" Jihave raised his brows.

"I think they saw how we became close to each other in such a short time. Perhaps they expected that our team up would break us more and cause conflicts, but we all came together nicely and were able to work out our differences quickly." She focused on his eyes. "I think they are afraid of the new generation. Our parents knew what war was like, and maybe believed in its cause, but we only tasted its pain. I think no one from our generation wants to feel that loss of war again." Salvanra explained.

"I still don't see your point. Even if this was a show of power, and they want to keep us divided. They can't truly want us to go to war. It's still their job to prevent it. My feeling is that they want entertainment. They may want to display their power, but all they are really doing is forcing me to kill an innocent soul to entertain their sadistic needs."

"They don't really need a war. All they need is that feeling of discontent. Families will find the loss of their loved ones by another faction member painful and downgrading. A feeling of sorrow will take over everyone no matter who dies. The factions of the fallen will work hard to rebuild their power so that never happens again. Some might even want to test this power, and they will want to test it on those who hurt them the most. There will be more division between the factions. And as we all know, the best way to keep everyone under your thumb is when you divide to conquer."

"So, what do I do?" Jihave asked.

"I don't know yet, but this is huge. We can't think about it alone." Salvanra summoned her eagle and sent it with a message to Bofrat and Maringrad who joined them as quickly as they could.

🌀🐢🪷🌙

The four of them tried to think of a way to get Jihave out of his predicament, but their only idea was that Jihave escape Mastoperia.

"Even if I was to escape, there's no guarantee they won't be able to find me. We know nothing of their true power and capabilities." Jihave sighed. "I'm also not sure they won't try to punish the entire faction for it or use you to push me to return. I can't put everyone at risk just so I can keep using my powers. Perhaps I should give in and accept the bracelet."

"The bracelet won't just take away your power. It will take away who you are. We are born with those powers. We don't just embrace them. Your Majestics are as much a part of you as your inner organs," said Bofrat.

"I know that, and I don't want to give them up. Each time I think that I could lose them, I feel something pulling my soul out of me. I would lose all purpose of living, but what else can I do. We have been thinking for hours and come up with no solution, and I don't think there is any to be found." Jihave fought hard to keep his tears caged, but one escaped.

"You can't lose hope now. We still have time to find a way out." Salvanra slowly rubbed his back.

"I think I can help you with that."

The four looked toward the forest line where they heard the voice come from. They saw a bright light with a shadow inside. They put their guards up as they moved closer, but the shadow never moved. They couldn't see who it was.

"Who are you?" Jihave squinted.

"It doesn't matter who I am or where I come from. All you need to know is I'm here to tell you the truth about the Forbidden Warriors."

"Kawan?" Maringrad asked. He knew his voice well.

52

Upon his return to Delphia, Kawan received a message informing him that he needed to appear at the Skeptic Room for another hearing. It was the third time he received such a message. He knew that the Skeptic Room demands were as strong as court orders and that ignoring them led to immediate reform measurements, but this time he ignored it.

He knew what was coming ahead, and no one had the power to prevent him from attending that fight. He went directly back home and searched his medicine cabinet for anxiety pills—or as they know them in Delphia, saiting relaxers because they ease their minds if they had to saite too much in a short time—but had none left. He rushed out of there and toward the hospital immediately.

"I would like a box of saiting relaxers, please," he asked the pharmacist.

"Can I see your prescription?"

"Since when do we need a prescription for that?" Kawan raised his voice.

"Calm down, Sir. I see you have already reached your annual free limit. To give you more, I have to see an official prescription." The pharmacist pointed at the transparent screen in front of him where Kawan's data appeared.

"I was on an important mission for the Forbidden City. It forced me to burn through my dose." Kawan kept his high tone.

"I understand that, Sir, and I'm not against giving you more. All you need to do is explain that to an official spectator, and they will give you the required paper."

"This will take days. I don't have time for this."

"Again, I'm sorry, but without a prescription, I can't help. I see here, you are scheduled to appear at the Skeptic Room today. I'm sure they can expedite the process."

Kawan stormed out of the hospital, charged with anger. He couldn't tell him he used his entire yearly dose to buy drugs before he left on the mission. He moved toward the ground market, hoping he could find another way to buy the drugs he wanted.

⊚ ✿ ❀ ◌

"Please, stop shouting. I told you the price for the smokes is saiting relaxers. If you have none, I can't help you," the salesperson on the other side of the smoking station responded calmly to an angry Kawan.

"What seems to be the problem here?" Gabrin placed his left hand on Kawan's left shoulder.

Kawan looked at him with fire in his eyes and said nothing. The seller then explained the situation to Gabrin who in return signaled him to let it go.

"Walk with me. I am sure we can find a solution." Gabrin nodded at Kawan to calm him down.

"I need to buy some of his products, but I have no more anxiety pills. Can you please help me find another way to get some, or arrange a different form of payment with him?" Kawan spoke with a broken voice.

"First, you need to know that everything here is mine. All those people work for me. Only I know how to get the merchandise. Second, I will definitely help our hero. I won't leave you in need before a deathmatch with an Averetti." Gabrin placed his open palm between Kawan's neck and shoulder.

"Thank you. I am very grateful." Kawan lowered his head.

"But as you know, I am also a businessman, and I can't just give you something for free. Other clients will be angry and demand similar treatment. You don't want me to lose my business. Do you?"

"No, I don't." Kawan shrugged. "What can I do to get the product?"

"How much do you need?" Gabrin asked.

"Enough for a week or more."

"I will give you a month's supply of product. Would that be enough?"

"Yes. More than enough. Thank you." Kawan's eyes widened as he looked at Gabrin.

"What you will do for me in return is simple. You will transfer the ownership of everything you have to me in case of your death. If you win, then you can keep it, but you will offer me something else."

"What would that be?" Kawan planned to agree no matter what the answer was.

"You will pull out the warriors from certain locations and allow us to trade more freely." Gabrin paused for a second. "Are you willing to pact this?"

"Yes, I agree. I like the concept of free trade anyway, and if I die, then none of my property matters. I will pact this right now."

Both men held their arms together, elbow to elbow before they connected both their foreheads. Gabrin pulled out a two-sided needled tube-string and planted one side in his arm and the other in Kawan's. Their blood flooded the tube and mixed. A few seconds after, Gabrin removed the needle and pulled a small sack of product out of his pocket.

"This should be enough for today. Tonight, you will receive the remaining quantity at your apartment."

Kawan nodded.

"So, tell me. Do the smokes make you truly see a future that isn't yours?" Gabrin asked, handing Kawan the product.

"They do if you know what to focus on." Kawan put the small bag in his pocket.

"Then I hope it helps you to see enough of the future to beat the Averetti. After all, nothing is better than doing what's best for our people." Gabrin smiled.

Kawan nodded again. He left the city of Delphia to go to a small forest that inhabited its southern border. He positioned himself near a waterfall and rolled the entire bag in a tree leaf upping his own dose. He coughed a lot while smoking it, but that didn't bother him. Within minutes, his mind was elsewhere, navigating the world of those he knows.

He reached for the one person who threatened his existence and navigated his life. In the beginning, he couldn't see clearly, as timelines changed quickly from one to another. He could no longer manipulate the timelines based on his personal decision since he wasn't saiting his own future. As time passed, the image became clearer, and every single timeline lasted longer. He didn't realize it had become night until the effect of the product vanished. He moved only to reach his apartment where he found a big carton of the product in front of his door. He grabbed it and moved back without paying attention to the notice on his door that required his immediate presence at the Skeptic Room if he wanted to avoid punishment.

Kawan sat for days at the waterfall, ignoring the need for food and water. He focused on nothing but the timelines he needed to see. His only movement was to roll a new patch and smoke it before he resumed his meditative position.

Kawan had a plan, and that plan required knowledge. He was determined to get that knowledge, no matter the expense. He focused as hard as he could to see as much as he needed, then suddenly he saw something exceptional. Far more exceptional than being able to see a future that wasn't his. Inside his saiting, he saw a shadow of a figure that spoke directly to him.

He was the first ever to communicate with his future self. Kawan believed he was the chosen one.

53

Behind the Forbidden City palace lay an arena that had stayed abandoned for decades. The arena that witnessed the fall of mighty warriors ended wars and started others. No one dared to step foot in it since the last fight, which ended with the death of more than half of the spectators and launched the last all-faction war.

On the day of the first fight, a new generation filled the seats to witness yet another deathmatch that would determine something that relates to none of them. It seemed everyone always cheered for death when it touched no one. They all feared death, yet it was always entertaining to watch.

The guards and their leader took their place in a darkened booth watching the two candidates as they marched toward the center of the field from both ends of the arena. Jihave wore nothing but tiny shorts that barely covered his genitals. The sheer number of Majestic tattoos that enveloped most of his large body emphasized his masculinity. His eyes remained focused on his opponent, uninterested in the massive cheering that followed his appearance.

Kawan wore his battle outfit, a white leather jacket, and pants with blue lines that ran around the edges, matching his blue pointy shoes made of the same material as his clothing. The leather was enforced with a special material known only to Delphians to form a high-quality armor. He carried his sword on his back as he paced slowly and steadily with his eyes focused on the location of his next step.

The two stood still at the edge of a circle that centered the field. Neither of them spoke. The sound of a ringing bell brought the audience to silence. Seconds passed between the first bell and the second. Seconds through which the two opponents realized their new reality.

Kawan grabbed his sword the instant he heard the second bell as he jumped a few steps to the rear.

Jihave stood in his place as if he was unbothered by the beginning of the fight. He took a deep breath before he launched his tiger, but the Majestic didn't attack. It stood in front of Jihave, mimicking his facial expressions, or more like their lack of existence.

Kawan slowly moved back and forth in a half-circle around Jihave and his tiger, watching as they did nothing but follow him with their eyes. The loud cheering turned into booing as neither of them threw the first punch.

Eventually, Kawan stopped and closed his eyes for a second. When he opened them, he found himself staring directly into Jihave's eyes. He nodded before he turned his large sword around itself at the same time, he raised it high in the air.

Sparkles ignited around the sword as it formed a small cloud of lightning surrounding the blade. His pace increased as he moved toward an unshaken Jihave.

The tiger assumed a charging stance when Kawan moved closer.

Kawan leaped into the air planning to use the tiger as a base for a bigger jump, but the tiger lunged toward him while he was in midair.

Kawan shifted his weight toward the ground by planting his sword into the soil and using it as an anchor to pass under the tiger. He pushed against the ground with both feet and swung his sword toward Jihave's left leg.

The sword landed on Jihave's leg but inflected zero damage. The beetle armor that appeared around Jihave's leg at the moment of impact rendered the attack void.

Kawan tried to pull the sword back, but it was stuck. With a quick glance, he noticed a snake surrounded the tip of the blade, trapping it.

The viewers shouted, "Leave it!" their voices harmonizing and gradually increasing. They believed that Kawan's only choice was to abandon his sword if he wanted to avoid his neck being detached by the approaching tiger fangs.

Kawan anticipated every movement and prepared for every outcome. He increased the lightning charge his sword produced out of its under-the-handle-motor and directed it toward the snake as he jumped toward Jihave carrying a smaller sword he hid within the first one.

Jihave launched the beetle armor around his entire body simultaneously. At that moment, Jihave didn't notice that Kawan changed his direction and attacked the temporarily paralyzed snake. He sliced the snake in half, grabbed the tip of the sword, and moved behind Jihave, twirling himself around twice while flipping the sword before throwing it at the heart of the tiger that was already in the air. The tiger dropped dead immediately.

Kawan took a few steps back and watched Jihave maintain his frozen stance. Pacing around Jihave with slow determined steps until he could see his face again, Kawan saw the tears make their way down Jihave's face as his armor retracted.

Jihave didn't move a muscle for several long moments. Eventually, he only moved his head to look at his fallen Majestics. It was then that both his ape and elephant found their way out of his two sides and charged Kawan who felt he was fighting against actual people with planned and organized strategies.

Their lack of decision-making made Kawan take longer to realize their next movement, yet he managed to defend himself against both Majestics.

What Kawan failed to realize was that Jihave was no longer standing in the same place. At the exact second Kawan launched a blow toward the elephant's head, he felt a chill rush through his body.

His hands let go of the sword as it was too heavy to carry, and felt Jihave's hand as it was extracted from his body. Kawan fought to look back as he fell to his knees. He could see Jihave's hand, but it didn't look normal. His fingers looked like claws. He raised his head to take a last look at Jihave's face, but everything turned dark before he succeeded.

Kawan fell to his death with unfulfilled plans, knowing that his ability to see the future was nothing more than a curse. Without it, he wouldn't have seen his own death thousands of times or knew that there was no changing it.

Jihave shed no more tears. He walked toward the edge where they locked their artifacts before the fight, grabbed both pieces and headed directly out of the arena disregarding all the loud cheering. He wasn't sure if it was worth it or not.

54

Rolakan walked into the red temple, passing from one section to another. He marched through the path of the warriors, paved by statues of ancient masters, to the vision chamber where they keep the magic crystal before he reached the training grounds where he found Rondai sitting on the sandy floor with his legs crossed together and eyes closed.

He moved up to Rondai, "Did you know?"

"Let me guess. Kawan lost the fight?" Rondai maintained his meditative position.

"I know he is physically weaker, but their ability to see the future always made them a dangerous opponent." Rolakan assumed the same seating position as Rondai.

"Was. He is dead now, and all factions are dangerous opponents, but the Delphians strengths always lied in their ability to win fights before they happen. If the fight starts, they usually lose."

"True, but they always carried tricks up their sleeves. I could never trust someone who knew what would happen before it did."

"It doesn't matter anymore. He lost the fight." Rondai displayed a faint of a smile. "I heard you will join the council. Congratulations."

"It should have been you." Rolakan paused, pressing his teeth against one another. "Or Ryn."

"Ryn will watch over us from the other side of the gates, it's a role far more honorable. As for me, my time will come, but now, my duty is elsewhere."

"How do you feel about that? Will you truly fight Evailen?"

Rondai took a deep breath and exhaled it slowly. "The benefit of the faction comes before personal gain. It wasn't going to work out, anyway."

"Spoken with real Kalanian cruelty." Rolakan sighed.

Rondai opened his eyes and shouted. "What do you expect me to do? Let her kill me and lose both my life and the honor of my faction?"

"I didn't say that, but I thought she meant something to you. Or were you fooling everyone?" Rolakan matched Rondai's voice.

"Watch your tone. You're not on the council yet, my rank is still higher." Rondai narrowed his eyes. "And she means a lot to me. I hoped it could be different, but this isn't her versus me. This is her versus my life and my faction. I ran the numbers, and they aren't in her favor." Rondai's heart raced in his chest.

"I honestly had high hopes for you, but it appears I was wrong."

Rondai lowered his head, speaking in a quiet voice. "Why do you care so much, anyway? It's not like the two of you are close to one another."

"I care because I thought you did. I care because you are part of a group that is trying to change this faction from within. I care because we lost the souls of not one but two of our members who worked hard to see all factions work together." Rolakan's voice grew sharper.

"Coming to your little gathering had nothing to do with changing the faction's values. It was a place to have fun, nothing more."

"It wasn't a place to have fun. It was never meant to be." Rolakan stood up, anger clear in his voice. "It was a safe spot where we could all come together regardless of our bloodlines. It was a place for people to see that we don't need all of those restrictions to be strong." Rolakan moved toward the exit.

"Wait," Rondai called to him. "What did you mean by two members? Whom else did we lose other than Ryn? Or do you consider Kawan to be one of us too?"

"Yasmina!" Rolakan shouted. "Or did you forget about your little sister too?" He stormed out of the temple.

Rondai had no idea what Rolakan meant by the word Yasmina. He had no recollection of her or of ever having a sister. Searching his mind for traces of Yasmina, he felt a strong headache take over his brain. The more he tried to fill the gaps in his memory, the stronger the headache became. Eventually, his persisting attempts to understand what his mind was missing knocked him unconscious.

In his dreams, he saw all the memories of them together. He saw Yasmina standing next to him watching their life. He tried to apologize to her but couldn't utter a word. His tears managed to find an escape despite his absence of conscious.

When Rondai woke up, he forgot about Yasmina once again. He thought he slept out of exhaustion and resumed his meditative position for another six hours before he finally went home.

⊛ ❦ ✿ ☯

Rondai wanted to take a break from his thoughts by focusing on his rap lyrics. The moment he knew he would fight Evailen, his brain split in half, each part fighting the other, opening the door for the first gate of magic to claim its payment. The price of the first gate is control over the master's darkest emotions. Rondai was angry and afraid, and the first gate amplified both, turning them into a drive for self-preservation and fuel for endless ambition.

He was aware of what was happening inside him, allowing his darkest desires to slip out in public, so others didn't see his weakness but fighting back when he was alone. Writing raps was one of the few things that helped him escape the prison of his mind in the past, but not this time.

It quickly became plain to him that there was no escaping his mind. If he were going to think, then it would be about nothing but Evailen. He kept telling himself that it was impossible to be in love so soon. That he didn't know her that well, and that she was a member of an enemy faction.

Perhaps it was a dream.... The thought of you and me

But now it really seems... We were never meant to be.

"No. No!" Rondai shouted before he scratched the lines he wrote. He wanted to convince himself that his feelings were fake. He believed there was no other solution.

Realizing there was no way out of his mind, he decided to switch his sad thoughts, with equally painful ones. He grabbed one of his old books and pulled a letter out. A letter he hadn't read in a very long time.

'My dearest Rondai,

If you are reading this, then the worst has already happened. I was never afraid of my end until the moment I met you. Holding your tiny body right after your mother birthed you renewed my faith in the world and gave me hope. You filled my life with happiness, but that also meant I had to make decisions I wouldn't usually make. I had to protect your world from those who threatened it regardless of my personal beliefs. If I can't be with you, I must at least make sure you will grow up in the safest environment possible.

I have no advice for you because I have no doubt you will be better than anything I could imagine.

I love you, my son, always.

P.S. forgive me for writing a short letter. Words were never my skill.

Your father,

Rakamai

Rondai tried to hold back his tears. He always saw crying as a sign of weakness, and he rarely forgave himself when it happened, but this time he let go.

He had no plan. No way out. No matter what happened in his next fight, it would break him entirely. He had only known Evailen for a short time, but he never felt the way she made him feel before in his life, and he had no control over it. Yet, he had a sense of duty toward his faction, which he spent his entire life enforcing. How was it possible that a simple encounter like that would make him question his loyalty and honor?

The pain was too much for him.

A simple knock on the door brought him to reality. He quickly hid the letter in his book and wiped his tears. He moved toward the door and adjusted his stance to portray a strong appearance. When he opened the door, he saw the last person he expected to see.

55

The moment Evailen heard she was going to fight Rondai to death, her legs became wobbly and her head too heavy for her body to carry. She knew she didn't want to fight him, but her bigger problem was the idea of a death fight. She never thought she would ever be in a position where she needed to take a life. It made her realize that being part of the Forbidden Warriors may require her to take even more lives later, and she wasn't ready for that.

"What do you mean you plan to lose the fight to him?" Cilia asked.

"I don't think I need to explain that. I will let him win," Evailen quietly answered.

"What I hear is that you are planning suicide." Cilia raised her voice.

"I am not. It is just—"

"You are letting him kill you. That's the definition of suicide. You are just choosing him as a method of execution."

"I told you I have no option. If I forfeit, then they will take away my seeds, and we both know that is a fate worse than death." Tears accumulated in Evailen's eyes.

"Death is death. There is no fate worse than that, but maybe you could think about… I don't know. Winning!" Cilia ran her hand through her hair aggressively.

"I will never kill a living soul. You of all people should know that about me." Evailen exhaled loudly.

"All of this for a crush? Come on, Evailen. You will meet someone else. It's your life we're talking about here. I can't believe we're even having this conversation."

"You are not listening, Cilia. It's not about him. I would do the same if it were someone else. I don't want to kill. Period," Evailen spoke loud and fast.

"Okay, okay. Calm down. Let's think about it. I am sure we can find another solution, so you don't have to kill or be killed."

"There isn't another way, Cilia. They made it clear that the only way out of there is in a coffin." Evailen's tears ran down her soft cheeks. "It's okay. I've made my peace with it. Our journey has to end at some point, anyway."

"Well, I haven't. You're young and full of potential. You have your entire life ahead of you, and you did nothing wrong. It's not fair they put you in this situation." Cilia kicked the furniture several times on her way out.

"Where are you going?" Evailen shouted.

"I don't know. I'm going to look for a solution. There has to be one. I refuse to be that passive." Cilia slammed the door behind her.

Evailen felt tired of explaining what no one else could understand. Being a Forbidden Warrior is the greatest honor any Mastoperian could receive, but no one knows what happens within the Forbidden City walls.

At that moment, Evailen realized that Rondai might not finish the job on his own. She feared the softness of his heart might take over his mask of cruelty. She wasn't sure if he could actually play the roles of the masks he wore in front of the world or if they were just that, masks, especially after she saw how the death of a member from his faction severely damaged him.

She couldn't imagine him taking her life. However, she had to make sure he did for the sake of both of them. There was no reason for the two to get punished by Kalita.

She contacted the one other Kalangou she knew and asked him to help her arrange a secret meeting with Rondai.

That very night she found herself standing in front of his door after Rolakan helped her sneak into Kala.

"What are you doing here?" Rondai caged his arms before they enveloped her.

"I wanted to talk to you."

"About what? Do you think it's wise we speak before the fight?"

"I don't think we would be able to speak after the fight." Evailen started to grin, but it quickly disappeared.

"I guess you are right." Rondai wanted to say a million words to her but chose not to.

"Are you going to leave me standing here? Won't you invite me in?"

Rondai opened the door for her to move in before he closed it behind her. "How did you get here, anyway?"

"A nice little place you have here. Small but cozy. I love it." Evailen fought hard not to think about how their future could have been.

"Thank you, but you still didn't tell me how you got here?" Rondai crossed his arms to secure the cage he built for them.

Evailen moved around the room, touching everything. "That doesn't matter now."

"Okay! Can you at least tell me why are you here? Are you trying to influence me or trick me?" His words didn't match his screaming thoughts asking him to just hold her in his arms and say nothing.

Evailen raised a single eyebrow as she stared into his face. "I'm not here to gain something for myself. In fact, it's the complete opposite."

"I'm listening."

"I want to make sure you will do the job. That you will finish me." Evailen shrugged.

"You want to make sure I will kill you?" Rondai paused to scream in his head. "I don't know what you are expecting me to say."

"I want you to tell me that what we have won't cloud your judgment."

Rondai's eyes reflected light because of the tears trying to escape, his heart unstable, trying to stop itself. "What we have is a mutual attraction and a short period of a good time together. Nothing more." He bit his tongue before it spelled the truth. "If you are worried that I will betray my duty to my faction for you, don't be. My faction comes above all."

"Thank you. That's all I wanted to hear. See you in a few days."

Evailen left before Rondai could see the tears rushing out of her eyes. He said exactly what she wanted him to say, but that didn't prevent her heart from breaking. Perhaps she hoped he would say otherwise or at least argue with her a little. Maybe she thought she would spend the night with him for a perfect goodbye. None of this mattered now.

The pain was so much that she did something she never expected to do. She removed her red seed from her chest. Her heart seed ripped her of all her emotions the moment she removed it. Her pain was gone, but so was her decision. On her way home, she thought about one thing only. No one was worth it, and she was no longer willing to give up her life without a true fight.

56

The sun centered the sky without a cloud in sight as though she wanted to see the events of the fight clearly. Hungry for death viewers once again filled the arena. The sound of their cheers for their favorite contestant echoed as they eagerly anticipated the screams of the opponent. Only a few knew what this fight meant for those who were about to step into the circle of death.

Cilia and Evailen stood in the fighter's preparation room before she walked into the arena.

"Are you sure you want me to hold on to this?" Cilia spoke loudly to make her voice heard over the crowd's cheers that shook the ground.

"Are you saying I should question my decision?" Evailen spoke firmly.

"That's not what I meant. I'm glad you are finally willing to fight and won't let yourself perish for nothing. I know you can win this. That you will win this. What I meant is, are you sure you want to leave your red seed with me instead of guarding it yourself?"

"I have to make sure I don't get swayed by his appearance or feel the need to put it back for any reason during the fight. That is why it has to be with you."

"I will guard it with my life." Cilia placed her hand on Evailen's shoulder. "And I will put it back myself as soon as you return after the fight."

"Let us not worry about putting it back now."

Cilia wrapped her arms around Evailen, but she didn't hug her back. Instead, she stood there awkwardly keeping her arms next to her body until Cilia detached herself.

Evailen moved toward the fighting circle and brushed her black seed for her armor to materialize around her entire body. She pulled her sword-gun out of her armor and grasped it with her right hand.

Evailen marched toward the center of the arena with sturdy legs. Her confidence gradually increased with each step she took as the cheering became louder and louder. That day was the one when she would show everyone that an innocent little girl could be tougher than those who consider themselves to be the strongest. She raised her sword-gun toward the sky and turned in a circle to greet the audience who went crazy for her. Even Delphians and Averettis were on her side.

She stood with her head held high waiting for Rondai to appear from the other side, but the longer she waited, the more she had time to think. First, her brain calculated different scenarios for the fight. She assessed what she knew about him and his power and what she could do to counter it. She remembered his fight with Jihave and his powerful Jackal attack. She knew that her armor would break if he used the same technique against her and thought about how she could avoid it. Noticing she had a lot of time to think, Evailen realized he was late, and her patience turned into anger.

"Where is that coward Kalangou?" she shouted.

The entire arena went quiet.

"Yeah... What is taking him so long?" a member of the audience shouted, breaking the silence.

"Coward Kalangous!" shouted another.

The Kalangous were notorious for their short tempers. They felt insulted by Rondai's absence, but that didn't mean they would accept any attack on their faction, no matter how small it was. Their response to the verbal abuse came in the form of a battle stance. Their thirst for blood was visible in their eyes.

Lunardis weren't ones to shy away from a fight either. In a matter of seconds, their side of the arena changed from a multitude of colors into a bright blue. They were a unified, fully armored unit.

The arena could have turned into a bloodbath that day if it wasn't for the three royal guards who launched out of their booth in a manner that grabbed everyone's attention. The first, Radaman, floated a few meters above the ground, accompanied by a major lightning storm that surrounded him and extended to the sky. The second, Amarin, stood above a tornado shaped monster that was almost as high as the top of the arena. The third, Takara, just stood in the middle of the arena, a few feet away from Evailen, holding her sword without moving but something about her scared everyone enough that they took back to their seats quickly.

"Unauthorized fights won't be tolerated and will be severely punished," Kalita raged from her shaded booth, her voice echoing through the arena. "I will expect everyone to be quiet while we find the reason for the tardiness. I won't remind you again that we prohibit inter-faction fights regardless of the reason behind it. Next time, the royal guards will interact immediately."

Evailen found herself surrounded by another level of power. A power she never heard of before. She knew the guards had to be much stronger than them, but she never imagined herself to be small in comparison until that moment. A part of her mind tingled at the thought of having all that power. "I could be the strongest to walk the world," she muttered to herself.

Radaman and Amarin suppressed their power as they stepped back on the ground before they moved simultaneously toward Rondai's side of the arena to see why he had yet to make it out as they knew he was present inside the arena that morning. Only Takara remained in the center. After the other two left, she raised her head and stared into Evailen's eyes.

"Perhaps not today, but one day you will have to make a choice between your heart and your world. When that day comes, I hope you choose wisely." Takara spoke directly to Evailen with a smile on her face.

Evailen opened her mouth to ask what she meant, but the voice of one of the other guards preceded her words.

"He's not there," said Amarin.

"Of course, he isn't. He is long gone by now," said Takara.

"Did you know about this?" asked Radaman.

"I know now," she answered with the same smile she gave Evailen earlier.

Radaman turned his face to Evailen. "This fight is over for now. We will contact you when we decide on another date."

The three guards disappeared instantly.

Evailen found Cilia waiting in her changing room.

Cilia placed her arms on Evailen's. "I'm happy to see the fight didn't happen. It's time you know the truth and why he wasn't there."

"He's just a coward who brought doom to his entire faction and possibly to our entire world," Evailen said with an assured tone.

Cilia felt annoyed by her comment and quickly forced Evailen's red seed back in its place above Evailen's heart, causing her to gasp for air as she felt an explosion of emotions in her entire body.

Evailen fell to the floor. "Or maybe he cared about me more than he could admit." She placed her head between her knees and surrendered to her cries.

57

"How could this possibly happen?" The ruler of the Forbidden Warriors stormed inside a wide room located under the main hall of the Forbidden Palace. The yellow stone walls stood naked with no decorations. The room had nothing but a long stone table surrounded by four stone seats which centered the round room perfectly.

Amarin moved closer to her. "We kept an eye on him until he entered the premises of the arena. After that, there was no reason for it. We had to join you at the booth to watch over the audience." He scratched his arms. The Majestic tattoos filling his body gave him a constant itch due to their nonstop movement.

"Obviously, that wasn't enough. He clearly knew we were watching him and timed his escape perfectly. How did he know that?" Kalita's six seeds blinked simultaneously.

Takara moved her eyes between Kalita and the other two royal guards, "What is everyone looking at me for? I had nothing to do with this."

"Maybe not, Takara," Radaman squinted, his tone cold, "but you had to have known about this at least."

"No, I didn't. I was focusing on the outcome, remember? The task she asked me to do this morning?" Takara pointed at the leader.

"Exactly my point. You should have seen that he wasn't there!" Radaman shouted.

"How many times do I need to explain to you that when I see a future that isn't mine, it's based on the scenarios I build in my head, not actual events? It will only become true if all the data I input in my mind matches the reality. In this case, I didn't expect he wouldn't be there. Therefore, I didn't see it. That bald head of yours isn't helping you get that point. Grow some hair, maybe it will amplify your intelligence!" Takara shouted before she shifted to face Amarin and winked.

Kalita narrowed her eyes when she saw Takara's wink. "I see you are not taking this seriously."

"I'm two hundred and seventy-five years old, and I'm the youngest of all of you. If you can't see the irony in what happened, then something must be wrong with you."

"What is that irony? Please enlighten us with your wisdom." Radaman clenched his fists.

"We were bested. We built the perfect scenario, and he still punched a hole in it and defeated us all."

"And you find amusement in this because?" Amarin quietly asked.

"Because we are the strongest beings in Mastoperia? I don't know. Maybe I'm bored that everything has been going our way for the past two decades or so, and we finally have a challenge. It will be fun to hunt him down and bring him back to the fight. He will become a great ruler, though. Maybe even stronger than you Kalita." Takara turned to face the leader.

"That will never happen Takara. No one has ever been, and no one will ever be. Stop telling yourself that one day you can beat me. I thought you would have grown out of this already."

"I don't want to defeat you anymore. We are about to pass our powers to a younger generation. Once we do that, then we will start to age again like normal people. I'm just looking for the next peaceful sixty-something years of my life." Takara glanced over at Amarin from the corners of her eyes.

"We are getting sidetracked," Radaman interrupted. "Shouldn't we look for him before he goes too far?"

Kalita shook her head. "We won't search for anyone. The factions will do it for us."

"Wouldn't that take a long time? They might even fail. If we look for him, then all of this could finish in a few days tops," said Takara.

"The factions need to know our grip on them is still firm and that everyone could pay for such an incident," Kalita replied, raising her voice.

"Isn't this a bit much? It wasn't the factions' fault he escaped. Why should we punish everyone for it?" Amarin ran his fingers through his long braids.

"It's not about the factions." Takara exhaled loudly. "She just wants to deny me the pleasure of the hunt. You should give it a rest already. It has been over a century."

"It's foolish of you to think I still care about you stealing Amarin from me. Though I won't lie, the added bonus of you being annoyed pleases me."

"You are the leader, Kalita. We will do whatever you ask." Radaman took a few steps closer to her.

"Of course, we will do what she wants in the end," Takara said as she moved toward the exit. "You don't have to be such an ass-kisser about it, though."

"Where are you going? I wasn't finished." Kalita raised her voice once again.

"You want me to summon the representatives of the factions to tell them about how it will go, don't you? I'm just going to make sure they come as soon as possible. Or would your majesty like me to stall that too?" Takara bowed in a sarcastic move.

Kalita moved toward Takara, her voice firm. "Speak to me like that again, and I will make sure you remain locked alone for the remainder of your aging life."

Takara knew that Kalita would enjoy nothing more than torturing her for the rest of her life, and she didn't want to ruin her final chance for a normal one. She apologized stiffly and froze in her place until Kalita gave her the orders.

Kalita waited for a few moments, watching as Takara stood still with her hands locked behind her back. "Now you can summon the representatives. I want them here as early as tomorrow."

"Consider it done." Takara was almost three centuries old and one of the strongest beings in Mastoperia. Perhaps the second strongest, yet, right now, she felt weak. It was hard for her to cage her tears as she walked out of that room.

58

The next day, the representatives of the four factions arrived. They waited in the main hall of the Forbidden Palace for nearly two hours until Kalita and the royal guards appeared before them.

"Why were we all summoned? Shouldn't you only be summoning the Kalanian Representative? Our candidate was present at the arena. We did nothing wrong," the Lunardis representative stated as soon as Kalita joined them at the main hall.

Kalita moved to her throne, her gaze inspecting the Kalangelle who kept her face downward, uttering nothing. "It's no one's fault he didn't join the fight. He arrived at the arena on the day and escaped while Evailen waited for him on the field. Either something happened in the period between his arrival and the time of the fight, or he planned all of it. However, regardless of the scenario, he wasn't alone. He received help, and that help came from other faction members."

"Exactly. Perhaps he was kidnapped." The Kalangelle jumped on Kalita's words, raising her head. "Perhaps someone was afraid they would lose the fight and orchestrated an operation to make sure they came out victorious."

"We would never do that. Evailen would have barbecued him easily." The Lunardis sharpened his tone.

"Enough!" Kalita shouted. "You are not here to argue and tell me what may or may not have happened. We looked at all the possibilities, and it's more likely he escaped."

"Then, why are we here? Why are we being questioned for the actions of a coward from another faction?" the Lunardis asked.

"Because he didn't escape with only one artifact. He escaped with two of the four pieces." Amarin quietly explained.

"We entrusted Evailen's piece to you when he didn't show up. So again, that's not our fault."

Radaman jutted his chest out before he crossed his arms in front of it, "As a Lunardis, you brag about being the smartest faction all the time, yet, right now you sound like anything but."

The Lunardis locked eyes with Radaman. "You may be one of the royal guards, but I'm a representative of my faction with a high level of influence there. You shouldn't be insulting me like that."

"I will do whatever I want." Radaman took a step closer to him with narrowed eyes.

"The piece you gave us was a fake one. Someone replaced it before she marched into the arena." Takara hid a little smile.

"That's impossible." The Lunardis raised his brows.

"Are you calling me a liar now?" Takara squinted.

"No, but if that's true, then it means we have a traitor among us." The Lunardis paused. "Is it—"

"No, it's not Evailen," Kalita interrupted.

"So, you know who is it?"

"The royal guards will handle the traitors. You don't need to worry about that."

The representative of the Averettis moved closer to Kalita with his gaze focused on his feet. "We would like a chance to correct our own errors."

"As I said, the traitors will be dealt with by the royal guards. This is not why we summoned you."

The Lunardis and the Kalangelle realized that there was a conspiracy, and it was bigger than they thought. The treachery extended to all the factions. Perhaps a Delphian member helped them too, but their representative stood at the back behaving as if none of this concerned him. The situation was bigger than they could handle, and instead of having the chance to bargain, they were now all cornered.

Kalita straightened her back on her throne. "Rondai committed not only an act of treason against us, but a betrayal against all the factions, and increased the risk for another faction war. We believe he is trying to stop this mission from completion to undermine our power. We are the glue that is holding all the factions from finishing one another." Kalita paused for a few seconds. "I know that you see us as harsh and mean, but we have to be like this to ensure the peace you all live in. Someone has to carry the hatred while being strong enough to stand above it."

She exhaled loudly. "None of you was present during the Great War but trust me when I tell you it nearly ended all of us. We need each other to survive. If we fail to deliver a successful succession, then everyone will see the Forbidden Warriors as weak, and before you know it, we will face another catastrophe. It's more important now than ever that the people see all the factions as a united front. One hand joining the Forbidden City against any who would think of crossing the line. Now more than ever," she stressed.

"What would you like us to do?" the Kalangelle asked.

"Announce Rondai as a traitor with a kill on sight punishment. The Kalangous council itself must declare the announcement to all factions. Citizens of Mastoperia need to see two things. First, that the Kalangous are not trying to protect one of their own, and that whoever crosses the line won't even find safety among their own people. Second, if you still cross the line, everyone will hunt you, not only the Forbidden Warriors. They need to know that traitors have no place to hide."

The Kalangelle nodded. "We already declared Rondai to be a traitor the second he decided to not show up for the fight. Anyone who proves to be a coward is no member of Kala."

"Well said Kalangelle… Well said," Radaman replied.

Kalita waved her hand through the air. "Now, you have your orders. Organize united search parties and find that prick. I don't care if he is dead or alive. I want his body here before the week is over and do not delay the announcement further than tomorrow. I will let you plan this part together. Now go. We have other matters to attend to."

The four representatives returned to broadcast the message to everyone. Rondai was an enemy to all of Mastoperia.

59

A few days earlier

"Why the gloomy face?"

Rondai jumped off his bed and focused his inner aura around his fists as he assumed his defensive stance. He stood in front of a blonde short-haired woman with vibrant blue eyes who wore a leather mask that covered all that remained of her face. A wide linen garment covered the rest of her body. The garment was similar to that used by the Kalangous masters, but the leather was a Lunardis specialty resembling their skin to cover their bodies.

"Relax. If I wanted to hurt you, I would have done it already."

"Who are you?" His tone was firm.

The mysterious woman cracked a muffled laugh. "I find it funny you would think I would answer this question after I went through all this trouble to not only hide who I am but also my faction of origin."

"What do you want?" Rondai ignored her sarcastic tone.

"Well… That I can answer, actually. I want you to not attend your fight and escape, but first, drop that magic parade. It will do you no good." She paused. "Trust me."

"You must be crazy or something. Why would I betray my faction and destroy my life for someone that is afraid to even show who they are?"

"Ah… but the why is the key." The mysterious woman ignored his tone of mockery. "You will do that to save the world."

"Big words backed with nothing." Rondai moved to an offensive stance.

"I was hoping this would be easy. I truly don't want to fight." She sighed. "Let me see what you think after I give you this gift."

The woman reached toward the floor with two open palms. Rondai tried to react quickly to what he considered a sign of aggression, but before he could move a muscle, she had already finished her actions.

He felt a cold hand climbing through his leg toward his back before it stopped at the back of his neck, and he lost control over his muscles. Soon after, his eyes closed on their own.

He saw flashes of events and memories passing quickly one after the other. When he regained control over his body, he realized what had happened. His body trembled, as his eyes grew watery. He tried to stand still, but his legs were too weak to carry the weight of his body, and he fell to the floor as his cries grew louder and louder.

"Your elders had no right to take those memories away from you. She was your sister, and they should have believed that her memory would have pushed you forward instead of bringing you down."

"Who?" Rondai struggled to form the question. "Who are you?" he asked.

"Again, you are asking the wrong question."

Rondai, however, couldn't ask any other question. His mind was no longer present. Instead, he was lost in his world of tears. The woman quickly realized that they wouldn't be able to continue the conversation like this, so she approached him.

She placed her palm on his heart and watched as he slowly calmed down. By the time he returned to the real world, she had positioned herself in the same spot she was before.

Rondai took a deep breath before he looked back into her eyes. His mind present, but his eyes filled with the ghosts of sorrow.

Now calmer, he closed his eyes and focused on why she claimed to be here.

"What do I need to save the world from them?" Rondai closed the fifth gate without realizing. Whatever type of magic she used, it temporarily cleared his mind of any dark thoughts, allowing him to feel more at ease with her.

"Now we can talk." She crossed her legs on the floor across from him. "The four artifacts you brought back are part of a single device that can enhance our magical powers dramatically."

"How?" Rondai copied her seating position.

"Centuries ago a Kalangelle created a machine. I'm not sure what her main goal was, but according to all my historical data, she was a pacifist. Nowadays she is only a caged memory by your council that no one knows about." She paused for a long moment as if her mind took her somewhere else. "Anyway, the device allows its user to utilize the power of all the factions and become the ultimate warrior. Personally, I think she wanted to give everyone even powers, so no one feels stronger than the other or something—"

"To have a better understanding," Rondai interrupted.

"Excuse me?"

"If she was a Kalangelle, then she wanted everyone to understand the pain we carry to become who we are. She obviously wanted to understand the others as well. If we could understand one another, then there would be no reason to fight. With similar powers, we would be one."

"Oh, Rondai. You are clearly delusional too if you think your faction is the only one who suffers because of their power. Everyone has their own pain, and just because theirs differs from yours, doesn't mean it's less agonizing." She paused. "Perhaps it's a good thing you think like that. Maybe it would help you understand what I have to say."

"At least now I know you aren't a Kalangelle either." Rondai displayed a wide smirk.

"Okay, Mister-I'm-So-Smart. Let me finish the story. The device caused the third all-faction war that nearly wiped us out. Each faction wanted control over it, but in the end, no one got control. A group of warriors from the four factions met together in secret and agreed that everyone was losing that war. They broke the device into ten pieces and hid nine in different places in the outside world."

"Hold on." Rondai's eyes widened.

"I know that you will say you only brought back four pieces, but that makes it even more dangerous. When the warriors divided the device, they entrusted the tenth piece to four warriors. That piece was an energy capsule that powered the device, but it was powerful enough to enhance the warriors' power tenfold as well as keep them at the same age for two hundred and fifty years."

"Why only two hundred and fifty?"

"I don't know. I'm not a scientist. I'm telling you the story I know." The woman inhaled a deep breath. "I think I heard that if they used the capsule longer than that, then their bodies would deteriorate. Anyway, the warriors thought two hundred and fifty years were enough for a user to keep their ideology, and not think of themselves as gods."

"So, what does adding the four pieces do?" Rondai tilted his head with narrowed eyes.

"With those four pieces of the artifact added to the capsule, our bodies can achieve immortality. The Forbidden City leaders will have the power to rule for eternity with nothing to stop them from enslaving everyone else."

"If so, then why not go for all the pieces?"

"Because the device was never meant to provide immortality. Its sole purpose was to give its user all four powers. It just happened that parts of it could manipulate our genes when used separately. You see, even though having all ten pieces would give them power beyond their imagination, they don't want it." She exhaled.

"Why seek too much power for a short time, if you could have more than enough for eternity?"

"Exactly." The woman nodded. "Do you see now why they can't have the remaining pieces?"

"What I don't understand is, why didn't the Forbidden Guards collect the pieces themselves? Why go through all of that trouble and risk exposing their plan?"

"Because they can't leave Mastoperia. The power of the capsule comes from the first civilization. It doesn't work outside the continent for reasons that remain unknown, and if they were to disconnect themselves from it now, then they wouldn't be able to reuse it."

"You seem to know an awful lot about this." Rondai stared directly into her eyes. "How do I know you're telling the truth? Your story sounds interesting, but it could be another trick to manipulate me. I won't forfeit the fight or escape." He stood up. "If the story you say is true, then we will stop them, but I won't deviate from my mission." He pointed at the door with an open palm.

The woman stood. "When you get to the arena, don't rush into the circle of death. Take your time. I'm confident you will see the proof of my words." The mysterious woman moved toward the door with confidence.

When she passed through, she held the door's handle for a moment and spoke to Rondai one last time. "You didn't have to be that mean with Evailen, you know? She only wanted you to comfort her. I have to say though; you handled it like a true Kalangou." Then she closed the door.

60

Rondai was the first to arrive at the arena. He wasn't eager to fight Evailen, but for the day to end. He convinced everyone but himself that this fight was more important than her. For him; Evailen wasn't just a girl he was attracted to or maybe in love with. She was the person who showed him the truth about himself. The one who made him realize he cared more about people than factional vendettas. The only person to pump emotions back into his veins and make him feel he was more than just an empty vase.

He stood in his preparation chamber alone, looking around the entire time without knowing what he was looking for. Pain was no stranger to him, but this time it felt different. He was the one who inflicted that pain upon himself without practicing any magic, or so he believed. He couldn't accept not being in control, so he tried to suppress his emotions. Denial had always worked perfectly for him until now.

As he heard the sound of people filling the arena, he felt his blood tremble and coldness crawl up through his feet.

How can I take her life? The question played itself repeatedly in his mind. He couldn't stop himself from questioning his reasons and realized he never wanted to be the leader of the Forbidden Warriors. It contradicted what he wanted to do. His entire life he trained for one goal, to avenge his father. If he were to be the leader, then he would have to prevent wars, not start them. However, he wasn't even sure if he still wanted that revenge after meeting his companions and learning more about their world.

The questions piled on top of each other without a single answer. He thought perhaps this could keep him from thinking about her but failed to realize that it was his feelings for her that swirled up that tornado inside his mind.

He kept adding more questions to the mix until he asked himself a single question, he felt a great need to answer. *Was the mysterious woman honest about her claims?*

◉ ❦ ✿ ◐

"There you are." Salvanra grabbed the wall of Rondai's preparation chamber as she gasped for air. "I was afraid I wouldn't make it in time."

"Salvanra! What's wrong? You are bleeding." Rondai rushed toward her and pushed on her side, blocking the wound with his hand to stop the slow stream of blood.

"Never mind that now. It's nothing serious. We have no time. You have to see this." Salvanra handed him an ancient book with Kalanian markings on the cover.

"What is this?" Rondai grabbed the book and flipped through it quickly.

"This is the book of Salinda, the creator of a machine that—"

"So the mysterious woman visited you too?" Rondai interrupted.

"Mysterious woman?" Salvanra raised her brows. "No, it was no one mysterious. Kawan could somehow see the future of the entire continent, and he told Jihave and me that the royal guards are trying to take control over Mastoperia and bring everyone to their knees."

"Jihave knew about this before his fight and still went through with it?"

"It wasn't that easy. When Kawan showed up to tell us, he claimed to be from the future. Jihave thought he was using a lame strategy against him and refused to listen, but I couldn't believe that Kawan was stupid enough to use such a cheap trick even if some of his words were absurd, so I investigated the matter further." Salvanra paused to catch her breath. "I'm sorry that I had to infiltrate your faction, but it was the only way I could know if Kawan was right or wrong."

"Is this why you're hurt?" Rondai asked.

"Yes. Some guards chased me and almost got what they wanted, but I'm tougher than I look." She tried to smile, but her pain won.

"Why me though, Salvanra? Why not show this to Jihave?"

"I did, but he refused to believe it. I can't say I blame him after losing his tiger. For him, the world is already lost. He said he didn't care what happens anymore." She blinked back a tear. "I've never seen him with such bleak eyes, and I don't know if he will ever find his sparkle again."

"Shouldn't you be next to him?"

"I should, and I will be, but right now, I'm the last person he needs." Salvanra took a deep breath.

Rondai looked at her with confusion in her eyes.

"Forget about this. You only need to focus on your own actions now. I doubt that you want to fight Evailen, anyway," she added.

"No, I don't want to fight her." Rondai sighed and flipped through the book again to discard his thoughts. "This book has a complete description of the device, but something is off."

"What is it?"

"The mysterious woman said they couldn't leave this continent, but that doesn't seem to be true."

"What are you talking about and what mysterious woman?"

"Never mind that now, everything else seems to be correct, anyway. We have to go." Rondai slapped the book shut.

"You are damn right we have to go, but we have to wait for someone first."

"Who?"

"Me." Cilia stepped into the chamber.

Rondai froze at the sight of her.

"Did you do it?" Salvanra asked.

"Yes, her lack of emotions focused her entire attention on the fight. She didn't notice as I replaced her artifact."

"Thank you, Cilia. You are amazing. I owe you so much." Salvanra placed her hand on her aching side wound.

"You owe me nothing, Salvanra. Go now, while everyone is busy. There may be no other window."

Salvanra grabbed Cilia's wrist. "Won't you come with us?"

"I can't right now. Evailen entrusted me with her red seed, and I have to give it back to her. One betrayal is enough. There is no reason to hurt the rest of her life."

"Okay, okay. That's fine. We will hide and wait for you, and then you can join us after." Salvanra moved closer to her.

Cilia held Salvanra's face with both of her hands. "I can't. You know that I have my sister back home. I can't abandon her either."

"Okay, then, we will bring your sister along, and it will be fine." Salvanra's eyes accumulated tears.

"It will be okay. Don't worry. I can take care of myself. You need to go now, or there may be no more Mastoperia to save."

Salvanra's tears carved their way down her cheeks.

"Would you give this to Evailen?" Rondai used the time as they conversed to put the words in his mind on a piece of paper using his magic. "Tell her nothing. Just give it to her."

Cilia nodded as she folded the letter and placed it in her pocket. She quickly turned to Salvanra and gave her a quick kiss, but Salvanra grabbed her closer as she tried to move away and pressed her lips against Cilia's for nearly a full minute.

"Be careful," Cilia said as she ran out of the room.

Rondai and Salvanra escaped in the other direction.

"What did I just see? I'm pretty sure Cilia looks nothing like Jihave in case you were confused." Rondai smiled as they ran.

"Now is not the time. We need to first get to safety then I can tell you everything, because if we don't then Cilia and I sacrificed everything for nothing."

61

Cilia quickly forced Evailen's red seed back in its place, above Evailen's heart, causing her to gasp for air as she felt an explosion of emotions in her entire body.

"Or maybe he cared about me more than he could admit." Evailen fell to the floor and placed her head between her knees before she surrendered to her cries. "I…I…almost…killed him."

"It's okay. Rondai understands, but I need you to listen now. I have something important to tell you and not a lot of time to do it." Cilia held Evailen close to her heart. "When I was looking for a solution to get you out of the fight, I ran into Salvanra, and—"

"What? How?" Evailen sniffed loudly through her blocked nose.

"That's not what matters right now. What you need to know is that we found clues about a large conspiracy organized by the Forbidden Warriors and the only way to unfold the truth required that we infiltrate a Kalanian temple."

"What?" Evailen wiped the tears out of her eyes and sat on the floor across from Cilia.

"We successfully infiltrated the temple, but before we could escape, we became trapped in an enchanted world."

"What happened?" Evailen grabbed Cilia's wrists.

"That is a long story, but the short version of it is that the minute we found the book we were looking for, a wave of energy burst through us. When we got out, the city was empty. It took time, but we eventually realized that there was no one but us in that strange world. It was a prison for those who tried to steal the book."

"Oh mighty lotus, that's awful. I am glad you found your way out?"

Cilia shifted her gaze to her feet. "I'm not sure we did," she muttered.

"I'm sorry you had to go through all of this, and I want to know everything, but why didn't you tell me sooner?"

"When I returned, you were missing your red seed, and I was afraid to talk to you."

"So, I'm not just an awful partner, but I'm a horrible friend too. I'm deeply sorry." Evailen cried again.

"Evailen listen. We were right. There is a very dangerous game going on, and it affects all of us. And there is something else." Cilia checked the time on her hologram watch. "I fell in love with Salvanra."

"What? Now you have to tell me everything about it. How? When? And that other conspiracy stuff too."

"I will. I promise you I will, but I don't have enough time right now. I wanted you to have the headlines of everything, and when I return, I will tell you all the details. For now, maybe you could read this." Cilia handed her the letter and left before Evailen had another chance to speak.

Evailen realized who wrote the letter, but she didn't read it until she was back in the comfort of her room. Something about being in her bed always made her feel safe, but not this time. Her heart raged like a tornado the moment she decided to read it, even before she grabbed it, but the band-aid had to be ripped off.

Dear Evailen,

I praise myself as being a master of words, but I have no time to craft something beautiful, so here are my thoughts as they pass through my mind.

I can't believe I was about to walk into that arena and fight you to death. I won't forgive myself for even thinking about doing it, and I don't know how I would have been able to live with myself after. You brought a new meaning to my life. You shattered my belief system and made me question most of my values. You are the most amazing thing that happened to me, and I'm sorry for choosing my faction over you.

I should have held you in my arms when you came to my door. I should have proposed that we run away together. Instead, I let you leave alone with a broken heart.

I'm so sorry that my stupidity and stubbornness get the better of me sometimes, and for breaking my word so soon. Unfortunately, I have to do it again now.

I recently learned that the leaders who claim to keep our peace are plotting to shatter it. I can't let that happen. I can't let them start another war, not when you are in this world.

For now, I don't know what to do except run away to the outside world with the pieces of the artifact I have, but I plan to return, strong enough to stop them.

There's no doubt they will hunt me. They might even demonize me in front of everyone, but it doesn't matter. I don't care what anyone thinks about me as long as you know that it isn't true.

I have no doubt that Cilia will fill you in, but please, when you know the full story, don't look for me. I repeat, don't run after me. Live your life and fill it with all the energy and happiness you made me taste in that short period with you. Find someone that will make you happy and put you first. Find someone that could do for you everything I couldn't, and I promise you I will do everything in my power to bring those so-called Forbidden Warriors to their knees.

I will show them they were wrong when they thought they could mess with us and that all Mastoperians are my people, not only Kalangous.

Be safe and smile always because the world is a better place with you in it.

I'm sorry I took all this time to realize the truth. The truth which is I love you.

May the gates be always open for you,

Rondai

Evailen shed no tears as she read the letter. The message was clear to her since the beginning. She placed the letter on her bed and stared at it for a few seconds before she got up to pack everything she had. She placed it all in a suitcase she reduced to the size of a pocketknife using her seeds. She then stood in front of a mirror to fix her hair as she hummed her favorite tune.

When she was ready, she looked toward her reflection in silence before she muttered, "Outside world… We shall meet again."

EPILOGUE

Three days after the factions declared Rondai an enemy of Mastoperia, Cilia traveled to Naradia's home to see her.

"Is it safe to meet here?" Cilia asked as she stepped into the living room.

"This is the safest place to meet. There's nothing strange about friends visiting one another." Naradia motioned toward the red and blue sofa centering the room atop a black lotus decorated carpet.

"You're right." Cilia sat down, her heartbeat irregular. "Did you get the seeds?" She turned to face Naradia as her friend moved behind the counter of her open kitchen.

"Don't worry. They will be here shortly," Naradia said as she pulled two glasses from the cupboard. "Can I offer you something to drink?"

"Water will be fine, thank you." Cilia did need something to soothe her dry throat.

"You know, I never properly thanked you." Naradia placed a glass of water on the round table in front of Cilia. "You took me in and saved me from the cruelty of our world. Without you, I wouldn't have had the chance to live in such a nice apartment." She smiled, glancing around at the expensive decorations covering most of her walls.

"There is nothing to thank me for. I gave you a chance, but you proved many times that you deserved all you got and more."

"True, but still. No one else was even willing to give me that chance." Naradia smiled, moving toward the door of her apartment after she heard the bell ring twice.

Cilia stood up quickly when she saw the two guests who walked in, her face turning pale. "What's the meaning of this?"

"Relax Cilia. We are here to help you." Takara smiled. "Naradia told us about your sister's situation, and we wanted to help."

"How?" Cilia's eyes widened as she moved her hand to her black seed so she could launch her armor quickly if needed.

Amarin moved around the room, checking its details, disregarding Cilia as he spoke. "You want six seeds for your sister. We are here to give you that."

"Since when do the Forbidden Warriors interfere in personal matters?" Cilia took a few steps backward.

"Since I want something from you in return." Takara sat on the sofa.

"I know nothing about Rondai if this is why you are here."

"I know, my dear. That isn't what I want. I'm here actually to tell you a story." Takara grinned. "Do you care to listen?"

"As long as you keep your distance." She looked at Amarin, who stood too close.

"Fair enough." Takara patted the empty space on the sofa, signaling Amarin to sit next to her. "I was the reason you went after the book of Salinda. I also visited Rondai before the fight to give him an incentive to escape. I knew that my explanation along with you showing him the book would persuade him to abandon the fight and leave the continent."

"Why?" Cilia's eyes widened.

"How could I tell him the royal guards are plotting to enslave Mastoperia when I'm one of them? It had to come from someone else."

"I meant why did you want him to escape in the first place? You're the ones who organized the fights."

Takara looked at Cilia with a smile on her face, saying nothing until Cilia understood that she didn't plan to answer that question. At least, not yet.

"Fine." Cilia shook her head. "Tell me the story then."

Takara nodded, her smile now awkward. "When I joined the Forbidden Warriors, I knew my power of saiting would somehow be amplified. What I didn't know was that I would gain new powers."

"Like what?"

"I became able to see the future based on my input, allowing me to construct whatever future I want."

"I'm confused. I thought this was what all Delphians did. You adjusted your own decisions until you saw what action will make the future you want to happen."

"Exactly. You're good, very good, but this isn't how my power works. Any other Delphian would see the future as it would normally happen if they did nothing to change their current course of actions. Then, using the power of saiting, they can see how that future would be if they did something different. However, the only variable is their own actions. For example, they can't see how the future would be if *you* decided to change it."

"How can I decide to change the future when I don't know what it is?"

"I did say she is good, didn't I?" Takara asked, elbowing Amarin before turning her gaze back to Cilia.

"You can't, but I can. I can see everyone whose actions affect my future. I can also see what would happen if any of those people changed their mind or did things differently. All I need to do then is manipulate the situation to make sure those people follow the path I want them to follow."

Takara moved her gaze from Cilia to Naradia who looked at her with a blank expression, then leaned forward. "Let's say there are ten pieces of dominos placed in an upright position on a table. A regular Delphian can only control one piece. They can move that piece around any way they want, and when they give it that little push to create the domino effect, they can only push that one piece. So if the other pieces are not already linked together, they won't be able to create a perfect sequence."

"That I get, but—"

Takara raised her hand, palm out, appearing to know what Cilia was about to say. "I can only push one piece to start the effect, but I can also move the other pieces to line perfectly together." Takara leaned back against the couch, her grin widening as if she looked forward to hearing what Cilia would say next.

"So, you can change someone's future by changing the future of a completely random person?"

"Exactly." Takara's smile filled her entire face.

"And you did something to lead me on the path you wanted?"

"Yes."

"Then, why me?" Cilia asked, taking a seat.

"In the original timeline, you kidnapped Evailen and locked her away for three days."

"I would never do such a thing to my best friend," she quickly responded.

"You would have. To make sure Evailen lived. Which allowed me to see you when you came to the arena and tried to speak to everyone about how the fights were cruel. I knew how far you were willing to go for your friend, and that was all I needed."

"I could have given the book to Evailen and not Rondai."

"You wouldn't have." Takara shook her head. "You knew the book would put the life of who has it at risk. You think of Evailen as your little sister, and you didn't want to endanger her life."

Takara paused, turning to look at Cilia. "Go ahead, you can ask the question again, I will answer it this time."

Cilia sighed. "Why go through all of that trouble? Didn't you do all of this to get the four artifacts? Why did you want Rondai to escape with them?"

"Because we need to go to the outside world. Like you, we are prohibited from leaving Mastoperia."

"By who? What power is stronger than you?"

"By the royal guards who were there before us."

"But they're long gone. How can they still have power over you?" Cilia raised her eyebrows.

"Do you know why there has to be a leader to the royal guards? Because when the succession happens, the leader remains as an advisor to the following group. The last ritual in the succession binds the leader in a shadow form. They become nothing but pure power that enforces the laws of the first pact on the royal guards."

"The shadow that stood behind Kalita when we first came to the Forbidden City. Is that who it is?"

"Yes. He is always watching our every move as long as we are inside the city. This is why we have to keep up certain appearances while we're there. To throw him off our scent."

"How does all of this relate to Rondai's escape?"

"According to the pact, we can only leave Mastoperia if we have to hunt someone who possesses more than one piece of the artifact."

"Is this why you also criminalized him? So, he has nowhere to escape and has to leave the continent?"

"Not really. We knew he would leave Mastoperia no matter what, but as I said, we have to keep up certain appearances in front of the shadow. We were simply following protocol."

"You don't want to enslave Mastoperia alone. You want to rule the entire world." Cilia squinted.

"We don't really want to enslave anyone, what we truly want is—"

At that exact second, Naradia forced a needle into Cilia's neck. Her friend hadn't seen it coming, so there was no struggle.

"Too soon!" Takara shouted. "You didn't need to do that. She knew how this conversation would end and accepted it the moment she sat in that chair. I was enjoying my conversation with her."

"You should have seen that then. Don't tell me you didn't know I would do that."

"Don't test my patience, Naradia. You're lucky I still need you for another mission, or you would be dead for denying me the time to finish this conversation."

"My…sister…" Cilia struggled to speak.

"Don't worry about her." Takara sat on her knees next to Cilia and held her hand. "The poison in your body will put you to sleep long before it kills you. I promise you that your sister will get all of your seeds. She will live normally and shine as you always wished she would."

Takara let her tears escape. "I'm sorry you had to die. We would have been great friends, but you're too smart for your own good." Takara stood. "I'm sorry you won't see the world we're building, but I promise you, the new age will be nothing you could ever imagine."

Teams and Phonetics

Teams	Phonetics	Faction
Evailen	**i vai lɛn**	**Lunar**
Yasmina	Jaz ˈminə	Kala
Bofrat	Bof ræt	Averett
Malani	ma læn i	Delphia
Rondai	**Ron daI**	**Kala**
Salvanra	sæl vanra	Averett
Enyo	Inyo	Lunar
Terqwan	Terq wan	Delphia
Jihave	**Jihav**	**Averett**
Cilia	Cilia	Lunar
Alinda	Alinda	Delphia
Rolakan	Rola Kæn	Kala
Kawan	**Ka wan**	**Delphia**
Maringrad	mɛrIn græd	Averett
Ryn	Ryn	Kala
Naradia	Naradia	Lunar

A word from the Author

Books available in The Forbidden series:

War Remnants

The Last Seed

Next in the series

The Book of Salinda

As a new author, I will appreciate it if you leave me an ***honest review***. Your feedback helps more than you think. It helps me grow, and other readers to decide if my books are for them.

If you want to learn more about the world of Mastoperia, the factions, and the complete details of the magic systems, check out:

www.mastoperia.com

where you will also find access to my discord server, where we can chat together.

For insigts and some world fun Follow:
@mastoperia on Instagram

Thank you for reading. I hope you enjoyed the story as much as I did writing it.

See You in the next book

MOUD ADEL

Made in the USA
Monee, IL
19 November 2019